SPLENDORA

SPLENDORA

a novel

EDWARD SWIFT

MEADOWLAND BOOKS
Secaucus, New Jersey

Published 1988 by Meadowland Books
A division of Lyle Stuart Inc.
120 Enterprise Ave., Secaucus, N.J. 07094
In Canada: Musson Book Company
A division of General Publishing Co. Limited
Don Mills, Ontario

ISBN: 0-8216-2001-0
Manufactured in the United States of America

*This book is dedicated
to Stanley Zareff*

The names used in this novel can, for the most part, be found in East Texas and are not to be confused with the actual people or places. Given such wonderful choices as: Overstreet, Faircloth, Lightfoot; Mid-way, Paradise, and Pluck—or, for that matter, Splendora—I could not resist using them.

The Author

". . . novels are works of fiction and works of fiction are never true; they only seem like they are."

Miss Jessie Gatewood,
Librarian

SPLENDORA

1

*Splendora: A small town
in East Texas near Louisiana*

It was the hottest day anyone could remember; around
July, near August; yes, that was it, on one of those July-
near-August days, each the hottest on record, the starting
up of dog days when the old-timers claimed that the creeks,
those that had not already gone dry, were poisoned on account of the weather; claimed that water stagnated in the
heat, foamed over with summer breathing hard down the
neckline, "The hottest breath ever," Esther Ruth Coldridge
would have said had she lived just a little longer; the hottest
because it marked the middle-going-on-the-last part of
summer; yes then, on one of those hot July-near-August
days when the creeks were dried up or nearly, the swamps
were parched and cracked, and every drop of ground water
there was had already evaporated and was holding up in the
air so the town of Splendora seemed to be enclosed inside a
blister, that day, and there were many like it that time of
year, but that day, that particular one, Miss Jessie Gatewood arrived on the afternoon train.

She had come to assume her post as the town's librarian,
although there was no library building and no real library

as such, only a battered-up school bus with shelves. She had come as the librarian of the school bus, had been hired by mail, through advertisements in educational periodicals and city papers. She had applied and was accepted and arrived looking like what she thought was expected of her, Miss Jessie Gatewood, director and driver and organizer of the new bus-bookmobile-soon-to-be, just purchased and waiting for someone with the knowhow.

She had gotten up early that morning and boarded the train in New Orleans where she had lived for many years. French Quarter nuns were chanting their way to early mass as she hurried through the narrow streets. She forced her way through their procession, got ahead of them in a hurry, and disappeared into an alley that opened into a green courtyard where her landlady lived. She deposited her apartment keys in the mailbox, and on perfumed stationery penned a fast note:

Dear heart,
 Thank you for your expression of confidence.
                              As ever,
                                   Jessica Gatewood (Miss)

"Thank the Lord I had the presence of mind to send my bags to the station last evening," she said to herself as she hurried once again into the narrow street and was trapped behind the same procession of singing sisters. Happily she turned a corner and left them behind; made her way as fast as possible toward Canal Street. Her eyes caught every clock along the way and made mental note of the discrepancy in time. "I must not be late as there is only one train that can take me there," she reminded herself, and, in spite of her lack of time, she paused for a few moments to admire herself in a shop window. Her reflection was pale, like a wraith, for she was wearing a dress of white eyelet through which could be seen all the furniture in the antique shop, Victorian furniture.

"It's my very favorite period," she had been known to say, just as though no one could tell by looking. That morning she had dressed beyond her thirty-three years in order to meet the town's and the committee's approval. She was well aware that her hemline fell halfway below her knees and a little farther still for good measure. She was secure in her dress of white eyelet over mint green cut with leg-o'-mutton sleeves, a high neckline, and trimmed with white silk ribbons here and there. She was almost a vision of white except for the green underskirt showing faintly through the eyelet. Her friend Magnolia had designed the dress and had carefully chosen the accessories: white silk, sweet-scented gloves, flowers at her throat, a pocket watch on a gold chain around her neck, and a white sash tied about her waist, giving to her dress a slightly blousy effect, so right for her role, she thought. From her elbow dangled a white linen bag, so practical for traveling, and on her wrist hung a beaded reticule inside which she carried a white lace handkerchief, her cosmetics, and a few cigarettes she had no intention of smoking in public. Her lace-up shoes with one-inch heels gave her the feeling of a matron, and her gold wire-rimmed glasses and Gibson-girl hair were just the right touches for a country librarian still living in days gone by.

How glad she was to be leaving the city. For the longest time she had dreamed of being able to live in a country town.

On Canal Street she boarded a trolley for a short ride to Lee Circle where she got off and walked the rest of the way to the train station. It was still early. A mist was rising off the Mississippi River and covering the city, "as though it is some poisonous vapor intent on trapping me here forever," she said to herself, fumbling in her purse for the ticket.

Fortunately she had thought to carry along a variety of things to occupy her mind on the long trip: a book of Victorian verse, a hoop of embroidery, a traveler's dictionary bound in leather, a box of assorted candies, a thesaurus, and someone to accompany her the entire way: Timothy John Coldridge.

They were almost inseparable.

Timothy John had grown up in Splendora. He had been of great assistance in helping Miss Jessie to be hired there. She was indebted to him more than she would admit. And in many ways he was also indebted to her.

It was over fifteen years since he had been home. He was nothing like the person he had been when he left, and he was not sure he was looking forward to his return. He did not look the same. His thinking was different, too. Although not that much different, Miss Jessie surmised.

Still, he could remember almost everyone and everything in the town. He knew the layout of the streets, the buildings, the houses, even the trees. In his mind nothing much about the place had changed. He had changed; on the outside, anyway, but inside he still thought of himself as the same; he had not changed much, only brought the inside that nobody could see outside where they could, and that to some people meant a change, but to Timothy John it did not. He was still the same except that he dressed differently and spoke in a voice that no one could possibly know him by, for in Splendora he was still remembered as Esther Ruth's grandson, Little Timothy John who left on a Saturday afternoon without letting anyone know; boarded the local bus and did not look back; did not think to.

"Dear heart, everyone will treat you like an absolute stranger," Miss Jessie said as the train left the city. "I am certain that your appearance is totally and permanently altered." She opened her dictionary and read a definition in his face. " 'To alter: 1. to change or to make different; modify. 2. To adjust (a garment) for a better fit. 3. *Informal*. To castrate or spay.'—Well," she whispered, closing the book. "I trust your experience has not been that extreme. I am especially referring to the informal part."

Timothy John did not respond.

When he left Splendora he had said that the town had been cruel to him, that he had no intention of ever returning. Little did he know he would return; little did he know he would want to return; little of all this did he know then. On a Saturday afternoon he had left, boarded the local bus south, and was not seen after that and was not heard from but once or maybe twice a year, at Christmas and on his grandmother's birthday; one or the other, sometimes both, he would write or call or send a box of something sweet.

"You have a different look about you," Miss Jessie said in a soft whisper, "a different face, a different set of clothes, and I would even go so far as to say that you have put on a little weight. I am ever so certain that you will have to tell everyone who you are, that is if you care for any of them to remember who you are. Chances are, you don't."

"I don't care for anyone to remember anything," Timothy John answered. There was tension in his voice. He settled back to look at the passing landscape.

"You are different, yet you are the same," Miss Jessie continued.

Lord, won't she ever hush? Timothy John thought.

She inserted a comfit without parting her lips and then spoke around it. "You are none other than Esther Ruth's grandson slightly effaced." Then she recited from her previous day's reading: "To efface: to rub out, or wipe out, eclipse; to make oneself inconspicuous."

"Completely rubbed out is more like it," Timothy John said. He was thinking of his friend Beasley, a landscape painter, and how he would rub out a pencil sketch and start all over again by using only the bare outlines of what had already been drawn there, thus creating a new picture on top of what was, or what had been and was not right, or creating anew on the surface of what should or could be improved upon.

That's exactly how I feel, Timothy John thought as the train approached Splendora. Rubbed out and redrawn.

2

On the morning of the day of their arrival, that hot July-near-August morning when it seemed that all of Splendora could instantly burst into flames without anyone knowing it, blaze up, and be gone so fast that no one would ever suffer or know what had struck; that morning Sue Ella Lightfoot woke up early and found two flat tires on her car.

Someone had punctured them with ice picks. They were still there; three ice picks in one tire and two in the other. There was nothing to do then but walk to work, she told herself; on such a hot day, too, and when only five days earlier she had had every tooth in her head pulled out and the dentist had warned her about getting too hot. "But what can I do about it?" she said and started out walking. She put the blame on her husband, Snyder, because he operated the icehouse and was always leaving extra ice picks stuck in the outside walls.

Now, who but me would have a man as ignert as all that? she thought, and then, just as though he was standing before her, she screamed, "How careless for someone who's supposed to be halfway educated; finished all four grades of high school and half a semester at some university some-wheres."

She thought at first that the culprits were some of the high-school boys who were working for Snyder that summer and that they probably had good reasons to get back at him for something. But what she could not understand was why they picked the hottest day of the year for their revenge; and why use the car for a target, since everyone in town knew that she was the driver and Snyder the walker. She did not immediately consider that the affront might have been aimed at her. She was usually quick to reason out such malicious attacks, had a nose for sifting through and com-ing up with anything aimed against her, and did not con-sider many people brave enough to take her on—or foolish enough—she could not decide which.

Sue Ella Lightfoot had lived through fifty-four summers in Splendora. She was fifty-four years old. She looked older. She was just at five and a half feet tall, slightly heavy. Wrinkles were beginning to run in concentric circles around her face. Her eyes were small and brown. Her hair, brown also but fading fast, was cut as close to her head as she could cut it herself, and her teeth had just been pulled out the week before and she was glad to be rid of them. She worked at the train station, had nearly all her life. She had watched many people come and go, many years come and go, and many summers, but this one, the one she was walk-ing in, was the hottest one there ever had been. She swore that it was.

Walking along that morning, walking because she had to, and not because she enjoyed it, she noticed that the streets, even the tree-lined ones, were bone-white and glistening. "A'ready," she said. "By eleven a-clock everything'll be burnt plum up." St. Augustine grass was curling on every lawn. Even the Johnson grass looked wilted. "A'ready!" Sue Ella remarked. "And here it's only eight-thirty. You

7

can bet no one'll stir the streets today without taking the sunstroke, but by evening, you better know it now, the porches'll be alive with rockers and swings going full blast."

It had been that way for over six weeks: absolutely unbearable. "The hottest ever," the old-timers said, always the hottest ever. Milford Monroe went around reminding everyone that he had predicted the heat wave back in February, and Lucille, his wife, went behind him saying that he had not been right in the head since his last stroke and not to pay any attention to his babblings.

Sue Ella approached her friend Agnes Pullen's house. A.P., as they called her, was four feet nine inches tall and more than eight sizes overweight. She was the inspiration behind The Miss Agnes School of Dance and Expression, and in spite of her size had managed to teach every young girl in Splendora how to tap-dance, tumble, and recite. That morning she was leaning out her upstairs window trying to get some air when Sue Ella shouted to her.

"It's cold washrag weather, A.P., honey. If you ain't got yours a'ready, you better get it fast. Wrap it up in wax paper like I do mine and you can take it anywheres you like. Mine's in m'pocket but it'll be coming out quick, I spec; never can tell in weather like this when you'll need a cool something to put to your face and neck, so you better get ready if you ain't."

A.P. went speechless. She had never known Sue Ella to walk to work before. "How'd you sleep last night, S'wella?" she managed to say, and all the time felt like she was talking to a ghost.

Sue Ella said something that sounded like "Poorly," said that she had taken the sick headache yesterday evening late and was up with it nearly all the night long and felt part of it still going on. "Dog days, dog days, dog days, why'd you come and won't you ever go?" Sue Ella screamed, lifting up her head like a rooster.

"She don't care if the whole town hears her crowing, I guess," A.P. said to herself.

There was a pause, but only for a moment. Sue Ella filled it up. She was good at closing gaps. She informed A.P. that she was walking to work because she had two flat tires and that she did not have one friend who was friend enough to offer to drive her to the depot. A.P. could not understand a word she said without her teeth so she just nodded her head in agreement, smiled sweetly, and said, "I guess not, S'wella," and hoped she had answered favorably.

Sue Ella thought, It's just like A.P. not to listen to a durn thing. She moved on pretty fast after that; anxious to get to the depot before the bad heat and also anxious to notify the sheriff about her tires.

The train station where she worked was across town from her house and at the bottom of a steep hill, steeper on the train side than the town side, way steeper. On the town side there was not much indication of a hill, but once at the red light the street started going down fast and did not level out again until it had passed the train tracks and was nearly out to the sawmill. Some people called it a bluff. The street running that direction was called Bluff Street. "So I guess it's a bluff and not a hill," Sue Ella said. "But it seems to me you could call it either one depending on what side you approach it from. Coming from across town it's certainly a drop-off, and that's a bluff, but coming from the station it's the steepest hill anyone around here ever put foot on." She was already worrying about how she would get home without having to make the climb in the afternoon heat. "There'll be a way," she said. "There's always a way, someway, somehow, even today."

Air conditioning had just made it to Splendora and there were two cool places in town: the bank, and the R. B. Goodridge mansion. R. B. presided over the bank and almost everything else in town. "He does what he pleases regardless of who says what," Sue Ella remembered her late friend, Esther Ruth Coldridge, having said many times. "Ruthie's been dead, let me see, I guess it's going on six months now, God rest her soul. Funny that I ought to be thinking of her today. Wonder what it means, if anything?"

On the opposite side of the street she saw Brother Anthony Leggett, the assistant pastor. "It's hotter than the hinges of hell, Leggett," she shouted. "Tell 'em that next Sunday and see what they do."

"It's worse than that, Sue Ella," he answered.

"A preacher ain't supposed to say something's worse off than hell," Sue Ella teased.

"I'm only saying it to you," he said, walking off toward the First Baptist Church.

"The only preacher in the world I ever cared anything about," Sue Ella said as she came to the icehouse where Snyder worked. He did not cross her mind as she passed. She went by Wanda's Ready-to-Wear with sale signs in the windows. "Who'd come out to buy on a day like this?" she said, hardly looking. Nobody was stirring. The stores did not open until nine or nine-thirty and some not even then, not that time of year. There was a white sale at the dry goods, and the hardware was running a special on sandpaper and house paint. At the corner grocery fryers were twenty cents a pound, and brooms two for fifty-five cents. "Who'd want two?" Sue Ella said. "I barely use the one I got."

Coming up the street she spotted a black-and-white dog walking along with his tongue hanging out. "Popsicle, what'er you doing this far from that icehouse? Get on back there and see what Snyder's doing. He's going to need you bad today, hot as it is." When she finished, the dog went running down the street as though it had understood every word she said. Then she continued on her way.

When she got even with the courthouse square she thought of Esther Ruth again and how much she had hated the courthouse building after R.B. had had it remodeled. She remembered Ruthie saying that she did not know why people wanted always to change things from the way they were to some other way that was certainly no better. "Ruthie, Ruthie, Ruthie, you could see everybody else's mistakes, but not your own, and you had plenty of them, too, don't forget," Sue Ella said, resurrecting her dear friend on the spot.

Out of the corner of her eye she caught sight of Milford Monroe sitting on the square and tried her best to hurry by before he saw her, but it was too late.

"I found the coolest place in the world, Agnes. You better come enjoy it with me before it's all gone," he shouted, as if flirting. He was, although he meant nothing by it.

"I ain't Agnes, so don't get all worked up for nothing," Sue Ella shouted. "Pore old Milford can't get straight on his names so he must be in for another sunstroke," she said to herself. "If Lucille had had her way, he'd have been locked up years ago for nothing more than accurately predicting the weather changes, so I suppose we should be grateful that she don't rule the world, only thinks she does."

She left the courthouse behind and approached the corner where the only traffic light hung, where the bluff started down, and where across the street she noticed that Clyde's service station was just opening up. Clyde Gingham, hosing down the driveway, pointed the spray toward her. "Too bad it don't reach all the way over here, 'cause I could sure use a good hosing down right now. Roasting alive a'ready and it ain't even noontime. Gotta flat. Two of them, and I'm aiming to get the sheriff after the guilty, whoever they are, and you notice I say *they*. I got leads a'ready."

Clyde smiled and waved her off, as he had understood very little of it. "Why'd the woman wanna go and have all her teeth pulled out for and not have any re-place-ments put in, I am not able to say, and it's too hot to even think about it."

There at the traffic light where the bluff started down, Sue Ella noticed that the street was already oozing asphalt and the sidewalk was slick as glass and hot as fire. "Hotter than the devil's breath," she said, still thinking about her friend Esther Ruth Coldridge who had been found dead in her nightclothes and stretched out under her lilac bushes. "Would have been eighty-nine had she lived to last March. God lov'er. Always complained of the heat; so I guess that's what put my mind on her, today of all days."

Milford watched Sue Ella cross the street and slowly disappear down the bluff. Gradually her body vanished from the feet up until he could see only her head bobbing up and down like fishing cork over the rim of the hill, if it could be called a hill. When he could no longer see her, his thoughts returned to the morning sky and what he expected the day would bring: more heat.

Halfway down the blufflike hill Esther Ruth popped into Sue Ella's thoughts again. "Now, what on earth are you doing cropping up at ever corner, Ruthie?" she said. A few steps farther her mind cleared, and a little farther still and she was once again seized by thoughts of her departed friend. "Yes, it must be the heat that keeps bringing her up. She hated it so and was never well this time of year, so I thank God she didn't have to live through this one as it would've killed her off for sure; melted her first. She always said she felt just like she was melting away in the summertime, looked like it, too, like she was made of candle wax, and the ony time she didn't was in her coffin, never looked more natural in her whole life than she did at her own funeral. Yes, it's better she went back in the winter when she did; better on her; better on us who had to bury her and choose the dress, the coffin and the songs; and better on the pore Nigras that had to dig her hole; yes, better on everybody that she went when she did."

Before she knew it she was at the train station. She opened her ticket booth, heated and poured her coffee left over from the day before, and sat down to a stack of detective magazines A.P. had already read and passed on. There was not much doing that time of year down at the depot. No one had gotten on or off the train in months. Hardly anyone ever came to Splendora that time of year, and hardly anyone ever left. She could not remember her last ticket, and Sue Ella always remembered her tickets, who bought them, where they were going, when they expected to get there, and on what train they were coming back. But tickets were slow that time of year and for weeks she had passed her hours with magazines, conversation with Duffy Jones, the porter, and with a subscription to all the weekly newspapers from the neighboring towns. She had them delivered right to her ticket booth.

That summer all the weeklies were full of the same thing; the murders of three men all found nude and wrapped up in barbed wire. Sue Ella thought it was interesting that their bodies were discovered out in the open or nearly so: one in Woods Creek where it made a turn and went through the part of town they called Little Splendor; and the other two by the side of the highway going toward Beaumont, one in tall grass and the other in a ditch.

Sue Ella finished her coffee, put down her magazines, and glanced over the headlines of that week's edition of *The Splendora Star Reporter*:

BODY FOUND IN WOODS CREEK

"Whoever it is doing it wants to be caught so bad he don't know what to do," she said. "Just dying to be caught so he can spill out all the bloody details and have a listening audience. Sure as anything doing it purely for the attention or else sexshul motives." Lately she had been reading about sexual motives, the most interesting things, too. Just about then, Duffy Jones showed his face at the door and Sue Ella said right off, "Reckon it could have been sexshul, Duffy?"

And Duffy said, "Not between you and me couldn't, Miz

Lightfoot, 'cause I sure don't believe in mixing up blood."
Then he went over to the sycamore growing so close to the
tracks it had to be trimmed every year to let the train by.
Duffy planned to spend his work day under it unless of
course someone needed something unloaded or loaded or
someone needed to get off or on the train, and that was not
too likely that time of year, but still it could happen, so he
was there just in case.

They had worked together for thirty-five years that hot
summer, Duffy and Sue Ella. Duffy lived over in Little
Splendor, the Negro section of town, and Sue Ella lived up
on the hill close to the businesses. That's what she liked best
about where she lived, she was close to everything; and
what Duffy liked best about where he lived was that he was
far away from the part of town where he was not comfortable nor very well treated. Little Splendor was still part of
Splendora, but no one who lived there thought that way.
R. B. Goodridge owned it all and had his hand in everything that went on down there. The streets were narrow and
unpaved. The main one curved around on three separate
levels before it reached the bottom of the hill. On each level
small dirt paths, hardly wide enough for a car, went off in
all directions to houses and stores. To Duffy, Little Splendor was his only home, and he hardly went outside its
narrow dirt streets except to go to work, which he did not
mind doing; he got along with Sue Ella very well, always
had. He knew his part of town and she knew hers and they
got together with what they knew; enjoyed each other that
way, Sue Ella and Duffy.

The sheriff's office did not answer so Sue Ella went on
reading well into the morning and then the afternoon, and
Duffy went on sleeping. It was the same every day unless
someone got on or off the train and late that afternoon,
much to their surprise, someone got off. It was someone
they had been told to expect but did not know to expect just

yet; the woman who had just been hired to operate the bookmobile, a librarian.

"God in heaven, why she had to show up today I'll never know!" shouted Sue Ella. "Wonder if we can tell her to turn around and go back till we cool off some?"

Even though she did not have a picture to go by, Sue Ella recognized the passenger at once. "Peers to me she's been pressed between pages for forty years, just like some old bookmarker. Thin as one, too." Then she shouted to Duffy, "Here she is four weeks early. You find out where she's going and I'll get somebody to help her get there, although it ain't going to be easy. You'd think a body would have better sense than to go traveling on a day like this."

3

It was on the afternoon train that Timothy John Coldridge arrived back in Splendora, and Miss Jessie Gatewood, the woman come to operate the bookmobile, arrived with him. Together they had traveled on the same train, in the same car, and on the same seat. They had looked out the same window and had made similar comments about the passing landscape. "How sultry it is today," Miss Jessie had said every now and again, using her hoop of embroidery as a fan to wave before her face. Luckily she had chosen the coolest dress she owned, a mint-green shift, overlayed with white cotten eyelet. She had worn it especially because she associated eyelet with the South, and she was a Southern lady. "So Southern," she said, as if out of breath. Her voice was always breathless, always soft, sounded like the wind in the pine trees. She was tall and slim like the pines Timothy John had grown up around.

Along the way she had busied herself with a hoop of embroidery: a lady in antebellum dress peering into a reflecting pool around which grew hollyhocks and larkspurs; the butterflies had not yet been completed, nor had the reflection. Only occasionally had she stopped her rapid needlework to allow Timothy John to bite his thumbnail. It was a habit she did not like and had tried since early morning to keep his fingers busy, his mind occupied with thoughts other than himself. "Do observe the butterflies going in," she had said, and Timothy John had answered like a spoiled child that he did not like butterflies except to pull their wings off. "How truly malicious I do believe you are," said Miss Jessie Gatewood, bringing her voice above her perpetual whisper. "I beg you, observe the butterflies this instant, for somehow I think it might be to your benefit. Now keep your fingers out of your mouth and don't disquiet my nerves. I find your uneasiness almost beyond endurance. Why, I'm hearing myself over and over: What on earth has eaten you up today?"

For a few miles longer Timothy John had settled back and Miss Jessie had been able to continue her stitchery, an anodyne for the contagious anxiety Timothy John had felt since their early departure. Having something to watch had always kept him from bursting into an uncalled-for action, one that might incriminate Miss Jessie Gatewood.

The afternoon train came to a slow stop and let off one passenger, a lady, from all Sue Ella could tell from her window inside the ticket booth. Right away she began searching for the woman's name. She had written it down on an envelope but could not recall what she had done with it, so she dialed A.P. because she had been on the committee that found and hired the woman.

A.P. answered on the first ring and Sue Ella shouted as though she were hard of hearing; "The bookmobile woman, if I've ever seen one, has just this minute stepped off the train and there ought to be a committee here to welcome her up the hill. And what's more, I can't find the creature's name where I wrote it down to save my neck, so you better get here fast and give her a welcome."

A.P. said that she would try to get dressed up and be

there, and Sue Ella said, "Never you mind about the dressing-up part. Come with whatever you got on, even though the library woman's wearing her best rags. I just wish you'd look at her. Dressed from head to toe is what she is. Wearing something long and white, got flowers on her neck, and the yellowest hair you've ever seen, and lots of it too, all pulled up so high on top of that head of hers it gives you the backache to imagine how she did it. Now get yourself down here; she's got off at the far end of the train and ain't made it to the station yet, has to claim her bags too, so there's plenty of time for you to get here if you hurry fast."

A.P. said again that she would try to make it as soon as she possibly could, but Sue Ella knew she had no intention of doing so. There was the usual ring of insincerity in A.P.'s voice that was always noticeable when she did not want to do something but was too embarrassed to say no.

She's occupied with something else and has no idea what she's about, Sue Ella thought, hanging up and dialing Lucille Monroe and all the time wondering if she should be calling Zeda Earl Goodridge instead. "One's about as bad as the other, I guess," she said hopelessly. Before the phone had rung three times she remembered that she had not asked A.P. the woman's name. "Lucille will come closer to knowing it than anybody," she told herself, and before the phone had time to ring again something told her that Lucille would not have the faintest clue what the woman's name was, nor would she be likely to find it in a hurry, so she hung up and dialed Zeda Earl Goodridge. "Zeda Earl will know the woman's name if she's got one," she said, waiting impatiently.

On the fifth ring someone answered and Sue Ella shouted through the telephone without giving herself time to distinguish the voice on the other end. "She's wearing white eyelet over pale green and has a bunch of yellow daisies pinned to her collar. Now what did you tell me her name was?" She thought that Zeda Earl for once in her life had picked up before the tenth ring, but she had not. It was the maid who shouted over a roaring vacuum cleaner and the radio turned up loud.

"That poor thing's white as a sheet except for that yellow hair balled all the way up to heaven, looks like," Sue Ella muttered to herself while waiting for Zeda Earl to come to the phone. Beyond the covered platform and far out on the end of the old wooden sidewalk she could see the library woman baking under the hot sun. "There seems to be some trouble indentifying the baggage," Sue Ella observed, and for once was glad of it as that would give her more time to find someone to welcome the lady and see that she got to wherever it was she was going up the hill. "Hope nobody is relying on me to get her up there on a day like today and without wheels to start on, but I am willing to run out and make a fast speech myself if I can find where the devil I laid her name down. It's written on back of an envelope. I at least got sense enough to remember that much." She fingered everything on her desk looking for it.

Miss Jessie felt her hair go limp in the humid heat, felt beads of water pouring from her face. She fanned herself with her hoop of stitchery while assisting Duffy Jones in finding her baggage. "No, no my good man, the other one, the other one, yes, correct. Correct again! I congratulate you! All the lavender ones are mine. There are seven of them, exactly seven and no more," she said, bringing a lace handkerchief up to her powdered and perspiring brow and then, with it wrapped around one finger, she patted it gingerly across her lips and cheeks. Timothy John had seen Esther Ruth do the same thing.

Duffy could see her lips moving but could not hear a word she was saying. "If you're talking you gotta make it louder than that," he said, to which Miss Jessie replied, "My good man, a lady never speaks above a whisper."

When the bags were all collected on a small wagon, Miss

Jessie asked if Duffy would be ever so kind as to see that they were promptly delivered to the Coldridge house. "Lady, you planning on living there or something?" he asked.

Miss Jessie tilted her head back as though looking at him through bifocals (although she was not, he noticed) and answered in the affirmative. "I have recently purchased the house from a charming gentleman, a Mr. Timothy John Coldridge, whose grandmother, I believe it was, bequeathed the property to him."

"Well, I guess so," Duffy said hesitantly. Although he found something singular about the passenger, he could not for the life of him determine just what it was.

"May I extend to you this small gratuity for your services, which I am sure will be accomplished with utmost punctuality?" Miss Jessie whispered. She handed him a one-dollar bill. Duffy smiled, showing gold, and said that he would deliver the bags right away, all the time not knowing how he would manage to do so.

Watching her step lightly down the old wooden sidewalk he realized what it was about her that was so unusual. "She be like the screech owl that come out in broad daylight just to see what's going on. Something almost unheard of, but sometimes known to happen."

If only I had remembered to board toward the middle of the train, I would not have been stranded in the direct sunlight, Miss Jessie thought as she made her walk like a beauty queen gliding gracefully down the wooden runway toward the depot.

Why is there no one here to receive me? she kept thinking as she approached the familiar yellow-gold station. No receiving committee, no mayor, no limousine, not even a battered-up yellow Ford taxi to take me from the depot. My letter posted last week must not have preceded me. My letter stating when I was to arrive, it must have gone astray as so many important letters seem to do—"Oh, why is there no one to meet me on this oh-so-propitious occasion?" she said and Timothy John answered her, "Why should there be?"

Miss Jessie drew her reticule up to her bosom and clutched it tightly there as if it were a shield protecting her, and in a sobbing whisper, said, "Why do you torment me in public places? Have you no mind?"

Timothy John answered that he had plenty of mind and Miss Jessie said that she was beginning to wonder if the sun had not burned it away. "If you keep this up, I can plainly see that I will need to give you a list of rules to go by," she said, approaching the station with the sun shining in her face.

They arrived together but no one knew it. They came in each other's company but no one realized it. They arrived and stepped off the train: Timothy John Coldridge, Esther Ruth's only grandson, and Miss Jessie Gatewood, wearing a dress of white eyelet over mint green, with leg-o'-mutton sleeves, and a nosegay of yellow daisies pinned to the neckline; wearing white lace-up shoes with one-inch heels, natural stockings with straightened seams, gold wire-rimmed spectacles and masses of flaxen hair pulled up and fashioned into a Gibson-girl roll bouncing beneath a tight bun held in place with invisible pins and combs. They arrived together but no one knew it. They came in each other's company but no one realized it. They arrived and stepped off the train and even Sue Ella Lightfoot saw only the one person: The woman come to man the bookmobile.

"There's only the one passenger, and that's the book-science woman come early and looking just as out of place as a person like that can look," Sue Ella screamed when Zeda Earl finally came to the telephone. "Now get yourself down here if you've got any kind of going-out clothes on and make a welcoming speech."

Zeda Earl replied in her usual made-up tones, "What ever are you talking about, Sue Ella Lightfoot? I am always dressed and ready to go."

"Well, hurry up then," Sue Ella screeched. "There's hardly any time left." She hung up and dialed Maridel Washmoyer, the florist, just in case Zeda Earl failed to show. "You never can tell what she's liable to do; A.P. either," Sue Ella said, drawing pictures of them both on the corner of the newspaper; while waiting for someone to answer, she took delight in stabbing their eyes out with her pencil. At that moment Miss Jessie, like a long wisp of smoke, floated before the ticket booth, and Sue Ella, deeply involved in disfiguring her friends, failed to notice her pass.

Walking will be a way of putting me right into things, she thought, but at the foot of the hill she paused a moment. "Precious Jesus lead me on," she said courageously, clutching her left breast with her right hand. Then she started up. It was a steep climb for anyone unaccustomed to walking in heels of any height. Miss Jessie, however, made the climb with very little difficulty except for the heat beading up on her face, painted like a china doll.

Timothy John said nothing, thought nothing, slept quietly, even through the heat; while Miss Jessie, with a certain surface equanimity, went gliding up the hill.

"Why is it that people like her always do manage to look out of place no matter where they choose to go?" Sue Ella said to the jeweled frog paperweight holding down a stack of weeklies on her desk. She listened to Maridel's phone ring a few more times and then, as if her statement had been put to question by the sparkling frog, she said, "Shut your mouth. I'm tired of listening to you." The frog's mouth was wide open because it was supposed to be used as a vase, according to A.P., who had given it to her, but Sue Ella used it for other things: paper clips, gum, rubber bands, and whatever she wanted to keep, newspaper clippings and such. "That's where I put it!" she screamed, hanging up just as Maridel answered, and digging what she thought was an old crumpled-up envelope out of the frog's mouth. The name was written on it and it was not an envelope after all, but a napkin.

With Miss Jessie Gatewood on the tip of her tongue and the napkin wadded up in her hand, Sue Ella Lightfoot went flying out of her ticket booth with intentions of welcoming the librarian to Splendora.

Milford Monroe, still sitting on the courthouse square, spotted the pale figure coming up the bluff and wondered who would be fool enough to pull such an incline on the hottest day he had ever predicted. The hill was steep and hard to climb in such heat, but Miss Jessie did not think on that. She thought only of keeping herself together until she could get inside again.

"Whoever she is, it looks like the sun's about to burn her up," Milford said.

For a few moments Miss Jessie stopped and stared at the courthouse. Timothy John was remembering how Esther Ruth had hated the building after R. B. Goodridge had had the outside structure completely remodeled.

"Esther Ruth was really something," he said. "She came from money and married into money and after my grandfather's death she threatened to use every dime he had left her to hire some poor Negro to come and chip away the stucco from the courthouse. She turned out circulars to that effect; passed them out in church, along the streets, in the bank, and grocery stores. She reminded everyone that the old Victorian structure with gargoyles and gothic windows, some stained and leaded, was still there, only hidden beneath the cement. She said that it had once been the most beautiful building in East Texas and all of Louisiana combined until R. B. Goodridge, Jr. declared the architecture no longer indigenous to the area or the times and took it upon himself to modernize it by covering up what was there and changing the shape to three cement blocks diminishing in size and with no sign of trim anywhere. 'It looks like a wedding cake without decorations, an eyesore beyond compare,' she went around saying.

"For years she said that the courthouse was like somebody hiding something that he had no business hiding, but was made to feel like he had business hiding it, so he did. She said that the courthouse was in disguise, like somebody who was ashamed of himself, or like somebody who was ashamed of what he looked like so he let everybody else make him over to look like what they wanted him to look like, whether he wanted it or not. She said that she felt sorry for the graceful old building all covered up and that Splendora should hang her head in shame for the way R. B. Goodridge was allowed to just take over and do what he pleased with the place."

Timothy John carefully studied the courthouse from top to bottom. He was trying to see beneath the cement to the original building and was wondering if anyone had eyes to penetrate such artifice.

From his bench on the square Milford Monroe was as much involved with Miss Jessie as Timothy John was with the courthouse. Because she just kept standing there and staring into space, Milford took it to be the first stages of sunstroke and stood up, about to shout, "Get inside somewhere, quick," but before he could get to his feet, Miss Jessie turned and entered a ladies' specialty shop. "A little shopping on the way strikes me as most agreeable," she whispered.

A.P. did not care to go all the way to the depot in such weather. Zeda Earl said she was coming but had not yet arrived, and Miss Jessie had already gone on foot up the hill. Sue Ella could not understand why Duffy had not kept the woman occupied until she got off the phone. "But she wanted to go a'foot," Duffy said. "There weren't no stopping her. Anyway, I don't reckon I'd know how to stop somebody like that. She wanted to go on up to her new place, so I told her, I said, 'Go, then,' and up she went. Going to that old Coldridge place, she said."

"So," Sue Ella said, "Ruthie's house has been bought, and, I reckon, paid for and everything inside it? Wonder what's going happen to her lace table napkins and china plates? And her satin glass? How I would love to keep it for her."

Zeda Earl Goodridge drove up in her black sedan and came to a fast stop, causing a cloud of dust to engulf her car and then thin out over the depot. She had composed a short speech and was carrying her notes with her when she got out wearing blue water-marked taffeta and looking in all directions for someone who might prove to be Miss Jessie Gatewood. Sue Ella and Duffy stood to one side and watched Zeda Earl high-step across the platform and pose. She held her notes in a black folder, straighted out her spine, and opened up her mouth as wide as it would go, like some church-choir soprano ready and waiting for her cue.

"You smell like an old box of facepowder," Sue Ella said.

Zeda Earl closed her mouth fast.

Then Sue Ella took charge. She told Zeda Earl to get back behind the wheel as there was no one to be picked up after all. She told Duffy to load the bags in the back of the car and to get in, that Zeda Earl would be so happy to give them both a ride home.

Zeda Earl looked over at Duffy and said that she was not offering anything of the sort, and Sue Ella said that she and Duffy would appreciate it just the same. They got in, closed the door, and were off.

Somewhere en route to Duffy's house, Sue Ella Light-foot, studying the day's events, said to herself that she thought it strange somehow that the bookwoman took off on foot just like she knew all along where she was going.

4

Speaking of the Victorians, Miss Jessie once said, "It took great confidence for them to add to such furniture styles as Sheraton and Hepplewhite; and the manner in which they expressed themselves, in what would now seem archaic phraseology, much of it hideous, also took great confidence."

Timothy John had heard someone else say the same thing, or he had read it somewhere, and even though it was something he himself could not express with ease, Miss Jessie had no trouble expressing it for him. She was able to let herself go, or he was able to let himself go through her; so returning to Splendora and his grandmother's house was much easier for him with Miss Jessie along than it would have been without her. He had confidence not in himself but in her; together they could go anywhere, even back to Splendora.

But as he approached the tree-lined block where Esther Ruth's house stood, his confidence in Miss Jessie began to weaken. A car passed and its passengers turned and shot glances of amazement at the stranger. Timothy John felt their stares go straight through him like bullets. Miss Jessie waved in return and continued walking at a leisurely pace. "It's going to be harder than I thought," he said. For a moment Miss Jessie stopped and looked around in all directions. "Absolutely nothing has changed," came his thin voice. "Even the trees are no bigger than they were." She strolled a little farther down the block but with a slower pace than before because Timothy John was dreading the first sight of the house he would live in again. He thought not so much about the Splendora he was returning to but the New Orleans he had left. Suddenly he found himself wishing that he was just passing through. He kept thinking of the day he had left fifteen years earlier when he had never been away from home in his life. He remembered leaving with a brown paper bag filled with a few changes of clothing, a wind-up alarm clock, a fifty-dollar bill pinned to the inside of his shirt, and a feeling inside his head that he was doing the right thing.

Esther Ruth had always told him, "If what you're doing feels right inside your head, then go ahead and do it, because it's the right thing, for sure."

In New Orleans he got off the bus and took a room in a boardinghouse run by a black woman on the edge of the Quarter. He did not make friends right away because he enjoyed the anonymity of being in a city. Just to walk down a street and not feel the need to speak to everyone was a pleasure. In Splendora everyone had known him, and he had felt that he could not think a thought without the whole town knowing exactly what it was. He had had many thoughts he did not want known, not in Splendora anyway, so he left. It was the only right thing he knew to do.

"And here, years later, I'm still harboring similar thoughts, and yet I'm back, and one minute it feels right and the next minute it doesn't," he said, almost slowing to a stop. A familiar cedar was growing close to the curb. "I simply cannot go through with this," he said, taking cover under the tree. The limbs were growing so close to the ground they afforded Miss Jessie a perfect shelter, so, while she regained her courage, he allowed her to smoke her first cigarette of the day.

The past fifteen years were divided by three inside his mind. There were approximately two good years, five bad ones, and eight good ones again. His first city job had been washing towels in a Turkish bathhouse. It was there he met a visiting professor of ancient history who was a collector of erotica and claimed to have been an East Indian prince schooled in the art of pleasing men.

"A likely story," Miss Jessie said, moving farther into the tree. "You'd believe anything, wouldn't you?"

"He never touched me without first asking permission," Timothy John said. "And after awhile I came to regard it as a nice but rather unnecessary bit of formality."

"Dear heart, you should consider yourself fortunate that you were not beaten and bruised your first time out," said Miss Jessie, holding her cigarette between her thumb and first finger.

"We lived together almost two years before he had to return to his country, but by the time he sailed he had passed on to me not only his vast collection of lecture notes, but his entire knowledge of the erotic arts as well."

"How extremely useful, I would say," Miss Jessie whispered. Then, from her delicately pursed lips, she very slowly exhaled a long thin ribbon of smoke.

"After he sailed there was no one who came close to replacing him," Timothy John continued.

"Well, I guess not, dear heart," replied Miss Jessie, steadying herself against a branch.

All during those first two years he could remember having thought, Never, even in her wildest nightmares, would Esther Ruth have dreamed I'd be living this way and feeling right about it.

Then he moved into a small apartment by himself and

furnished it with Victorian couches, chairs, and love seats, numerous love seats. And it was shortly after that when the bad years set in. During that period he was unable to find suitable employment. He went back to the bathhouse but found that he did not belong there anymore. Then he became a messenger, a waiter, and a professional shoplifter for a large department store, where he worked in Loss Prevention. It was his job to determine how difficult it was to steal garments from the various sales clerks. Everyday a new plan for shoplifting was decided upon and everyday he was caught with the merchandise. After two weeks he was fired because he called too much attention to himself. His employer said, "We've got to stop all this shoplifting, and the only way we're going to do it is to find out how it's being done. We need somebody who looks like the average person for this job and you don't. You've been caught every time. All the clerks remember what you look like. So you'll have to go. We can't use you anymore."

It was then that he began to realize that even in the city there were people who stared at him the same way they had in East Texas. He looked into the mirror and for the first time admitted to himself what it was that caught their attention: he was beautiful. Everyone in Splendora had told him so all his life but he had never come to the direct realization of it before. Suddenly it seemed to him that all the stares he received were negative.

"When you were sequestered away with that delightful collector of erotica you did not notice these things," Miss Jessie said. "But the minute he left, your sheltered little mind opened up. The stares you were suddenly conscious of receiving seemed negative because they were negative. Up until the time you discovered me, that is." She deliberately dropped her cigarette, ash end first, to the ground, and buried it with the toe of her shoe. "In most places men are supposed to be handsome, not beautiful," she continued.

"And little boys are never supposed to wear bangs, remember?"

During those years he rarely left the Quarter. He felt safer there than he did in the world beyond Canal Street. To avoid receiving too much attention he attempted to make himself look ugly, but there was not much he could do. Not even bad haircuts, baggy clothes and dirty hands seemed to do any good. Under favorable circumstances, he discovered that even men who had never considered loving another man gravitated toward him. He realized that because of his good looks most of them did not consider him a man and therefore were able to handle the situation without feeling threatened. Without guilt or shame he gave himself freely, but not once did he find anyone else who gave him the right feeling inside his head.

"Everyone wanted me to play a role then," he recalled. "They wanted to strap me to the floor or hang me from the ceiling. They wanted to play slave and master, or man and wife, or they wanted me to pretend that I was being raped. I didn't see the point in all that. I also didn't see the point in small talk and discovered that because I had not practiced it in so long that I had completely forgotten how to do it."

"There is a certain danger," Miss Jessie said, "in falling in love early in life. Now this is not going to be a lecture, but allow me to say just this: Had your first experience not been so positive, everything else may have seemed glorious."

"That's not the way I care to look at things," Timothy John said. "I have never been one for playing roles and that's what everyone wanted me to do. I just wanted to be myself."

"So then you discovered me," Miss Jessie said, taking out her compact and removing the last traces of Timothy John from her perspiring face. "May I remind you that I too abhor chatty communication and rarely give myself to it, yet my manner of verbal expression has not been labeled archaic and artificial as yours so often was." Then with a smile she added, "I can help you through the rough places. That's why I'm so important to you. That's why you need me. I command more trust from people; and besides that, everyone says I'm too charming for words."

Sinking into deep thought again, he recalled the first night he met Magnolia, the Black Queen. "You think too much, honey," Magnolia said. "You got to let yourself go more and learn to enjoy life. You scare everybody away by seeming to know more than anybody else. It's like you can see straight through everybody you meet, and take it from me, nobody these days wants to be known inside and out. You may be pretty to look at, but your talk don't match up with it 'cause you're too high and mighty. You got to loosen up and be more down-to-earth in your conversation or you'll wake up and find yourself standing alone in every bar you go to. Sometimes your mind runs too deep, you talk about things nobody's ever heard of or cares anything about."

"Well, I'm not exactly someone you might have a chat with in your local drive-in grocery, because you will never find me there," Timothy John protested. "Nor are you likely to come across me bending over the frozen foods in the supermarket, so why should I force myself to talk about such things as that? I'm not a T.V. dinner, nor am I a laundry-mat conversationalist. And to be quite honest, I am sick to death of meeting men who have no ideas, no drive; who are vapid, unintellectual and unrefined, vulgar, low, uncultivated, unpolished, and uncultured, as well as ill-bred, ill-mannered, inelegant; boorish, raw, crude, and coarse. Suddenly the world seems to be full of them. And the ones who do possess the right qualities of mind are usually snobs of the worst sort. Am I looking in the wrong places? Or is it just me? I have always felt quite different from everyone else."

"That's because you *are* different from everyone else," Magnolia said. "And I want you to know, there's nothing wrong with that if you can get away with it, but it seems to me you ain't got what it takes to be able to. So I say we make you over from head to toe, starting right now. Create a new you, is what I mean; somebody you can feel more comfortable with and everybody else can feel more comfortable with, too. You've got to cut loose and learn to be more accepting than you are. Wouldn't hurt you none, you know, 'cause not everybody out there is as bad as you say."

Miss Jessie removed a tortoise-shell comb from her linen bag and retouched her hair. Daphne Hightower strolled by on her way to the Post Office but did not notice anyone standing among the branches. "Daphne hasn't changed a day," Timothy John thought. "She still looks the same as she did twenty years ago when her husband disappeared on a hunting trip. I wonder what ever happened to him?" On the opposite side of the street Dudley Lock came out onto his porch to spit and then went back inside again. He too was unable to see Miss Jessie standing within the branches while she regained her courage for going on.

Timothy John returned his thoughts to New Orleans and to the night Miss Jessie was born. It was Halloween eve, and it was not entirely he who thought of her, but Justice Dodson, better known in the Quarter as Magnolia, the Black Queen, who assisted in drawing her out.

The Jessica Gatewood years flashed before him as though he had no control over their resurgence, as though he were experiencing himself on film.

Mangolia helped Miss Jessie feel comfortable with herself; helped Timothy John feel comfortable exposing her. It was Magnolia who put the finishing touches on the metamorphosis occurring like a miraculous birth in one of the small back rooms of a hotel on Ursuline Street where Timothy John had come to live. Magnolia chose a late Victorian look, a long skirt of dark gabardine, a white shirtwaist with a high neckline and leg-o'-mutton sleeves. She contrived to add the proper jewelry, cameos, and opal brooches, and fashioned his hair into a bouncing roll circling his head and held in place by a tiny bun on the very top center of his head.

"You ain't quite thirty yet and already your beauty is fading fast, honey," Magnolia sighed. She was not about to admit that he was as good looking as she thought. "Still, you ain't too bad to look at, though. You ain't no Magnolyum, that's for sure, but after all, few people is. Now don't go get me wrong or nothing like that, for your beauty is still there, only better from certain angles than others, so it's best that we go in the direction of making you look interesting and not in the direction of making you look beautiful. The beautiful part is reserved for only a select few of us girls."

Magnolia was forty-eight then, although she did not show it and was proud of the fact. "Looks to me like I'm aiming to stay young and beautiful all the rest of my life, and I'm sure glad to know it, too, since that's how it is I'm paying my way." She was black as the inside of a stovepipe, had no blemishes, and was fond of wearing long dresses of black satin, bringing attention to eyes that already seemed larger than they should be. She was tall, had hard muscles in her arms, almost always exposed, and in her legs, almost always covered, for she was hardly ever caught without a long clinging dress revealing the hardness of her body. Before she became Magnolia, the Black Queen, she had been Justice Dodson, a professional basketball player, the most graceful on the team. In those days he had frequented the gymnasiums and public baths. "But I soon found out it's all right, honey, for big men, they just love their big tall women, and with some of them, the bigger they come and the stronger they get, the better they is liked, and I don't have to tell you either—that spells Magnolyum."

She wore black satin dresses with spaghetti straps and

long straight skirts slit up the side. She made them herself. Since leaving her job with the telephone company she could wear whatever she wanted whenever she wanted it; to her it was the supreme luxury. " 'Number, please,' is no more for me, honey, because I got me a Sugar-foot that won't quit. He gives me plenty just for being around ever' once in awhile, and the rest of the time is mine, all mine, and after this new you we're installing, you is likely to have the same luck, even might be some competition for ole Magnolyum here," After a pause she added, "You notice I say *might*."

With a rattail comb she gave the hairdo its final touches, examined the makeup job carefully, and then handed Timothy John a mirror. "All done, honey," she said. "Now when you go out, you won't have to be scared to death that somebody's gonna mistake you for a woman, 'cause you just this minute became one, just like me. Only this way it's better than having your parts cut on and rearranged, 'cause if you ever want to go backwards again there's nothing to it. Although I don't think backwards is anyplace you're gonna feel like going anytime soon. What's nice is that now it will all seem right when people show you how much they like looking at you. There won't be no mistakes unless you want there to be. Of course there's always room for mistakes, but what Magnolyum here means is you are right now better equipped to take care of some mistakes than you was before, so from here on out you believe Magnolyum and it'll all seem easier, just like it seemed for her. I tell you for sure, I thank my lucky stars and count my blessings I had a helping hand when I did, for now I got no more worries. It gets easier and easier; got that telephone 'Number, please' job the first try, and after that I soon found out I didn't have to work at all, because I got everything I wanted first try. Magnolyum, she got it all figgered out. Magnolyum, she be flying high these days and, once and for all she sure do believe in heaven on earth, but like Mamma always told my sisters: Honey, all in this world you gotta do is keep your cookie clean and you'll be sitting up big as you please. But first off, we got to find a name for this new you we've invented."

It was Timothy John who came up with the name Jessica Gatewood. He found it in the New Orleans telephone book. Magnolia said that it was a perfect name, not too pretty, but interesting.

That was the new beginning of things. Gentlemen had always offered their seats to Timothy John and with Miss Jessie they did likewise. But now it was different. Miss Jessie accepted their gallantry without embarrassment. Magnolia watched with pride what had been partially her creation. "Every day you gets a little better and a little better still," she said. "One of these days soon we'll have to put you to the final test so you can go out and start making a living off who you are, for this thing sure ain't no good unless you can use it properly."

Everything became easier. He had always thought of himself in the feminine, was more comfortable with what everyone said were feminine stances and gestures. He had never been comfortable as Timothy John, but as Miss Jessie everything, even going to the laundry was easier. She was waited on hand and foot in all the stores. She was spoken to in a kinder voice. People did not seem to be skeptical of her as they had been of him. She was who he felt he should have been all along. She was who he had wanted to be from the very beginning, but he had not known how to go about correcting the error he thought had been given him to live with the rest of his life. Miss Jessie was easy, she could go into any district of the city and not be noticed as an oddity, but admired as an example of a style long passed and still remembered as a graceful period when ladies were still ladies. Rarely did her hairstyle change. Magnolia insisted that it was perfect. Together they shopped for dresses that had the flavor of the period but were still modern and could be worn in search of employment. It had always been difficult for Timothy John to hold a job for very long, and he had never gotten the jobs he really wanted. It had always been his experience to be turned away by would be employers who were not sure who he was, what he was, who were afraid of him, or who were mistrustful of a man so delicate in appearance that it would seem that he was both man and woman at once. With little or no effort he confused the two selves, fused them so thoroughly he could not at times tell where or when one merged into the other. It seemed to him that Miss Jessie had always been with him, yet in hiding. Or was it that he had always been in hiding from her? There were times when a confusion swept over him and he could not tell who had come first, Miss Jessie or Timothy John. There were times he did not care who had come first as long as Miss Jessie was in command. She was soothing. She made going out into the world easier. He learned to dress her so she could blend into most any crowd and still be noticed. He thought of her as a jewel when he thought of her, but most of the time he preferred to believe that she was doing the thinking for herself. Gradually she took over like a long wave that builds up in momentum until it sweeps over everything in front of it, and eventually breaks.

At the beginning he wondered if what he was doing was destructive, or was it merely nature taking care of itself the best way it could? He often felt as if part of him had been hibernating and finally woke up, but gradually something else took over, and he no longer consciously thought these things. It was as though there was present some other mind or some other eye that saw them both. Some impartial existence saw them, as if from above. Miss Jessie, the solid figure, was always out front and Timothy John, more transparent, was either standing to the rear or to one side. At one time, long before Miss Jessie's existence, it had been the opposite, for he had felt her, who at that time had no name and no form, standing behind him, or to one side, or inside, he could never be sure, but was certain that with every step taken he had carried with him an apparition in the feminine form.

In practically no time at all Miss Jessie became so comfortable with herself that she began attracting a variety of admirers who treated her with tenderness. "Just like I told you, honey," Magnolia said. "This way you'll attract the right crowd, and pretty soon you'll have so many men around you, you won't know which one to choose and which one not to choose. You're getting steady with it now, so I suppose it's time to go out and try for some kind of all-the-time employment. A steady job is the best medicine a woman like you can have at this particular time in her life, for it teaches her that she could do all the time what it was she thought she'd never be able to do."

Timothy John did feel a noticeable change, but it was difficult at first for him to say what it was. Miss Jessie had given him a freedom he had never known before. She was made welcome wherever she went, and Timothy John, for the first time in many years, felt what it was like to be at ease. Miss Jessie began searching for employment that had dignity to it. She set her goal to work in a bookshop and had no trouble at all being hired. She looked the part. All her friends said so. The shop was in the Quarter and specialized in out-of-print books and fine bindings. "I have always liked anything in a fine binding," Miss Jessie purred to the owner of the store when he interviewed her. She went to work the next day and stayed with the job until she left for Splendora. She was liked and admired; "an asset to the bookstore," the owner said. She recommended and quoted titles and passages, spouted publishers and prices without having to look them up. She had special customers who refused to be waited on by anyone else. At the shop everything was going well. There were no clashes in her social life, either. Magnolia and she had become extremely close and were frequently seen in the Quarter with their following of fashionable men who enjoyed fine company and pleasures. They usually referred to Magnolia as a real woman, and to Miss Jessie as a real lady. Timothy John's world had expanded just as Magnolia had said it would, and once again he was beginning to enjoy the pleasures of companionship that he had once thought would be denied him forever.

He did not think of Miss Jessie as a role he was playing. He thought of her as himself. From time to time Magnolia issued advice: "You can't forget who you are, nor the fact that you ain't exactly who you seem to be on the surface, but that's all part of the fun of it. It's like a masquerade, only it works overtime, so it can seem like you're at a party every day of the week if you don't let yourself get too mixed up with really wanting to be who it is you seem to be. Ever' now and then you ought to let yourself go more than you do. Don't try to be so made-up all the time. Let your hair down once in awhile and it'll be a breather for you. Who told you you had to take yourself so seriously anyway? That sweet Miss Esther Ruth, I 'magine."

On a warm spring evening not long after Miss Jessie's birth Magnolia—smelling of old dresser drawers where cheap perfume had been left to evaporate and powder had been carelessly spilled and not wiped up—was sitting on the corner stool, her stool, in a bar downstairs from her apartment, when Timothy John—wearing Miss Jessie's hairstyle and tight-legged jeans together with a camisole top flaring out around his waist, a string of pearls, and silver lamé heels—came strolling into the bar and took a seat on the next stool just like she owned it. Magnolia took one look. It was all she needed. "You don't seem so much like a cartoon no more, honey," she said. "You been taking lessons from the right person is all I can say, and there ain't nothing left for me to do but pronounce you 'graduated with honors.'"

It was then that Miss Jessie bought a second-hand piano and began practicing. She started out with all the pieces Pristine Barlow had taught Timothy John when he was a child. Before long she was giving concerts in her apartment. Her concerts developed into Friday-evening salons for artists. Her evenings at home became popular with the intellectuals of the Quarter. The talk was clever and stimulating. She enjoyed most especially the company of the young romantic poets and often invited them back, one at a time, to visit her in private.

She saw herself in tradition with all great salon hostesses, was on intimate terms with her "regulars," and excelled in being able to bring out the best in each. "Do give us that little phrase again," she would ask a poet, or: "Dear heart, do repeat the last movement of your sweet little concerto. I feel there is so much there we cannot possibly be expected to grasp it *all* during one listening."

When Esther Ruth died and her city lawyers informed Timothy John of his inheritance, the salon period of Miss Jessie's life came to a rapid close. The decision to return to Splendora was instantaneous. "What a lark it will be," he said, and at once began making preparations in the name of Miss Jessie Gatewood.

"I tell you, it couldn't be more perfect," Magnolia said. "That darling Esther Ruth dropped dead and left a pile of money just when the town was in desperate need of somebody with the library know-how. It's a miracle for sure, and goes to prove that you gotta live right and not hurt nobody, and everything you want, you just set your mind to having it, and it's yours, all yours."

Six months after Esther Ruth's death Miss Jessie Gatewood boarded the train for Splendora and with her she carried a set of false references, a false degree from an unheard-of-university, a pair of false eyelashes, a set of plastic fingernails, and a purpose the town could accept and be proud to support.

On the eve of Timothy John's return Magnolia had said, "Honey, I can't wait to be your very first houseguest, because two stray women like us will fairly more take that little town by storm, believe you me."

On hearing her words again, Timothy John came to his senses and discovered that Miss Jessie must have summoned her courage, for he was standing in front of Esther Ruth's house; as Lucille Monroe, who had been spying through a hole in the cane patch for over fifteen minutes could have told him.

5

Timothy John Coldridge came home. Esther Ruth had left him the means to do so. She had left him all her money as well as her Victorian white-frame house located on the main street of town. Fortunately he had no living relatives to challenge his position in the house; fortunately he had no living relatives anywhere that he knew anything about; at last he could do what he pleased. Esther Ruth had left him money and a house and everything that was inside it: her prized chaperon couch, her carpets, her tapestry curtains. He inherited an assortment of tables, chairs and settees, cabinets filled with china plates, camphor glass, satin glass, crystal and flatwear. She had left him her Tiffany lamps and vases, her hats and hatpins, her antique dolls, her brooches: diamonds, rubies and sapphires; all her dozens and dozens of cameos, all her Victorian bedsteads, her mattresses and monogrammed sheets. She had left him everything; her money, her house, her electric bill, even her organza dresses.

On the walls she had left framed photographs of people in various and sundry costumes and poses, but at her death she had little idea who many of them were. Some, of course, were snapshots of Timothy John. But she had had trouble remembering the others. Perhaps they were lost admirers, perhaps lost relations, or perhaps they were people whom she had never known, or had only slightly known, or had caught a glimpse of from the window of a train and for some reason or other snapped their picture. Such had been her way of doing things.

The house had gone empty for several months before Timothy John became its occupant and owner. Though he didn't know it, Lucille Monroe, his next-door neighbor, watched him arrive. She was wearing a shift of polyester double knit, bright orange, contrasting brilliantly with a frosty blue bouffant and a face that was caked with coloring; she had just returned from an appointment with Junie Woods, who advertised herself as Splendora's most original beautician and makeup artist.

"Oh, how happy, happy, happy we are that you've arrived at last," she shouted, fighting her way through the gardenias and cane bordering their property. "We've waited such a long, long time for somebody like you to come help us out. Zeda Earl just was here with your suitcases and told me to look out for you, said that you were going to be living in our dear Ruthie's old house. Oh, how wonderful for you, and for us, and especially for me, since I'm just next door."

Miss Jessie managed to whisper a polite "Hello," and then mentioned that she had purchased the house from a charming gentleman, a Mr. Timothy John Coldridge, whom she did not know, only met briefly.

"Oh yes, Timothy John," Lucille said, with an unhappy look on her face. "I must say I am surprised to hear that he's still alive. Suppose we sit right down and let me tell you a few things about that young man, the way he was when I knew him, that is."

How can she still be the same after all these years? Timothy John thought.

"Oh, how sweet of you to fill me in on a thing or two,"

Miss Jessie whispered, wiping the dust off a porch chair with a tissue taken from her linen bag. "Won't you please sit here?" Lucille sat. Miss Jessie cleaned off another chair and sat also. They faced each other directly. "Do please continue your story about the gentleman who once lived here. I'm interested in everything I can know about the past occupants of this old house as it is my belief that something of their spirit still lingers behind, and the more I know, the easier it will be for me to settle myself. Now, as you were saying about the charming Mr. Coldridge . . ."

"Ruthie had to raise him up after his father, her only child, killed his wife for running off with another man, and I guess you'd do the same thing too if you had the mind for it," Lucille said as fast as she could. "Killed the other man as well, and then, big as you please, called the police on hisself, and just as they arrived, what did he do but commit suicide right there in front of them, while that child, bless his sweet heart, was off in some motel room somewhere fairly more crying his eyes out. But the saddest part of all, and S'wella Lightfoot will tell you the same, the very saddest part of all was when Ruthie snatched up that grandbaby and carried him home without asking anybody what was right and then commenced treating him just like some kind of doll baby. Only in Splendora County would you hear of such things happening, and only R.B. and Zeda Earl Goodridge have ever come close to topping it, and who's to say whether they topped it or not. Now take their two girls, for example, one is dark-colored like Zeda Earl is, part Indin', they say, and the other one, who's fair, looks so much like R.B. nobody can stand looking at her, washed-out and faded just like some old bedsheet, white all over, almost, plum scary looking, well, she, the light-colored one, is off living with some tramp in the city dump because she likes it better than her fine, fine home, and the other one, the dark one, looks so much like Zeda Earl you just want to cry for it, well, she's off doing something so sorry God his-

44

self don't have no name for it. Zeda Earl will not for the life of her even so much as mention their names in public, and R.B., he refuses to allow them inside the city limits, but I say, at least they haven't committed murder, suicide, or been thrown in the pen, but who's to say what their father's done and covered up, and their mother, Zeda Earl, well bless her poor ignert heart . . ."

"Excuse me," interrupted Miss Jessie. "You were telling me about this house and its past occupants, I believe."

"Yes," said Lucille. "My point was this: Zeda Earl had no business trying to raise a family in the first place, and if you want to know something else, neither did Esther Ruth, but nothing would do Ruthie but to try again, so she got that grandbaby, Timothy John Jr., and was tickled to death to have the opportunity to start over. Comes a time in life when everybody wants to start over, so I'm told, and that's what must have been in Ruthie's mind when she got him, not even a year old at the time, and commenced raising him up like she knew what she was doing, and I'm here to tell you that she did not. Her first mistake was that she allowed him all the freedom a boy ever dreamed of getting, and what did he do but run off the first chance he got, and I say it all started when Ruthie denied her right as a grandmother and insisted the little thing call her Esther Ruth because grandmothers were too old and dried-up looking, like she thought she wasn't."

Lucille paused, grabbed a breath, and then went on.

"Now, I guess you wonder how I happen to know all this, so I'll tell you truthfully, I didn't live next door for nothing, and at that time the cane between our houses had not grown up so thick and I could still see and hear from my porch swing. Just last week in fact I had some of it cut back again so I could keep a better watch over Ruthie's dear house. It's so lonesome without her. After all these years, I mean, and then one day she's gone. Well, I just can't tell you how empty I feel not having her around. So I took it

45

upon myself to keep an eye on her place until it passed into good hands once again. That's what good friends are for, you know, and we were the best friends ever; just like you and I are going to be. Oh, it's so exciting to have you here at last. I just know you're going to love being next door. We'll enjoy each other often, too. Oh yes, I just know we will."

I know you haven't stopped talking a minute since I left, was all Timothy John could think.

Miss Jessie gave a little moan and slumped into her chair. "I trust you will forgive me for changing the subject, but I seem to have taken leave of my senses at this moment. It could only be the heat, I'm sure," she said, knowing fully well that it was not. "I feel as though a cat has just sucked the very last breath out of my body. Cats have been known to take your breath away, you know."

"Yes I know, but that's only with babies," Lucille said.

"Still, I'm afraid I must retire now for a little rest. The fatiguing train ride, you know, that, and the heat combined. And now your charming company. It's more than I can endure in a single day."

Miss Jessie stood, hoping Lucille would do the same. Reluctantly she did so.

"Right *now* I feel the necessity to lie down for a little while. I hope you don't find my behavior too forthright or in any way shapeless," came the librarian's delicate whisper.

"Oh my good heavens, no!" Lucille said. And then she thought, The nerve of the little bitch. Here I am only trying to be a good neighbor. And then she said, "I understand how awful traveling can be sometimes, so I'll just leave you to get your rest." And then she thought again, Asking me to leave this way. What absolute nerve.

Miss Jessie apologized. "Dear heart, it pains me to have to behave this way. One of these days soon we'll have to get together, and I trust you will tell me what it is you do to your hair to achieve that stunning shade of frosty blue. Why, in the direct sunlight it's nearly mauve."

"Oh, I'll be so happy to," Lucille exuberated. "It pleases me so much that you like it. Junie Woods, my beautician, has been doing it for years and I'm sure, if I mention it to her, of course, she'll be happy to give you an appointment also.

So Junie Woods is still at it, Timothy John thought.

The two ladies waved good-bye. Halfway to her yard Lucille said to herself, "Well, how sweet of her to pay me such a lovely compliment on my hair. I think it looks extra good today myself. Oh, I'm so happy to see that we're going to get along just fine."

Miss Jessie watched her go. She realized that Lucille had not said too much about Timothy John, but it really wasn't necessary; he remembered quite enough himself. He stood on the porch for a long time after she had left and recalled Esther Ruth as though she were still alive. He remembered how she had always managed to know so much about everyone else and hardly anything about herself. Even before he left home she refused to remember how she had pinned ribbons in his hair, had sewn dresses for him to play in, and had painted his fingernails bright red. She had many strange ways about her, he recalled; many likes and dislikes. Among her likes she mentioned: men with long thin noses and chin whiskers and women with bustles, even though they were, and had been since her early womanhood, out of style, and she would never again be caught wearing one. She liked silk organza and brass buttons, butterfly sleeves, scalloped necklines and anything cut on the bias. She had been born into New Orleans society, and almost all her married life she entertained thoughts of returning to it.

From her dining-room window Lucille could see Miss Jessie leaning against a column and staring off into space. "Now just what can that woman be thinking?" she wondered. I thought by the way she talked she was going straight to bed.

Miss Jessie thought nothing; she stood motionless, her hands resting on the banister, her eyes clouded and still. But Timothy John could not stop his thoughts. He felt a sense of astonishment to be thinking of Esther Ruth in so much detail; he had been in the habit of recalling her with such distance between them that she had seemed like a character in a book he had read long ago. But standing on her porch, *his* porch, he felt her presence looming over him.

He had spent many afternoons eavesdropping on Esther Ruth's party line. He recalled how often the ladies in the town had said that Ruthie's marriage had been so successful because money had married money, and it lasted over fifty years and legally terminated when Jonathan Edward died of natural causes. Esther Ruth said natural causes ". . . probably . . ." making it sound all the more murderously suspicious by spacing the word out and lifting her voice up to a crackle when she got there. She loved to do that with her voice. The hospital had not been able to determine the exact cause of death. One doctor had said that he was old enough to have died twenty years earlier, but Esther Ruth had not been satisfied with that answer and went around saying that it was the hospital that killed him, Jonathan Edward, the only husband she would ever have. Agnes Pullens had said that Ruthie and Lucille should stop trying to prove that a killing had occurred in the county hospital. "Hospitals are for making you well, not doing you in—silly things."

It was Sue Ella Lightfoot who finally had to remind her to go back and reread more carefully all the detective magazines as well as the local headlines from the past year and she would see that there were murderers to be found everywhere, in all professions and in all walks of life. "But that's not what happened to Jonathan Edward," Sue Ella had said. "Ever since the day he married Ruthie he was given an improper diet, so it was a miracle that he lived as long as he did. Esther Ruth, if you want to know the truth, starved him to death on one meal a day, that's what. She never did like cooking, and with all the money they had, it does look like they would've had sense enough to hire a housekeeper, but no, they were two of the stingiest humans who ever walked the earth. So naturally it came as a surprise to most when Ruthie went all out on his burial, funeralized herself nearly 'bout to death and everybody else right along with her."

Now just how long can she hold that pose? Lucille thought as she pressed her nose against the windowpane until her whole face flattened out like A.P.'s little Pekingese dog.

Miss Jessie was lost in Timothy John's thoughts. He was thinking of Esther Ruth and how for years after Jonathan Edward's death she declared her dislike for the hospital. She professed great disfavor for the local bank as well; carried her money on the bus to the next town is what she did, and also declared her contempt for the courthouse building as well as the wobbly bridge over Woods Creek and the diesel trucks and whoever it was that routed them down her street in the middle of the night. She hated wasps nesting in the eaves of her porch, hated crickets, hated hummingbirds swarming on her blooms. Each year they came by the hundreds and settled in her flower gardens. There was something blooming in the woman's yard the year round. But if by some chance something refused to issue forth a blossom, she had on hand a supply of artificial flowers which, after dark, she would carefully place in various flowerbeds and pretend, even to her best friends, that they had bloomed overnight. "Doesn't she think we have sense enough to know the difference?" he could hear Lucille ask and Sue Ella answer, "No! Ruthie was not blessed with common-everyday sense, which is one of the reasons why she's a more interesting person that most."

Lucille Monroe, still staring out her dining-room window, decided that Miss Jessie had been in the same pose too long and that something must be the matter with her. "She's paralyzed. I swear to God she is," Lucille said, tapping on the windowpane in hopes the racket would bring Miss Jessie back to her senses. She did not move. "What must I do for her?" she said. "Should I call the doctor or the ambulance?" Miss Jessie tilted her head slightly. "Oh my God in heaven," Lucille exclaimed. "Did she move or am I just seeing things?" She could feel the tension mounting in her shoulders and neck.

Timothy John, staring up at the mimosa still in bloom, was remembering how Esther Ruth had hated a bare yard and refused to have one. And if it wasn't a bare yard she hated, it was somebody, and if not somebody, a hummingbird. In the spring it was the hummingbirds she hated most of all; said that they made her nervous, swarming like darts going out of control. There was no dodging them. There was no escape. They drove her crazy in the spring of the year and at that time her thoughts dwelled solely on how she could set about to annihilate as many as possible. She tried setting mousetraps with flowers as bait; she tried shooting them down. She kept a pearl-handled pistol cocked and loaded. She tried keeping cats and at one time had as many as eighteen. But most people agreed that her most ingenious method was a huge sheet of plate glass propped up against a tree. They dashed themselves to death against it. It was a spectacle she enjoyed observing, but she said that that was not good enough and found that her best plan was to set out saucers of sugared water and arsenic. On a single afternoon she killed sixty-eight hummingbirds (she counted them), and all eighteen cats, who for days had been dying of thirst. She never had much respect for cats after that; said they were dumb as donkeys for not knowing better than to eat poison. She disposed of them at night by dropping their bodies into Woods Creek, and the hummingbirds, after she had plucked them clean and stored their feathers away in jars, were thrown into the street where stray dogs ate them up and died in agony. Such were her ways, Timothy John remembered. She had devious notions, yet a big heart, and was known for such things as buying up every stick of firewood from any poor soul who came knocking at the door and finally, when there was no place left to stack it all, she ended up paying to have it hauled to the city dump and burned. It never occurred to her to give it away.

He remembered her as a delicate, fine-boned woman powdered with lilac and attired in organza dresses with butterfly sleeves, always butterfly sleeves. She tinted her grey hair to a pale lavender-pink, curled it with an iron, wore tight chokers and cameos centered on her bosom. All her dresses had buttons that sparkled. All her gloves were scented. All her hats were covered with feathers from her collection. She was remembered as dainty and frail, with a face that was delicately painted. Her temperament seemed to be amicable; graceful like her attire, but that was not always gospel, for she was a woman of strong opinions when she had any at all, and once put to question could be irascible or "downright hard to get around," as Milford Monroe once put it. He also said that Jonathan Edward Coldridge finally took the good sense to die, and that he did not understand how the man had managed to live in peace with Esther Ruth all those many, many years.

Miss Jessie shifted her weight. Timothy John came out of his trance and started toward the front door. "The heat is such that it can only be cooler inside," she said.

Lucille expelled a deep breath and cried out, "She moved! She moved! I saw her for sure this time. Oh, thank God she's still alive. Had she died standing straight up what on earth would I have done?"

Esther Ruth Coldridge's white frame house of two stories stood on an overgrown lot on the main street of town, some two blocks from the businesses. Her street was also Highway 190, the truck route, although it had not always been. She had blamed the city council for allowing such a thing as that. "Diesel trucks, and at all hours. I guess they leave Zeda Earl's street alone. I guess they know better than to fool with Mrs. Zeda Earl Goodridge. This used to be the quietest street in the world, and now look!" She thought that the smoke from the diesel trucks had caused her house to look dingy grey, said that she was going to have it repainted and send the bill to the city council, and that everyone on her street should do the same. "The trucks could use the other highway and would, were it not for the fact that the Goodridge mansion is over there and they won't stand for the noise day in and day out; not the way we have it over here. It's been a judgment upon me. I tell you, a judgment has been placed upon me upon this earth. That highway, and that city council, and that R. B. Goodridge, they have all taken it upon their shoulders to be a judgment upon me upon this earth."

At Esther Ruth's funeral Sue Ella Lightfoot remarked that it was fortunate that she died when she did as things were not getting any better, and were, if anything, progressively worse.

After fifteen years, Timothy John returned. To him nothing much had changed. Lucille certainly had not. And the house, as far as he could tell from the front porch, was also the same as he remembered it. The front door was massive oak, carved with an oval window of cut-glass foliage reflecting a tintype image of Miss Jessie half in shadows and standing erect as though expecting to be welcomed, but she was not; was not even thinking. It was Timothy John who was thinking, reflecting on how it seemed to him that he had left only the day before and come back. It was as though a paralyzing spell had been cast over everything before him, as though there had been no passing of time.

In the years he had been away he had extended all the things Esther Ruth had taught him, had formed her opinions to his needs, her style to his desire. Even after her death he was ambivalent in his feelings for her, and at once both loved and hated her and could not decide which because there was too much of her inside him. She was forever present; he knew that, and could not always determine how he felt about her being there, but, depending on the climate of his mind, he had come more or less to accept that side of himself and to extend it as far as possible.

"What am I doing this for?" he asked, and Miss Jessie answered him, "Because of me you are able to be here."

"But that's not an answer," he said, entering the front hallway.

He had forgotten the redolence of the old family home, but was instantly reawakened to it. The moment he opened the front door he felt himself enveloped by the sweet fragrance of lilac hanging heavy in the hot summer air like the last breath of his grandmother lingering behind to fill the rooms with that still-warm, sickly-sweet essence he had forgotten, or possibly had never consciously noticed because of its proximity, and therefore had never realized, except on return, that it was and had been the character of the place, the whole house: oozing with sachet wrapped in white silk, tied with pink ribbons and dropped behind the curtains and inside closets, hampers, and bureau drawers, so the visitor on first arrival would be overcome with fragrance, and Esther Ruth would say (Timothy John could still hear her) that it was her flower garden coming in through the windows. "Seeping in through closed windows," Lucille Monroe had often observed, and wondered why the woman could not be truthful, for everyone knew that she had perfumed her house from roof to foundation, had perfumed it so thoroughly there could never be any hope of ridding it of the odors as the sachet had settled into the cracks, had molded behind the curtains, had become damp in the upstairs closets, and had filled the rooms with an embalming essence, which lingered on as if to preserve the house and everything in it from decay.

He wandered through the scented chambers without actually seeing but feeling as though he was walking through the past, veiled with an essence rising like a fog behind the sofas and chairs, the curtains; steaming from the rugs and staircase runners. From room to room he floated like an apparition inside Miss Jessie's clothing. She brought her lace handkerchief up to her nose when Timothy John felt faint. It was on entering the parlor that he felt his body sway. The walls there were covered with pictures of himself framed in carved wood and tarnished silver. Something inside him did not want to identify with the child framed there from infancy to six. He was pictured with long curls tumbling down his shoulders, and long slender fingers, legs and arms so perfect he could have been a doll. "He's *my* little doll, that's what he is," he could still hear Esther Ruth saying.

She had liked dolls, had collected them nearly all her life, but after her son left home to do what she called dirty work, her collection grew, not only in number, but to life-size proportions. At the time she was horrified at the thought of any child of hers leaving such a well-appointed home to go off with a band of bridge builders. Jonathan Edward came out of himself long enough to say that it was as good a living as any, and then he drifted back into his private world, his room and his books.

At that time she began collecting life-size dolls with porcelain heads, hands, and feet. They were dressed in costumes from foreign lands and occupied every room in the upstairs except Jonathan Edward's. Each doll was given a certain chair or sofa and was not to be removed by anyone other than Esther Ruth. (She did not like anyone touching her things.) The life-size dolls she thought of as permanent houseguests. She entertained them with tea and cake, gave them full names to match their distinct personalities, and sometimes carried her favorite ones on short strolls through her garden or around town. At night they were each tucked into various beds and kissed good night, and at times she even read them bedtime stories. On one night alone she read "Rapunzel" four times in four different bedrooms to four different groups of dolls all wearing nightcaps and gowns and waiting patiently for their good-night kiss. She would allow only four or five dolls to a bed, but she thought nothing of mixing the sexes, as they were mere children who knew nothing of such things as physical intimacy and would not until they were at least twenty-five years old, the proper age for those things to be discussed.

"What a little doll he is." Timothy John could still hear it being said as he left the parlor (Miss Jessie fanning her nose with lace), and sat upon the carpeted stairs. A wind from the front door, left open, whipped through the house, ruffled the curtains, stirred the smothering essence with outside air, and seemed to bring new life with it. The double parlor doors slammed shut. It was some relief to Timothy John that they were closed. As he sat there on the stairs—Miss Jessie silent, her eyes glazed, hair tumbling down her shoulders—he listened again to his grandmother's gatherings of lady friends who had used to come for tea and cake every Thursday afternoon. All her parties had been the same. All had merged into one inside his memory, even their voices had blended into one voice, the one he had always been able to hear inside himself, and finally paid it attention, and allowed it freedom. Sitting on the stairs—Miss Jessie quietly humming, her skirts pulled up, the parlor doors blown closed—he could hear them again, his grandmother and her flock of lady friends talking about him, always about him, his looks, his beauty, his sensitive gentle charm. "What a little gentleman, but more than that, what a perfect little gentleman, so perfect that he is too perfect, and what a complexion, and what fine hair, and what eyes and lashes. Why, if Timothy John had been born a girl, he'd be the prettiest one I've ever seen. Don't you all agree? The very prettiest one?" And somewhere above all the collective and blending voices came one that he could recognize unmistakenly as Esther Ruth, one like a mockingbird agreeing, "Yes, yes, he puts us all to shame. He's too pretty indeed; too pretty to be alive and too pretty, yes much too, to be a boy, much too pretty to be a boy."

Timothy John buried his face inside Miss Jessie's skirts to

shut out the multitude of shrill voices that were echoing inside his head.

After a moment, Miss Jessie rose, straightened her dress, and started up the stairs. The wall leading up was paved with photographs of Timothy John from the age of one through his high-school years. All the stages were there, all the different costumes, all the different faces, yet the same face changing yearly, becoming more and more doll-like, more like a china figurine, and progressively more delicate, even fragile. Timothy John tried not to look but could not help it. By his tenth year he could see that everything that had been said about him was beginning to plague his eyes, wrinkle his brow, droop his mouth. Everyone had noticed him, had pampered him, had made over him as if he might break, as if he could not be real, and if he were, should not be. "He ought to be a French bed doll," Esther Ruth had said. She had then taken to worrying about his state of health and his life's vocation. "He's so precious, so fragile. Who will take care of the darling little thing after I'm not here anymore?" she had worried.

But Lucille Monroe relieved her mind by saying, "With his kind of looks it won't be hard to find most any kind of guardian, young or old."

Timothy John ascended the stairs from one photograph to the next. The costumes he had been dressed in were all pictured there. Each Sunday he had been given something special to wear for going to church, usually something that had come from one of the life-size dolls living in the up-stairs rooms. He recalled how Esther Ruth would disrobe a doll, conceal its nakedness in an empty quilt box, and dress him in the removed costume, usually something from a foreign land. She would get herself done up as well and off to the First Baptist Church they would go.

For years Lucille Monroe talked about it: "Ruthie attended the Baptist church every time the doors were opened, has a certain pew way down front that was hers alone and not to be occupied by anyone else. She always arrived five minutes late just so she could parade herself in front of the whole congregation; loved showing herself off, and that grandboy too. She always had him dressed up just like a doll. No wonder he left home the first chance he got."

Esther Ruth had given the largest donation to the building fund and because of that she thought she had good right to choose and keep the pew of her choice.

Regularly, she had taken him to the House of the Lord, his golden curls flying, his big eyes brown and bashful. They would arrive, she in silk organza, he in satin, lace, or tulle as Pierette, a fairy princess, Pocahontas, or some dainty character such as Cinderella, Sleeping Beauty, or a Spanish infanta, anything that struck Esther Ruth as fanciful or cute. But during the Christmas season he had always appeared in Chinese dress honoring Lottie Moon, the American missionary who had served China the word of God, and who, each Christmas, was remembered with a special offering for the on-going of her good work.

Brother Eagleton had often remarked that attendance in his church would have dropped off long before had it not been for Esther Ruth and her grandson being so faithful and flashy in their love of the Lord.

Timothy John remembered it all and the memory of it was painful.

"He did not receive his first pair of store-bought pants, poor thing, until the day he went to school, totally unprepared for the kind of adjustments he would be called on to make that year and all the other years to come." It was told around town that the principal had personally sent Esther Ruth a copy of the codes of dress. The first month she had not allowed him to attend class due to it being against her wishes to comply with the regulations, but, on the urging of such friends as Agnes Pullens, Lucille Monroe, and Sue Ella Lightfoot, who spoke the loudest and made the first approach, Esther Ruth bought Timothy John his first boy clothes, cut his hair, and wept bitterly after doing so. "Petticoats are so much more civilized than pantaloons," she had said. "Why can't everyone else see that?"

He heard their voices coming from every corner of the house:

"You can tell that he's not too comfortable in his new clothes, but his looks have not been spoiled. Even with his short hair he's still everything he has always been: too pretty to be a boy."

Looking carefully at each photograph, he continued his climb. "All these pictures have got to go," he said. "I just can't stand looking at them." He broke away and hurried to the top of the stairs. The second floor, however, was no escape. An angel holding a trumpet and a cluster of lilies flew through a leaded glass window at the end of the hallway. The late-afternoon sun carried the angel's shadow through the hall and traced it upon an oriental runner so old there was hardly a design left but for the angel shadowed there, outlined with scarlet splotches of light "where the Lamb of God had been slain," or so said Esther Ruth. The sight of the window gave Timothy John pause. He recalled the angel doll. It had been one of his grandmother's favorites; one of Brother Eagleton's favorites as well. She had insisted on suspending the doll above his bed as a reminder that everyone had a guardian angel.

It was still hanging there.

The upstairs rooms were entered from the hall and were all joined either by French doors or arches draped with heavy curtains. The windows were also heavily draped as was the door leading out to the balcony. The stained-glass window allowed the only light into the second floor. Esther Ruth had liked it that way. "It's more peaceful to live in semidarkness," she had said. "Bright light is too harsh on the eyes, besides making everything look so cheap."

Tucked away in the dark rooms were dolls of all sizes and nationalities. They were sitting on beds, tables, and chairs. Most of them were old, mildewed, flaking about their eyes and mouths; some were bald or nearly bald; all were dusty, faded, covered with spider's webs; were all broken down, all dying from neglect, for their mistress in her last years had been unable to provide for them and had left them suddenly without remembering to dust their clothing or polish their waxy faces, without even tying their shoestrings when they had come undone. Miss Jessie thought the scene was too much like a cemetery, for in every possible sitting place there was a doll with a broken neck or arm just sitting there collecting dust and memories for one who did not care to remember such things: Timothy John Coldridge. Their eyes seemed to penetrate his thoughts as if they had known all along that he would return, as if they had expected him to come back and care for them, mend them, wash their clothing, comb their tangled hair. Esther Ruth had been so negligent in her last years. They had suffered so. Their eyes told him this. He even had the feeling that they recognized him instantly.

He wandered from one room to the next. Miss Jessie unfastened her dress along the way. In one of the middle bedrooms the Irish doll disrupted his composure. The green wool skirt with crisscross straps that she wore had been his favorite. He had insisted on wearing it everywhere: out into the yard, down the street or roller-skating through the main part of town. The wool had scratched his legs and made them sting and itch. He could remember enjoying the stinging sensation and crying on discovery that he had outgrown the skirt and could not have another. All of Splendora had seen and commented. Some had been no more than amused. Others had been horrified and let it be known. Even the Baptists had begun to think that the dressing up had gone a little too far and that it could very likely have a perverse effect on the child. But Esther Ruth had felt that there could be very little harm in allowing him to wear what he wanted.

Sue Ella Lightfoot had reminded her that boys were not girls and could not be raised the same way.

Years later she was still talking about it: "He wore that green skirt every day but Sunday, right up to the moment he went to school, and then, and only then, did Esther Ruth exert some authority and insist he take it off during school hours, but by that time it was too late, for the damage had already been done him." Sue Ella had often told Duffy Jones that she would forever consider it a terrible crime, even worse than anything she had ever read about in her detective magazines, because Esther Ruth, whether she meant any harm or not, saw to it that the boy would be sawing against the grain all his life. "It will be uphill for him all the way, Duffy, don't you see it?" she had said and Duffy had agreed: "Yessum, seen it a'comin' way long time a'fore it ever hit."

"It was cute for awhile only," Lucille Monroe had added. "But after he started getting up bigger it was no longer cute to anyone but Brother Eagleton; shows you where he keeps his mind, does it not?"

Milford had told her that in olden days men wore skirts and nothing but skirts, and Lucille reminded him that olden days were dead and gone.

"He's getting too big for the dollhouse," Sue Ella, Lucille, and even A.P. had advised Esther Ruth, and at first she had not agreed, but later, through their constant harping, she broke down and bought him his first boy clothes, or had them made by ladies who sewed only for ladies, so what he wore was usually marked with an unmistakable style: big-legged pants with wide suspenders sewn on, shirts of organza with silver buttons, mittens of the finest cashmere, and shoes that he could slip right into without the effort of lacing and tying. She spent good money for knit hats and bow ties that were more like sashes. "They came from the girls' department of Wanda's Ready-to-Wear," Lucille had said. "I know for sure because my daughter, Juliet Ann, bless her *dear* heart, saw the labels and told me so. She's gone and bought him rings and watches from there too. Also pins engraved with his initials. He's got a different book-satchel for every month of the school year, and every day comes to class smelling of lilac water. The poor little thing never uses a comb, always a brush, and she makes him carry that to school too. Now, have you ever heard of such?"

"Well, at least she's made some improvement," Sue Ella had commented, "even though she's gone too far improving it."

"Still, it's a pitiful sight," Lucille had said. Her *dear* Juliet Ann had been in his class then and had come home saying that everyone was making fun of the little Coldridge boy for coming to class in what looked like a girl's blouse and big-legged pants so much like a skirt you couldn't really tell any difference since he never took big steps like the other boys did. She had come home and said that the teachers were hardly able to correct his papers without him crying, that he did not play with the other students, and that everyone thought something was sure the matter with him because he did not.

Lucille had always had a lot to say about everyone. Timothy John could still hear her as though she were standing behind him.

"The only thing the matter with him is that Esther Ruth lets his mind run loose, pays not one ounce of attention to how he entertains himself, and if she does, she says she can't see any harm in any of it. Now don't get me wrong, I do realize that children will be children and will make up playmates when they're lonely, but that Timothy John Coldridge has gone much too far. He's invented, I want you to know, a little-girl friend to the sole exclusion of everybody else including my *dear* Juliet Ann."

"Her name was Sallee Ciffry and she took my loneliness away," he said, not in Miss Jessie's windy voice, but in his

62

own. "She was the only real friend I had, and she was not real but imagined, yet she seemed real, more so than anyone in my class. She did not play make-believe as they did. I knew exactly what she looked like. She was my size, had my hair, wore little round tortoise-shell glasses, and like myself spoke in a grown-up fashion. We both found it difficult to converse with children of any age, but had the ability to treat adults as equals.

"Sallee Ciffry dissipated my loneliness then," he said, wandering back into the hall. Miss Jessie, combing her hair along the way, made no comment. How lonely the house felt to him, just as it had years before when he had needed a friend and had created one in total sympathy to his needs. "Sallee Ciffry was the only one capable of giving me what I needed; she understood me totally," he said, gazing into the blue mirror at one end of the hallway and seeing Miss Jessie Gatewood listening attentively, returning his intense stare. He saw her differently there than she had appeared only minutes before reflected in the front door. Her hair was down; she was softer. Her dress was unbuttoned; she was more seductive. "Sallee Ciffry swept my loneliness away. She went with me everywhere and was always given lengthy introductions to everyone we met. Milford Monroe enjoyed her most of all. I would usually begin our conversations by saying, 'Mr. Monroe, Mr. Monroe, I would like for you and my dearest chum, Sallee Ciffry, to become acquainted. Don't you think her dress is pretty today?' Then Milford would repeat his usual rejoinder, 'Well, how do you do, Miss Ciffry? May I take my hat off to you this fine morning?' At that, he would bow low and I would remind him that he was wearing no hat and that it was not morning but afternoon and that Sallee Ciffry was standing behind him, not in front of him like he thought. 'Oh no!' he would say, turning around fast and repeating his polite 'How do you do?' in the opposite direction, adding to it something about her pretty dress. Usually he would ask its color, to which I often replied, 'Oh, Mr. Monroe, Sallee's dress is mauve; surely you are well acquainted with that splendid color, are you not?' Then I would skip off and look for someone else to introduce her to, but no one ever enjoyed her quite so much as Milford. Often he was introduced to her several times a day, and whether he wanted it or not, at least he pretended that he did."

"And what was Sallee Ciffry's appearance?" Miss Jessie asked. "Dear heart, do give me that part again, as I think I adore the little thing, so petite, so precocious, and her little round glasses are simply darling. Now, did you say that her hair was the same shade as mine, or by some remote chance am I imagining things? Oh, how I do appreciate the way she spoke up to the adults. As a child that was my nature, too. Now, am I right in thinking that Sallee Ciffry and I have a great deal in common? Correct me if I'm wrong, and should you do so, then I will stand corrected." She spoke in a faint whisper and in the blue mirror she watched herself braiding her hair into one long plait over her shoulder.

Timothy John answered that she was not wrong. "I created her in my own image and always described her as looking exactly like me. Sometimes we even wore the same clothes. Lucille Monroe thought that was the most absurd thing ever. She often made the comment that it was just a pity that I needed to invent a playmate when the whole town was full of children just crying for a friend. But none were as clever as Sallee Ciffry, I told her, and therefore would not be suitable friends. 'Not even my Juliet Ann is good enough for you, I guess,' she said, and I replied politely that her Juliet Ann giggled too much just like her mother."

"How mischievous you were, and what a caustic little tongue," Miss Jessie said, tying off the end of her braid and then pinning it down from ear to ear and back again.

"There was little else to occupy me," he said, still gazing hypnotically into Miss Jessie's eyes. "I had already read everything in the house and there was nothing left for me to do except play with Sallee Ciffry or listen to Esther Ruth and her gaggle of lady friends."

"The prevailing atmosphere of femininity in your young life seems to have produced a retrograde effect upon your emotional growth," Miss Jessie diagnosed. "Whereas mentally you seem to have been highly capable, emotionally I would say you were enormously retarded."

"That's because I only had Esther Ruth to talk to for the longest time," Timothy John said. "And although she wasn't exactly what you call an ideal companion, she could be wonderfully entertaining. She would tell lengthy accounts of the odd members of her side of the family, 'the fungus on the family tree,' she called them, and would regale me for hours with stories of her Uncle Raymond alone. All her kin had slipped through her fingers, she said; had no idea where any of them were and could not care less, as she thought them either too old or too eccentric to behave in a civilized manner.

"Her father's brother, my Great-Uncle Raymond, had once lived on the 'Dark Continent,' as she told it, and when he returned to New Orleans he still insisted on living by Johannesburg time, which necessitated his arising at ten in the evening and going to bed shortly after noon the following day. She said that the servants did not like him at all, as you may very well imagine, and were relieved when the idiotic schedule killed him; so were most of his kin, Esther Ruth included. 'Somehow it was much easier to explain Uncle Raymond after he was dead and gone,' she always said."

Timothy John could hear Esther Ruth speaking inside him. Miss Jessie could hear her too:

"Raymond was forever appearing suddenly in his pajamas during luncheon, tea, or garden parties, and it got to be the sport for some of our neighbors to sit up past midnight just to see him dressed in his business suit and strolling down St. Charles Avenue. Always, but always, he carried an umbrella because he was certain that the street lamps emitted vulgar light rays that were most unhealthy for a gentleman of his age. He was no more than forty-seven or eight then, and died on his fiftieth birthday just like he said he would. Oh, Raymond was dear after you got accustomed to him, but he was becoming much too much the talk at your better dinner parties and teas, so when he died I could not help saying, 'Thank the Lord for it, the Garden District just could not absorb another fool, especially from our family.' Death was absolutely the only conventional thing the man ever attempted, and, because it was impossible for him to have a say in the matter, his funeral was most dignified and quietly celebrated at home with only the family in attendance. We thought it best not to announce his quietus until three days after his burial, but somehow word of his death got out and the whole city of New Orleans, it seemed, lined up for ten blocks outside our house; everybody said they'd die if they didn't get one last look at him. Well, there was nothing to do, you see, but to send one of the servants out to tell everyone to go home because we had already planned a closed-coffin service and were not about to change our minds. And to this day I still thank God we didn't decide to open up his casket and let them all come in, because we'd still be sitting there and they'd still be lining up outside. Of course we used St. Louis Cemetery #1 in those days and I suppose it's still being filled up with those of us who are left."

For a moment Esther Ruth left him. Miss Jessie urged him to go on. "Oh, do continue," she said. "And, pray, why have you not told me these stories before?"

Timothy John lapsed back into his natural voice. "Uncle Raymond had three brothers, one of whom was Esther Ruth's father; and, of the three, only her father attended Raymond's funeral. The other two had run off years before, one to scale the world's tallest mountain and the other to live on the Great American Desert, and both probably never lived to see their dreams accomplished. Esther Ruth could not even remember their names, but, of the four brothers, she was certain that her father had been the most level-headed up until the last sixteen years of his life when he went to live in the attic and even took his meals up there until his wife died, and then he came out and stayed out until he followed her to the grave five years later."

"And that darling Esther Ruth with her lavender waves and butterfly sleeves, where, might I ask, was she during this season of mortification?" She slipped out of her dress. She was wearing her favorite slip, the straps of which were so narrow they could scarcely be seen.

"Esther Ruth had already married and come here to live with my grandfather, who was also from New Orleans, but had once passed through Splendora and thought it pretty as a picture and could not resist moving here. For years they kept up their city connections and even considered moving back, but neither wished to be surrounded by what was left of their families."

"And the Coldridge side. What were they like, pray tell?" Miss Jessie said, taking off her shoes and stockings but still managing to keep her face visible in the mirror while doing so.

" 'They weren't much good anymore,' Esther Ruth said, but just what was wrong with them I have never known. And because Grandfather Coldridge died when I was in the first grade I have very little memory of him except that he was tall and emaciated, had hair as black as jet, skin the color and texture of a brown paper bag, all crumpled up, and eyes that were green as glass."

"Should I see him floating around the premises, I will no doubt recognize him by that engaging description," Miss Jessie replied.

She moved away from the mirror and into another room also populated with dolls. "Do you mind if I lie down for a moment on this lovely old bed? I do adore canopies." He did not answer. She chose to lie in the center of the bed between two dolls, a geisha and a cowgirl. After she had positioned herself comfortably with pillows beneath her head, she continued her train of thought. "And your grandmother, dear heart, how it must have troubled her that neither you nor your father imbibed her values or her attitudes. So, rather than having more children, which, of course, was probably impossible by then, she seems to have adopted the next best method: the acquisiton of lifelike dolls, the lives of which she could not destroy. They were dependent solely upon her, were not as troublesome as children, and could not lash out against her, so I'm sure her preference for them was immense. The whole troop as you have portrayed them is a most disconcerting lot, if you desire my unbiased opinion." She crossed her legs at the ankles in what Timothy John thought was a most ladylike manner, and then continued. "Now, it seems to me from this vantage point that Sallee Ciffry gave occurrence to the only degree of intelligence around you. She was the most plausible one of all, and you were right to befriend her, as there was madness encompassing you at every turn, and your grandmother's friends were no better, just more of the same. Heaven forbid that I should have to acquaint myself with any more of them. Lucille is quite enough for one lifetime."

"Lucille is *more* than enough for one lifetime," Timothy John said, and lapsed into a long silence inside which he found himself sitting on the parlor floor playing with his dolls as he had so often done, while above him Esther Ruth engaged herself in entertaining her Thursday-afternoon friends. He remembered that the topic of conversation would always drift back to him, and Esther Ruth would say, "Now, close your ears, Timmie dear, because we're discussing your welfare."

"The other ladies would usually be scolding her for not buying me boy-things to play with, for not trimming my hair, and for dressing me in petticoats. And Esther Ruth would always defend herself by saying, 'Timothy John likes his toys and the way I dress him, too.' Then, after all the ladies had spoken their warning, someone, usually Lucille, would slowly work the conversation around to the facts of life, and each in her own way would ask Esther Ruth whether or not she had talked to me about the birds and the bees, and each time she would answer them the same way. 'No, and will you stop asking me that ridiculous question, please, as I have already informed you of my views, and they do not change from week to week. Now, I'll say it only once more. When the time comes he'll know precisely what to do. Won't you, Timmie honey? For it's no different than birds flying south in the winter. Even if they've never flown south before they still know which way it is and what it's going to be like when they get there.'

" 'Well, just you mark my word, Ruthie, you're going to have some trouble on your hands unless you explain a few things to him,' Lucille had warned and Ruthie had once, and only once, admitted that she did not think she could explain the mysteries of life herself, but maybe her butcher could. She had suggested him because she liked his manners. He had been the first person to pop into her thoughts. The suggestion, however, planted itself in my mind that all butchers were sexual maniacs."

"I would not be surprised to find out that some of them are," said Miss Jessie, getting up and going toward the window. The sun was setting, and the whole town looked as though it had come off a picture calendar.

"I never felt comfortable here," Timothy John said, looking out over the town. "At school they made fun of the way I spoke and dressed. They said that my voice was soft like a girl's and that my pants looked like skirts, my shirts looked like blouses, and that my ties were not ties but ladies' scarves. As I remember, they were right, too. Naturally I stayed as far away from them as possible. So, to compensate, I became a good student, excelled in everything except physical education. The coaches acted like we were supposed to know the game rules before we got there and, of course, I didn't know anything and no one was about to teach me. I couldn't pitch, catch, bat, tackle, or dribble and didn't show promise of learning. I was regarded by students and teachers alike as highly abnormal, so, to keep myself out of everybody's way, I feigned illness. Finally, I really was sick—asthma, general malaise, coughing fits—so, during the P.E. hour I was sent to the piano teacher, Pristine Barlow. She said I had a natural ear and a good sense of rhythm, which everyone in my class interpreted to mean that I was crazier than they thought.

"I was much the topic of conversation then. And because of the party lines I often heard more than I should. Esther Ruth had arranged to have all her friends put on the same line so they could pick up simultaneously at four o'clock each afternoon and would not even have to dial a number. Every day they would all be on the same line, all trying to talk at once, until there were many different discussions cross-firing. Esther Ruth claimed that she was able to listen to all the discussions and keep hers going as well. She often would hang up and leave the others connected. Once I listened in after she had hung up and heard Sue Ella Lightfoot say that she had studied it a long time and that she was convinced that something went wrong somewhere, and it all had to do with Esther Ruth—'There's something about the boy that's both boy and girl,' she said. 'And both parts show up, sometimes at once, sometimes separate. It's like he has no control over what he's doing, like he almost has no mind to go on, or has two to go on, so maybe that's his problem, he's got two to go on and not just one like the rest of us seem to have.'—Then A.P. asked distressfully, 'Could it be?' and Sue Ella answered, 'Well, what else, then? The boy just loves that green skirt, simply will not take it off, screams when he has to, yet he is a boy, physically, I mean, but only realizes it part-time.'—No one will ever know how clearly I can still hear them," Timothy John said. "Their voices are forever coming through keyholes, under parlor doors, and over party lines."

The green skirt, the lilac hanging heavy, the dark drapes closed, the angel flying low through the center hallway, and all the broken-down dolls: it was almost more than he could endure. He could not help remembering how he had been as a child, how he had gotten his way almost always, how he had worn the green skirt and nothing but, its straps criss-crossing his bare shoulders, and had paraded skipping or skating around the town. Roller-skating down the hill had been his favorite pasttime. He had learned to gather so much speed going down until he appeared to be nothing more than a flash of blond curls and something green that did not stop until it was past the depot, the sawmill, and was almost out to the Splendora city limits.

But he did not enjoy dwelling on such memories. It was evening. The house was growing darker, and he felt uneasy in the dim light. Going from room to room he turned on every lamp on the second floor. While doing so he noticed that all the beds had been slept in. He had almost forgotten that Esther Ruth had kept all the rooms for herself and the dolls, had slept in every one of them, and often had wandered circuitously from one bed to the next several times during a sleepless night. Many nights he remembered having been awakened by her, by sound or by sight, dressed in one of her long white gowns, a ruffled sleeping cap, and satin slippers.

"On such ramblings through the dark house she always carried a flashlight that was not turned on. She would step lightly, but would be given away each time, for there were many weak boards in the old house, many rattles about the windowpanes when one came too near; many rusting hinges and creaking bedsprings, falling slats, and always a table or chair to bump into, for she had been one for moving things around and leaving, as if on purpose, an obstacle in her path; something that would come crashing down during the night and give her away as if she had desired for someone to come take her by the hand and lead her someplace where her mind would give her rest. The nights had all been long, their approach slow and painful. Often she stumbled into my room and related her dreams to me, not knowing she was doing so. Recurrently she dreamed of Jonathan Edward and how pitiful she thought he had looked in his coffin, even though she had hired the best undertaker in the region to color his face. And if it was not Jonathan Edward and his expensive funeral that plagued her sleep, it was my father who shot himself over love. Over and over they would come to her and send her fleeing from one bed to the next.

"Holding her unlit flashlight before her she often stumbled through the house and into my bed to continue her dreams. She would embrace me in her half-slumber and call me by my father's name, or her husband's name, or by the name of a dead poet I can't remember. So many times she held me tightly and told me how she had failed them all and was being tormented for it in her dreams. She had often said that hers had been a marriage without union, that there had never been any kind of love involved, that only their combined capital had constituted the marriage, that it had been arranged in New Orleans, had been drawn up by fashionable lawyers and both their fashionable families.

"I can still hear her ranting: 'It was a horrible day. The sun threatened not to shine upon us and when it did it came out so strong that every flower in the yard, every rose on the arbor, every daffodil, even the tropical plants that thrived on heat, wilted in the garden where the ceremony was pronounced blunderingly by the preacher who seemed to have lost his senses. It was a ceremony unbelievable, unwanted, unblessed by heaven, blessed only by the fashionable families, the fashionable lawyers, and the society page of the *Times Picayune.*'"

He could almost see her dragging a bedsheet from one room to the next, for she was still lingering behind like one of her nightgowns hanging on a bedpost, like the vapors in an old medicine bottle, like dust on a marbletop, lingering like the scent of rosebuds and lilac preserved in mason jars and transferred to her best satin-glass vases. He could almost hear her speaking in a solemn and pious tone as if giving her testimony in church.

"I don't know how many times she told me the details of her wedding day. She said that the union was not smiled upon by heaven or by earth. She wore her wedding slippers on the wrong feet; the hired soprano forgot the words; the preacher stumbled through the prayers; the best man dropped her ring in the grass; the flowers wilted along the arbor; and a long black snake crawled through their exotic garden and crawled between them, husband and wife soon-to-be. She said that for seven days thereafter the sun was not seen, that the grass turned brown in the garden where she stood, and that her hair suddenly began to thin. She told me all these things during the long nights when her somnambulistic journeys and soliloquies kept me awake until dawn. The nights had been long for us both; the dawns too slow in arriving."

He came out of his reverie staring at the closet where her nightgowns were hanging. She had owned the prettiest gowns ever. Miss Jessie liked them all. She chose a long one with full sleeves. Difficult to sleep in, Timothy John thought, but wonderful to wear around the house. She put it on, went into the hall, threw open the doors to the balcony, and went out. The evening air was warm and fragrant. A moonbeam vine, flowering, grew up the columns, circled the banister, and nearly covered an outdoor lounge. She reclined upon it as though it were a funeral bier, folded her arms over her breast, and slept. All the world, it seemed, was balmy with an earthy humidity; somewhere down the street grass had been cut that day; honeysuckle drifted in from nowhere; the moon came up; the white flowers opened; candle moths fluttered around the streetlights, and off in some remote corner of town a whippoorwill could be heard begging the world to be still.

7
～

To Sue Ella Lightfoot's way of thinking, the Sheriff's Department was not worth a dime; neither were the Fire Department, the Chamber of Commerce, the churches, the bank, the school system, the hospital, the Department of Public Safety, and the Justice of the Peace; even the postal service was not what it had been. The Ladies' Study Group was the most boring thing she had ever slept through, the Garden Club was for frustrated old ladies, something she would never become, and the motion picture house only opened twice a week, Friday and Saturday. In short, to Sue Ella Lightfoot, all of Splendora was either already there, or on its way to the dogs. She wondered why it was that she was the only one who had figured it out that everything was either crooked or falling apart, for it did not take much sense to realize it.

The day after Miss Jessie arrived the Sheriff's Department was still closed and Milford told her that the doors had been padlocked for two days running.

"That's law and order for you," Sue Ella said. "That's what we're paying for, mind you. That's how it's gotten to be around here, I want you to know it, and if you don't a'ready, I don't know how come."

She wanted to report the flats on general principle only. She had already discovered who was responsible. She had figured it out only the day before when she returned home and found that her tires had been taken off and patched up. "Snyder did it," she said. "His mind got to troubling him over it and so he thought he'd make amends by rectifying his crime, but he can't fool me. I can tell his work over anybody elses's. Sloppy! I see he dug holes under the tires so he wouldn't have to jack the car up very far to remove the wheels. What a way of doing things. Didn't even fill in the holes before letting the car down again. Was trying to get back at me for something is what he was doing."

Again she had been right. Snyder had gotten fed up with her once more. This time it was because she had had all her teeth pulled out and he could not understand a word coming from her vacant, cavelike mouth. He was tired of eating soft food, and hearing her say that if he would only get his teeth pulled out too, then they could both eat soft food together, and that if he didn't want to do that he could just get up and fix whatever it was he could eat, for she certainly was not about to, was tired of cooking what he wanted and only what he wanted, and decided to please herself for once. So for revenge he had gone out and put ice picks through her tires, deliberately, to make her walk, and later in the day began to think how he might feel if on the way to work she suddenly took a sunstroke and died. He believed it was silly of him to think that way, but he could not help it. It was just his way. He was always considering how he might feel if something bad happened instead of something good.

Sue Ella was pleased to have wheels again. The moment she arrived at the depot she heard the telephone ringing. "God in heaven!" she said. "Give me time to turn the motor off." She got out with her arms loaded with maga-

zines and made it to the phone just as A.P. was about to
hang up. She called to say that they were planning to visit
the new librarian that morning and thought Sue Ella would
like to go too. "Can't go driving up and down that hill all
day long for everybody," Sue Ella said. "I got other things
on my mind. Am dee-termined to get through to the sheriff
if it's the last thing I do. Take Leggett in my place. He
needs to step outside that church ever' once in awhile and
ought to enjoy that bookwoman a lot. I was picturing them
in my mind all night long."

Esther Ruth's house had not seen visitors since the day
she died in the dead of winter among the shrubberies in her
backyard. She had been determined to make them bloom
that past winter even if it was against their nature. So
shortly after dark she stalked out wearing only her nightclothes, and was in the process of attaching paper blossoms
to the lilac bushes when death caught her in the act. Since
then the house had gone empty and was the loneliest thing
in the world to look at, Lucille Monroe thought.

"Presumably the property has been purchased by the new
Miss Gatewood," Zeda Earl said when she arrived with
A.P. and Lucille at the Coldridge house. They had gotten
themselves all dressed up to pay their first call on the librarian who had just been hired. Zeda Earl was president of
the Ladies' Study Group that year and already had it in her
mind to persuade Miss Jessie to give a talk in the not-too-
distant future.

The three ladies, out to impress in their Sunday dresses
and summer hats, each took turns with the knocker, but no
one came to the door. On the balcony just above them,
Timothy John was waking up to their voices. It sounded
like one of Esther Ruth's Thursday gatherings. "Don't they
know to allow a woman her rest?" Miss Jessie whispered,
rolling over on the lounge. They knocked and knocked and
then came a long pause, and then they knocked some more.

Surely they'll go away soon, Timothy John thought. His face had not yet been shaven; his clothes had not yet been pressed. Miss Jessie's hair had not been done; her face had not been applied; her fingernails needed touching up, and her traveling bags were still sitting in the front hall. She could not have gone to the door even if she had wanted to. Again she rolled over on the lounge and again came a loud knocking, and then A.P.'s voice carried up the moonvines to Timothy John's ear: "Well, I guess she's still sleeping, don't you?"

Of course she's still sleeping, Timothy John thought, and if you had any idea what you looked like, you'd be home sleeping too. When they finally went away, he hurried to get ready for their return. They had only stepped next door to Lucille's house. "Probably to stare out the windows until they see the first sign of life over here," came Miss Jessie's hoarse whisper. It took her awhile to find her voice each morning. "They won't be long returning, I'm sure. Women like that never are," she said, pitching her voice where it ought to be.

When to expect someone to come calling and when not to—it could be a problem, Timothy John thought. He would have to be ready at any given moment to receive unexpectedly. He could never let his hair down for very long. Miss Jessie must be ready at all times.

An hour later when the three callers returned Miss Jessie was dressed for receiving. She had also found time to make additional preparations. The parlor furniture was dust-free, the pictures on the walls removed, an anthology of Victorian verse was left open on the table, and fresh flowers, larkspurs and bachelor buttons, had been picked from the backyard and arranged in all the vases. Miss Jessie Gatewood—dressed in dotted swiss of a pale lavender with long raglan sleeves and white lace ruffles running around the shoulder seams, collar, and cuffs—answered the door with a dustcloth in her hand. Her hemline was again longer than was the style in Splendora that year and her shoes were the same white lace-ups from the day before.

That's the oddest-looking dress I've ever seen, thought Lucille Monroe. Now who would ever have thought of putting dotted swiss and raglan sleeves together? Why, the fabric is much too sheer to be patterned that way, if you're asking me, and those ruffles running from under her arms to up around her neck are simply out of place, and that's all there is to it.

"Oh, what a lovely dress," Zeda Earl said after introducing herself as the banker's wife.

"Yes, I was just thinking the same thing," Lucille Monroe added sweetly, while A.P. tried to notice what, if anything, had been changed in the part of Ruthie's house she could see.

Miss Jessie whispered the ladies into the parlor. "Dear hearts, please enter."

Zeda Earl, trailing a long scarf behind her, swooped into the room like a bird of prey, posed against the baby grand piano, and announced her intentions: "We are members of the Ladies' Study Group and we meet once a month for the most interesting little socials you've ever seen. You must understand that we are a dignified group, and that, of course, limits our enrollment to only a handful. We accept only the best there is and we never pressure anyone to do anything except give a program every now and then. As this year's program chairman, I am pleased to invite Miss Jessie to give us a little talk in the near future. It could be a talk on just anything at all really, but if I may make a few suggestions, I do think it would be most appropriate if you could speak to us on a book you once read, an idea you once heard, or maybe even thought of yourself, or even on the significance of a single word, just any word at all, as long as it is an English word, of course, and preferably something that derives from American soil."

"I will be so happy to prepare a little sermonette on the importance of the glottal stop," whispered Miss Jessie.

"Oh, wouldn't that be attractive," said Zeda Earl. "I don't think anyone has ever spoken to us on that subject."

Seeing that no one was going to introduce her, A.P. decided to do it herself. She gave a little curtsy and then said, "Hello, my name is A.P., and that stands for Agnes Pullens, and I teach Expression right here in Splendora."

"Yes, and I'm sure you're very good at it, too," Miss Jessie said. "Won't you please be seated?"

As they sat, Miss Jessie apologized for the disarray, the dust, and the poor lighting. "I was just doing some cleaning and straightening," she said. "In fact, when you arrived I had just finished running a damp mop upstairs." A.P. wondered if she always dressed so fine to do her housework. Zeda Earl suggested that she get herself a cleaning woman. And Lucille promised to send hers over the next day. Miss Jessie completed the round of conversation, declined the offer. She explained that she had just purchased the house at a most reasonable price from a young man who said he was leaving the country and seemed anxious to be going. "I believe it was his grandmother's property and he came into it after her death; is that not right? Do correct me if I have it wrong. I know you will," she said, looking first at Lucille Monroe and then at Zeda Earl Goodridge, and before they had time to answer she said that the young man was most singular in appearance and gracious in speech, and that she could not imagine why such a gentleman had not wished to keep the lovely old house.

"Well, if you'd known him, you'd understand," A.P. said. "He once went into my backyard and let loose on all of Splendora two dozen layers, plus a pen of rabbits I was fattening for stew. We never did find them all, either. Niggers made off with them I 'magine. Well, he was nearly 'bout crazy is what I'm trying to tell you. And if S'wella had come along and not gone to work today, she'd have told you so plainer than I can. S'wella, she can nearly 'bout always make sense out of anything, especially something you wouldn't naturally think had much sense to it."

"My, isn't that a good thing to know," Miss Jessie replied.

Zeda Earl said that she had been convinced for years that Timothy John was dead, and Lucille said that she did not understand how he could have stayed alive all this time because there was something unhealthy about him.

"He wasn't a bit o' good, and that's all there is to it," A.P. said, digging in her purse for a Cloret.

"Surely he had some good inside him somewhere," said Miss Jessie softly. "It's troubling to think that he did not."

Lucille Monroe wrinkled up her forehead and straightened out her spine again. She said that there was some truth to the statement but that the child was doomed from the very first day he arrived to live with their recently departed good friend, Esther Ruth. "Ruthie was a good woman, as all the rest of us are, but she surely did have her faults, and plenty of them, too," Lucille said, letting her forehead relax so all her wrinkles fell down around her eyelids.

"And may I be so forward as to ask what some of them were, her faults, I mean?" Miss Jessie said without having to feign interest.

The three ladies of Splendora exploded all at once. A.P. said that Ruthie had been mean and stingy and had acted hateful toward her more times than she could count. Lucille said that she had been the kind of woman who had to have her way all the time regardless of what was right, and Zeda Earl said that Esther Ruth had been jealous of everyone in town, including her housekeeper, but they all agreed that they were lost without her, missed her terribly, and still counted her as their dearest friend even though she had been dead for six months. A.P. said, "I still find myself talking to her all the time." And Lucille and Zeda Earl agreed that they had never had a friend quite like her and felt fortunate to have spent so many lovely years together.

Zeda Earl told Miss Jessie that Ruthie had been the founder of the annual Crepe Myrtle Pageant and Parade held out of doors the third Saturday in May and that she was happy to serve as program chairman for the next year. Hearing that reminded A.P. she was scared to death that Zeda Earl was not going to ask her dancing girls to perform again. The Miss Agnes School of Dance and Expression had been represented in the pageant for over ten years and A.P. thought it would be a shame to break the record.

Miss Jessie said that she understood that Esther Ruth had been one for fighting for the preservation of historical landmarks, and that she had always wanted to restore the courthouse to it's original splendor, and Zeda Earl asked, "Now, just who gave you that piece of information?" and Timothy John, trying to cover Miss Jessie's blunder, replied in a delicate tone, "The name escapes me."

"Sometimes you sound just like Esther Ruth," A.P. said. Miss Jessie ignored the comment.

"Oh yes, there were plenty of good things about her, even though some believed she nagged her husband to death," Lucille continued. "Milford swears it's the truth, but I believe there was a little more to it than that. Lots of us believe there was more," she said, lifting her eyebrows high enough for everyone to see that her eyelids had been carefully colored a bright green, calling attention to the bluing on her hair as well as the fact that she had no eyelashes, to speak of.

"Ruthie was as good as gold, when you come to think about her," A.P. said. "She took such pride in her home furnishings and decorations, inside and out; always had the prettiest Christmas lights of anybody in town and took the first prize for them nearly 'bout every year, until she was asked to judge, and even then she was going to give herself the prize until somebody stopped her. She said that nobody matched up to her tinsel angels with lavender hair and blinking eyes. Finally she was forced to give the honor to another yard. I forget whose it was that year—Dorine Shinn's, probably."

"I beg to differ with you," said Zeda Earl. "It was Laura Lou Handcock who won that year. Remember? She decorated her big cedar tree with blue Milk of Magnesia bottles."

"If my mind hasn't failed me completely, you're exactly correct," Lucille said. "But, of course, last year Ruthie's yard won again and then—before you knew it, she wasn't here any more."

"Thank God she won the yard prize her last year of life," Zeda Earl said prayerfully. And then she thought, Well, she surely will not be winning the prize this year and not just because she's dead, either. This year it's my turn. She had already visualized her own prizewinning yard display and it was only the last of July.

"What's the best book in the whole world?" A.P. asked.

When Miss Jessie answered, "None of them," A.P. asked what on earth she had gone to library school for. Miss Jessie tried to explain that the question was relative and could not be answered except from a specific viewpoint, but A.P. disagreed by declaring that all questions could too be answered, because her third-grade teacher had told her so and she thought it was the most important thing that she had ever learned.

"Well, what do you consider the best book in the world, then?" asked Miss Jessie.

A.P. thought for a moment and said, "All are good, but some are better." Then, on second thought, she said that she guessed that it would be *The Secret of the Apple Orchard*, because she had read it over five times in the last two years.

"Oh yes, I'm inclined to agree wholeheartedly with that choice even though some consider *The Wedding of Sarah Wiggins* to be a far more important novel," Miss Jessie said, making direct eye contact with each lady as though she were instructing a class on the fine points of literature. A.P. wanted to know if Wiggins was the woman's name before or after she was married, because she once knew a Wiggins girl after she was married, but did not know her very well and had no idea who she had been before she took her husband's name. "It might could be the same one I was thinking," she said.

"Hardly," Miss Jessie answered, "because novels are works of fiction and works of fiction are never true; they only seem like they are." Then she explained: "To fictionalize: to make into, treat in the manner of, or regard as fictitious.—You see? Oh yes, I know you do, and besides that, the character's maiden name had been Wiggins, and after she married she became a Simpleton."

With a sharp edge on her voice Lucille said that she once had known a set of Simpletons in Splendora, and Zeda Earl, looking straight at her, said that she had known many but did not like to call names.

The two ladies glared at each other. A.P., wishing for an opportunity to rummage through Esther Ruth's house, changed the subject. She said that Miss Jessie must have found lots of interesting things upstairs. Miss Jessie said that she had been told before buying the house that it was full of odd pieces, so she came early to sort it all out and rid herself of what she did not need. "Now, if you will be so kind as to recommend some good strong young men, I will have them take what I do not intend to live with into the yard the next pretty day and will sell it all at accommodating prices." Lucille quickly scanned the room. Her eyes fell upon a lamp with a bristol-glass base. She coveted it immediately, said so, said she would be so happy to take it off Miss Jessie's hands, relieve her of it, so to speak, but Miss Jessie said that it was one of the few pieces that was worth keeping.

"Well, we'll just have to come back on the day of the sale

and see what you have for us," Zeda Earl said with her eyes on a blue mirror and a smile as thin as a clothesline stretched out from ear to ear.

A.P. said that she was burning up and ready to go. Lucille thought, If you'd only lose some of that weight, you wouldn't have that problem.

Miss Jessie stood up, hoping her guests would do the same. They did. Timothy John felt a sigh of relief as Miss Jessie saw them to the door. As they made their way off the porch she said, "Dear hearts, your lively interplay of thoughts has been most rewarding. Do come again. My house is always open to ladies of fashion. We are the condiments of life, you surely must realize."

What a way she has with words, Lucille thought. How fortunate I am to have her living just next door.

As soon as they left, Miss Jessie glided into the kitchen and came out with a cold glass of mint tea. Then she went upstairs and out onto the balcony to relax again.

From her upstairs bedroom Lucille Monroe looked out and saw her there sipping her drink. "Now why didn't she offer us some of that?" she said, closing her venetian blinds as hard as she could.

What on earth am I doing back here? Timothy John could not help thinking as Miss Jessie curled up like a calico cat on the outdoor lounge. Is it really necessary to return to the hurt and start all over again?

While Sue Ella was pouring over her new batch of *Police Gazettes*, A.P. telephoned to say that they had just come back from visiting Miss Jessie. Sue Ella said that she wanted to hear all about it, but first things first. "How did Leggett like her?" A.P. said that he refused to go along because he didn't much like the idea of anyone else living in Esther Ruth's house. "They got to be awfully close right there at the last, you know." Sue Ella said that she knew that, but even still, she thought A.P. should have used a little force, to which A.P. replied, "I have never forced a preacher to do anything in my life."

After they hung up Sue Ella said to Duffy, "I can see that this is going to be just like everything else around here. If I want to get those two together, I've got to do it myself, because nobody else is going to lift a finger."

8

Miss Jessie Gatewood stood on her porch and shaded her eyes with a Vacation Bible School fan made out of a paper plate and a popsicle stick. A small child had given it to her in church the Sunday before. The plate had been painted to look like a sun in the middle of which had been written in blue crayola: *Jesus Wants Me for a Sunbeam*. Miss Jessie fanned herself often and made a point of being seen doing so. She said that the fan was the loveliest present she had ever received.

"Let me fan your neck a minute before you do any more heavy lifting," she said to Snyder Lightfoot. It was the day of her yard sale and everything she did not care to keep was being carried into the yard by Snyder and two of the high-school boys who had been working for him all summer.

"You will never know how much I appreciate all your help," she said, fanning into his collar. "Dear God, I do hope this yard sale is successful," she added, as if destitute for money. "If I don't sell everything, I don't know what I'll do. There simply isn't room for it in the house."

An assortment of dinette tables and chairs were scattered

all over the front lawn. There were boxes and boxes of fruit jars, flashlights and radios that did not work, dozens of mixing bowls in all colors, cups and saucers from Oatmeal boxes, casserole dishes, gooseneck lamps and miniature spoons from every state in the union accompanied by ashtrays from their capital cities. There were nine plastic wastepaper baskets, one with an oil painting of flamingos that had been badly smeared, and twelve T.V.-dinner trays with foldup legs that would surely be purchased the first thing, Timothy John thought.

One table was covered with salt and pepper shakers shaped like dogs, cats, and birds painted bright colors; another was stacked edge-to-edge with ordinary clear-glass vases made to look prettier with felt flowers and animals glued on and outlined with black paint. There were dozens of praying hands of all sizes and colors, and several ceramic Bibles with half the Lord's Prayer printed in gold.

What Esther Ruth had in mind when she decided to keep all these hideous dust-catchers, I'll never know, thought Timothy John. She certainly had an eye for good furniture and glassware, and yet she saved every jam and jelly glass she could find and accepted every stick of furniture anybody would give her.

"I just don't see how the three of you managed to carry everything and not give out completely," Miss Jessie whispered when the last table was removed from the house and a mangy moosehead with antlers on only one side was placed on top of it. The yard looks like a junk shop turned inside out, Timothy John thought, opening a box to find it filled with Scotch-tape dispensers while the one next to it was stuffed with tangled-up twine. I suppose she had a purpose for all this, he thought. Knowing her, she would.

Miss Jessie poured lemonade for Snyder and his helpers: Jo-Jo Wiggley, Bubba Wiggley's boy, a quarterback, and Sonny Week's son, J.W., a lineman who wanted to be a cheerleader, but no one would let him. His father said it would not look right.

"I'm real glad I got to help you out," Snyder said, drinking the lemonade. "The boys are real glad, too, even if they don't look like it. All they got their minds on this time of year is kicking that football. Ought'a get S'wella out there to show them how to do it, is what they ought to do."

Timothy John was studying Snyder's face carefully. I can't decide what it is, he thought, but it seems to me Snyder has grown to look more like Sue Ella or Sue Ella has grown to look more like Snyder.

They had the same height, weight, and complexion. Their faces were aging with the same pattern of wrinkles, too, concentric circles, like ripples in a pool of water. Snyder, however, still had his teeth and planned to have them in his coffin. Everyone knew him to be good-natured, agreeable, not much of a talker, and dependable. He could always be found at the icehouse with his old dog, Popsicle, a mixed breed.

Before Snyder and the boys went back to making ice, he mentioned that Sue Ella was looking forward to attending the sale. "She's bringing that preacher, Brother Leggett, with her," he said, winking at Miss Jessie as though he knew something that she did not. "She thinks you two ought to get to know each other; and I guess she feels awful strong about introducing you, because I ain't never known her to go anywhere with a preacher. Leggett's different, though, so she says."

"I am looking forward to meeting the man," Miss Jessie whispered, and did not give the matter another thought.

When she was alone again she sat on the porch to wait for her first customer. In *The Splendora Star Reporter* she had announced that the sale would begin at two o'clock; it was one-thirty and the first car had pulled up out front and stopped.

"I always come early because I wouldn't get nothing good if I didn't," came a voice out of the parked car. "I sure hope you don't mind me being here this soon."

It was Hibiscus Bee Simms. Timothy John recognized her at once. Her husband was the preacher in Little Splendora.

I might have known she'd be the first one to arrive, he thought. She's collected figurines all her life.

Miss Jessie met her halfway down the sidewalk. "My name is Jessica Gatewood. Everyone calls me Miss Jessie. I am delighted that you have arrived early."

"I just love you since I met you, I'm so glad I did," sang Hibiscus. For over forty years her husband had been the only preacher in Little Splendor, and she had led the singers each Sunday. She had always had a natural vibrato and used it even when speaking. Throughout Splendora County she was known to be the first to arrive at every yard sale and was often the last to leave. "I just love my knick-knacks," she said to Miss Jessie. "Everybody know I do too. When you come to my house you don't see no walls, just solid knickknacks everywhere, but there's room for plenty more."

"Come see what's on the porch," Miss Jessie said.

Hibiscus followed her across the lawn. The tall figure walking before her was wearing a dress of pongee. It was beige and had two large pockets on either side. Miss Jessie called it her "simple housedress" and was fond of it because she had purchased it from a Salvation Army store.

They went up on the porch and over to the corner where two rockers sat still, nestled among the moonvines racing to the balcony just above. Some house wrens were fussing in the vines and a brown lizard sunning itself on the banister saw them coming, leaped onto a leaf, and turned a bright green.

Over on one side of the porch were five boxes of glass figurines of all sizes. "I have separated this glassware from everything else," Miss Jessie said, "because all the pieces are interesting. It's difficult for me to decide whether or not to sell them, but should you want all five boxes, they are yours for the asking. And at the end of the day everything in the yard that has not been sold can be yours too, if you like."

"Oh, you are the nicest thing I ever met. And I'm so glad I know you, I don't know what to do," Hibiscus sang. "I know where I can borrow me a big truck."

"It is especially important to me to know that the special pieces will have a good home," Miss Jessie said, motioning for Hibiscus to have a seat on the rocker. The two of them sat facing each other. The lizard that lived on the porch leaped onto the banister again and turned from green back to brown.

"That ole lizard thinks he looks like a dried-up something nobody has eyes enough to see," said Hibiscus.

"All living things have ways of protecting themselves," Miss Jessie added, her eyes fastened to the lizard as though it were holding her in some hypnotic trance.

How gradual the transition is from one color to the other, Timothy John thought. "How practical to be able to do such a thing," Miss Jessie said, clapping her hands so only the tips of her fingers touched together and chimed like muted bells.

"Everybody in this world," Hibiscus said, "that goes for every man, woman, and child of us, ought to sit down and watch that lizard, for there is always two sides to everything and I guess he right now proved it too."

A wave of tranquility rippled through Timothy John, came out in Miss Jessie's face as a warm glow. She fanned herself for a moment, then looked out into the yard. There were a half dozen browsers, a family of five had just pulled up in their car and Lucille Monroe, wearing what might have been a kimono, was fighting her way through the gardenias and cane bordering their property.

From the far end of the yard, Lucille stood on tiptoe to peer over the porch railing at Miss Jessie and Hibiscus. "What on earth can the woman mean by entertaining a Nigra on her front porch?" Lucille said, and then turned her attention to what Miss Jessie was wearing. There were three cameos pinned to her bosom. "That is certainly not the kind of jewelry to be worn with that nothing-of-a-dress," she said to herself. "Wonder where she got the thing and if they have another one like it, only in blue or maybe rose?"

Although she saw none of the items she had hoped for, she decided to buy something anyway, just anything so she might have an excuse to go over to the porch and chat with Miss Jessie. She picked up a pair of salt and pepper shakers that had no tag on them and went straight as she could to ask how they were priced.

Miss Jessie took off her garden hat and fluffed up her hair. The bun had once again been twisted to the very top of her head but the hair around it billowed loosely over her forehead, her ears, and formed a bouncing roll circling her head.

Just like the way Mamma used to wear her hair way back then, Lucille thought, coming up the steps. Now I just wonder what the two of them have to say to each other? She came a little closer. Miss Jessie saw her coming but did not ackowledge her presence until she was nearly upon them. Lucille, like Hibiscus, could not pry her eyes from the made-up figure sitting there.

Lucille noticed that Miss Jessie's fingers seemed to be twice the length they ought to be and were circled with opal rings matching the ones dangling from her ears. There was a run in the librarian's dark stockings, and her shoes were peculiar somehow. Flats with buckles, like something that came over on *The Mayflower*. Now just what on earth can the woman mean by it all? she thought, while asking what the shakers were worth.

"They are porcelain and are worth considerable more

than I am asking," said Miss Jessie. "But I think a dollar will be just fine."

"Well, I don't think a dollar is going to break me," said Lucille, digging into her summer basket-purse. It was plastic made to look like straw, and had two handles with a nylon scarf tied around one of them. The scarf was the same color as Lucille's hair.

She handed Miss Jessie the dollar and told her to drop in for a visit so they could get to know one another better. "You have so many pretty things out for sale," she said, closing her purse. "If I did not already have so many pretty things myself I would buy my heart out." Then she untied the scarf, wrapped it around her neck, and tucked the ends into her collar.

Miss Jessie waved her off by wiggling her ringed fingers.

The yard was beginning to fill up. Three cars stopped out front. Lucille was leaving but had intentions of returning a little later. Sue Ella had not yet made it, nor had A.P., but Zeda Earl Goodridge was coming up the walk as fast as she could. She was wearing a dress of pink-voile eyelet with ruffles going off in every direction. The sleeves were long, the neckline high, and the hem fell way below her knees. Her seamstress had been up all night putting it together and had just completed the last-minute alterations so it could be worn to the yard sale.

When Lucille arrived at her porch she sat down to watch the activity in Miss Jessie's yard. As soon as she was comfortable she spotted Zeda Earl. The sight of her brought Lucille to her feet again. "Dear heart!" she said right out loud. "That is certainly not the proper dress to wear when you're going to buy something off the grass. And that hair, I do wish you would look at it, done up so much like Miss Jessie's it's a shame and a disgrace to this world. Zeda Earl thinks she has to imitate everybody she sees; suppose I'd better tell her she must learn to imitate herself for a change." She applied a little more color to her lips and cheeks and then walked over to her neighbor's yard again.

Hibiscus, seeing Zeda Earl near the porch, decided that it was time for her to go because she did not like tangling with R.B.'s wife. "She's always got something she wants me to do and won't never take no for an answer," Hibiscus said, getting up to leave.

"Remember to return at the end of the day," said Miss Jessie.

"I'll be back," she said happily. "I just love to get things give to me. Just like a baby at Christmastime sometimes. You need anything, you find me; I'll come quick, because since I met you, I just love you, I'm so glad I did."

Zeda Earl stopped at the largest table. She was looking over some glassware but saw nothing that she cared for and concluded that Miss Jessie had not put any of the fine things out for sale. Lucille sauntered up to her, and, with a breathy whisper she was unconscious of, said, "Well, well, well, I just wish you would look at that! Mrs. Zeda Earl Goodridge, I do believe. And am I right in thinking that you have yourself a new hairdo? Yes, so it is, and what an old-fashioned look you've come up with too. Now I just wonder, I just wonder, just wonder to goodness, what Miss Jessie will think of the effort you have gone and made?"

"Go and get over yourself the best way you can, Lucille Monroe," Zeda Earl said, giving her visual attention to a vase she might like to purchase. Lucille said that she thought the vase rather antiquated, like Zeda Earl's new hairdo, and Zeda Earl said that Lucille's choice of words and tone of voice was vaguely reminiscent of someone else, but she refused to say who for fear she might be wrong.

"Well, I will not stand to be talked to in that pretentious manner of yours," Lucille said. "If you are trying to insinuate that I'm out to make myself over like Miss Jessie, I would like for you right now to go stand before a mirror and ask yourself, just ask yourself where you got the idea to wear pink eyelet and a skirt as long as that, when I swear to

God, as long as I've been knowing you, I've never before seen you in such an unoriginal state of dress."

"Well, I suppose your lace-ups are not exactly like the ones Miss Jessie wore yesterday," Zeda Earl hissed.

"They belonged to my mother, I have you to know," said Lucille.

"And you never thought of wearing them since the day she died in Mexico until you saw Miss Jessie had a pair too," Zeda Earl replied, through her nose.

"How many times have I told you never to mention Mexico around me again!" Lucille screamed.

Miss Jessie interrupted them. "How delighted I am to have the honor of receiving two such splendid ladies. I do hope you're both enjoying the sale as much as I am enjoying giving it."

"Oh my, yes, we have had the best time already. Why, Zeda Earl and I were just saying so before you slipped up on us," Lucille said with a tight smile on her face.

"Yes, we were just saying how pretty your yard looks today, too," said Zeda Earl, holding her purse up to her forehead as though shading her eyes from the sun, but her true intention was to cover her new hairdo. Lucille had made her think that she was a little too obvious in her admiration, and she was afraid Miss Jessie would take offense.

"Isn't Zeda Earl's hair pretty today?" Lucille said. "Turn around, Zeda Earl, dear heart, so we can see it from all sides."

Zeda Earl did a small and nervous turn around, and Miss Jessie whispered that she had never seen anything like it.

"How kind of you to say that," Lucille said with obviously feigned sympathy.

At that moment, A.P., wearing ballet slippers and a long straight skirt with a high-neck blouse, arrived carrying Gusset, her little Pekingese. She cuddled the little dog up close to her face, and every so often gave it a big kiss right on the end of its nose. She had decided for the first time in months to start wearing her glasses again and had them on. They were little round wire frames that hugged the bridge of her nose. "I don't believe I've ever seen them before, A.P.," Lucille said. "Did you rush right out and get fitted so you could read all of Miss Jessie's good books, or did you have another reason, I just wonder?"

Miss Jessie said that she liked them very much and Zeda Earl said that it was kind of her to say such a thing.

The yard began to fill up with new arrivals. Hortense Gladly and Maridel Washmoyer were both wearing cotton eyelet. Daphne Hightower wore her hair up for the first time in her life, and Junie Woods sported a new dye job that was as close as she could get to Miss Jessie's golden blond.

Bertha and Beth Miller, identical twins, were again wearing matching dresses, but this time with long puffy sleeves and blousy bodices as opposed to their usual tailored look. The sight of them gave Timothy John pause. Beth had been his high-school English teacher and Bertha had attempted to teach him mathematics. He remembered how she had wept because he had been unable to grasp mathematical concepts with ease. Timothy John thought, There they are, still together like a subject and predicate. Miss Jessie added, Like a perfectly balanced equation.

She sure is going to be a trend-setter, thought Milford Monroe, who came home from the courthouse square just to see what was happening. There are more long skirts and high necklines than you can shake a stick at, and I ain't never seen so much rick-rack in my whole life. He sat on the porch swing and stared across the yard.

He looks just like some kind of manaic, Lucille thought, turning her back on him and addressing Miss Jessie. "Where on earth are all those lovely dolls? Surely you're going to part with one or two."

"I've become so fond of them, I've decided to keep them all," she answered.

"Well, I do hope and pray you don't start carrying them piggyback around town like Ruthie used to do all the time," said A.P.

Miss Jessie brought her right hand up to rest delicately on her cheek. "Oh my, no, I would never consider doing such a thing and hope to be committed to some restful institution should I ever behave in such a pathological manner."

"I thought you would say that," Lucille said sweetly.

"If you want a good rest home for the mentally disturbed, I can recommend the one my sister's in," said A.P. "But are you sure you're ready for it right now?"

At that moment Sue Ella Lightfoot, carrying a shopping bag filled with detective magazines, came bounding down the street with Brother Leggett in tow. Before they reached the sidewalk to the Coldridge house she turned to him and said, "For the last time, Leggett, will you put that Bible in your pocket? You're not going to preach a sermon, funeral, baptism, *or a wedding*—not yet, anyway; you got to meet her first."

Miss Jessie's eye caught Brother Leggett at once. He had led the responsive reading in church that past Sunday and she had admired him from one of the middle pews. In fact, she had not been able to take her eyes off him. He was originally from the little community of Imagination not far north of Splendora. He had attended a Baptist university in Abilene, and a seminary in Temple. There was a medieval look about him that Timothy John liked at once. He was slightly taller than Miss Jessie; his face was angular, his eyes deeply set, and his hair, brown and closely clipped, lay flat on his head like a scullcap. Although he was wearing a white summer suit, Timothy John could not help seeing him in long flowing robes.

He's beautiful, like a Franciscan monk, and has the look of intelligence in his eyes, he thought. And although there's an outward calm about him, there's something restless coming from within.

Sue Ella made the introduction and then left them alone for a moment; encouraged Zeda Earl and Lucille to do the same.

"Dear Heart, I stand amazed in your presence and know not what to say," Miss Jessie whispered. "The language fails me."

"It is often difficult to find the words that truly express our deepest feelings," Brother Leggett said.

"Your vocal rhythms bring to mind Gregorian chants, gothic arches, and cloistered existence," Miss Jessie replied, extending her hand. "Do you appreciate Early Music?"

"I think it's a shame that it's not used in churches around here," he answered, taking her hand in both of his. And then, afraid he was becoming too intimate, he released her at once. "Forgive me for seeming too forward," he managed to say with great embarrassment.

"Have no fear," Miss Jessie whispered demurely, and placed his withdrawn hand in both of hers. "I have always given myself freely to physical communication."

"Not too freely, I hope," Brother Leggett said nervously.

"Freely, but not too freely," Miss Jessie answered with eyes cast down.

Not knowing where to go from there, Brother Leggett managed to say, "I hope to see you in the congregation this Sunday." It was all he could do to get the words out. Miss Jessie's presence had taken him entirely by surprise. He wanted to stay and he wanted to leave and could not make up his mind which to do.

"I will attend this Sunday and every Sunday thereafter, as long as I can see you behind the pulpit," whispered Miss Jessie.

"You must excuse me if I rush off," he said abruptly. "I

have another very important visitation to make this afternoon."

"Do please, go and make it," she replied. "I am certain that your party is anxiously awaiting your arrival as I would be. But remember, my house is always open to men of intelligence and breeding. I would be disconcerted to learn that my name had been omitted from your visitation list."

Brother Leggett took a small book from his pocket and wrote *Miss Jessie Gatewood* on the next available line. "I am including you," he said, "not only on my visitation list but on my prayer list as well."

"How pleasing it is to encounter such fine reception," Miss Jessie whispered.

Slightly dazed, and with a heart thunderously beating, Brother Leggett left the yard, and Miss Jessie followed him with her eyes up the street until he entered his automobile and drove away.

Miss Jessie stood there perfectly stunned. When she finally came to herself again, Sue Ella Lightfoot was standing two feet away and staring directly into her eyes. "I thought you'd like him," she said. "Now all we got to do is convince Leggett that he's not as bashful as he thinks."

Timothy John recalled A.P. saying that Sue Ella could figure anything out. He felt himself pinching up inside, but Miss Jessie took over. "How pleased I am that you brought him along," she intoned.

"That ain't all I brought along," Sue Ella said, lifting up a bag of detective magazines that she thought Miss Jessie would enjoy reading because they contained a lot of interesting facts about people. Miss Jessie said a polite, "No thank you," said that she did not care to read detective magazines, and Sue Ella replied that she ought not to turn her learned nose up in the air, for they could provide her with necessary insights into individuals. "And believe you me, and you better know it now, around here if you ain't got insight, you ain't got nothing, because they'll twist you around and do with you anyway they can, especially if they think they can get a drop of blood or a dime, and that's not all; around here you better mind your P's and Q's because things happen right fast, and I don't mean maybe, and when they do it's all at once right here on top of you, just like this summer, for example, the hottest on record; just this past month, to be exact, three murders alone in this county and all of them as unsolved as they can be, and will go on being unsolved too because around here that's just the way things turn out. You want to commit murder, rape, or robbery, you just come right on to Splendora, and you can do it and walk out a free person. Seen it happen a million times. Flatmore flabbergasting, ain't it? Just last month: One body mutilated to death, found right here in Woods Creek, right here next to where you and me, we happen to be calling *home*, and the other two scattered all about, slung every-which-away between here and Paradise, but if you want to know what it is I think, just listen: You and me, we ain't got nothing to worry about in this case, because all the victims were men. Looks funny, don't it? Makes you wonder, don't it? Makes you want to ask the question, Was there any kind of sex involved? don't it?"

"I strictly forbid the discussion of such topics in my presence," Miss Jessie whispered. Feigning embarrassment, she fanned her face with her fingers and began to choke and gasp for breath, believing that this might hush Sue Ella long enough for her to extricate herself from all the talk. Sue Ella got all beside herself and apologized for talking that way in front of a lady. "I guess you ain't used to hearing people talk just any and every way imaginable, but you'll get used to it quick or you won't last long, because around here people don't never know when to stop."

Miss Jessie excused herself to find a buyer who needed her help, and Sue Ella decided to take the magazines back home so she might have some reference material if ever she needed any. She did not want to buy anything at the yard sale after all because it looked to her like nothing worth having was left, or was ever put out, one or the other. "I guess it was the word *Sex* that tore her up," Sue Ella said as she left the yard. "You'd think for sure that anybody brought up inside a library building around all them books and all would know enough not to get completely unstrung over a few facts and findings of an unsolved case."

Everything was stirred up because Miss Jessie arrived ahead of time, way ahead of time. All the carefully laid plans had been spoiled. "The welcoming, the luncheon, the party in her honor have all been called off," A.P. said. She liked nothing better than to have someplace to go besides down the street or out to work in her garden.

"Miss Jessie, it is plain to see, don't want no big todo made over her," said Sue Ella. "It's easy enough for me to see that she ain't the type who would appreciate it, probably would be embarrassed to know that a committee had been appointed to go to a fuss over her arrival, as she seems to want to just slip right into things like she's lived here all her life; don't want to be made over, and to tell the truth, I'm just like her, so keep it in mind, and when I die, just put me in a pine box and haul me off to the nearest cemetery without service, song, sermon, or prayer one."

"But we can't give you a shoddy funeral, S'wella. Just think what everybody will say if we do."

"They'll say it if you do and they'll say it if you don't,"

Sue Ella said. "Even if my casket was inlaid with gold and diamonds, all of Splendora would find fault with it and say, 'Poor thing, having to rest in peace in that sorry excuse for a coffin.' And no sooner than it could be covered up six feet worth, grave robbers would be hot to get their hands on the thing and dump poor me out, and that R. B. Goodridge would be the first to have his hands on a shovel. All I'm trying to get across to you is this: When I die, don't make no fuss over me, because I'm just like that library woman, I want to just slip right into things like I been there all the time. Now let me ask you this: Why do you think she came so early for, anyway?" She paused, giving A.P. time to answer, but she did not. "Well, if you don't have no idea, I'll tell you for sure, so listen: It all goes to prove that she has more common sense than most people around these parts, for she didn't want no small-town committee chasing after her and parading her around through town and showing her off like she was something pretty on a stick. The woman's got dignity and pride. You can smell it a mile away, and what's more, she's got something else about her; I can't decide just what it is yet, and that's the mystery. Makes her more inner-resting than most, wouldn't you say?" Then she stopped talking and scratched her elbow.

"If you can kiss your elbow, you'll turn into a boy, I always heard," said A.P.

"Ain't nothing to that ole saying," Sue Ella replied. "I'd done been one if it worked."

Miss Jessie stayed so busy getting her house in order that hardly anyone could catch her except on the move; on her way to the grocery, the laundry, the drugstore, or the Post Office. "There's such a dreadful amount of work to be done at home before I can assume my position as librarian," she was constantly heard to say. And even after the yard sale she was still complaining of a prodigious amount of furniture and wall space she did not know what to do with.

"She certainly does have a bundle of energy in that frail frame of hers," everyone was thinking or saying.

She took the town by surprise. All in all they were delighted to receive her; just a little put out that she did not allow anyone to know she was coming sooner than expected. It was plain to everyone that she was cautious of receiving more attention than necessary and even refused to have her biography printed in the local weekly. Mr. Albert Posey, the paper's editor, assured her that it would not cost a dime from her purse, but she said that it was not a question of money, but of privacy. "Then you've come to the wrong place," Albert said. "In Splendora there's no such thing as privacy."

Still Timothy John was determined to keep Miss Jessie at a distance. He knew it was important for her to be seen, but not seen too closely and not caught by surprise. She did not attempt to make close friends right away. Everyone watched the librarian come and go, but no one felt the freedom to call on her without an invitation. Every day she walked wherever she needed to go. On wet days a black rain-cape and umbrella covered her up almost entirely, and on sunny days she carried a ruffled parasol to protect her sensitive skin. She did her own shopping, had nothing delivered to her house, and carried her clothes to the laundry in a picnic basket. Maga Dell Spivy said that she had the most beautiful underthings she had ever laid eyes on.

After much thought she even opened an account with the Splendora State Bank.

When R. B. Goodridge saw what a sizable account she had to transfer he offered to be of service in advising certain worthwhile investments. He had a steady gaze in his eyes when he spoke. His tone was solemn, his words overpronounced, making everything he said seem to be aimed at the attention of a slow learner.

"I do not choose to take risks with anything, particularly with my money," Miss Jessie said. "And should I choose tomorrow morning to withdraw every dime of it, I trust that it would not be in the least bit difficult for you or your able assistants to find it tucked away in the back of your strongest vault."

"Most assuredly," R.B. said with a smile that was no more than the stretch of his mouth. "Let's not come to a falling out over it."

"No let's not," Miss Jessie said. "I did not come here to participate in an altercation, even though I am perfectly capable of doing so."

It was not two days before everyone in town learned that Miss Jessie was one of the wealthiest citizens in the county. When R.B. learned the status of her purse, he told Zeda Earl that she ought to make friends with her at once. "Do whatever you have to in order to get close to her," he said. "She's got money." Zeda Earl, determined to find out everything she could about Miss Jessie, called A.P. to ask what she knew about the librarian's likes and dislikes, and while discussing the issue she could not help letting it slip out that Miss Jessie was one of the wealthiest women the county had ever seen.

So the word went this way: R.B. told Zeda Earl and Zeda Earl told A.P. and A.P. told Lord knows who, including Sue Ella Lightfoot, who informed Duffy Jones right away and Duffy Jones spread the news to his side of town that the new bookwoman was one rich sister, said that it was obvious from the start by the way she carried herself and did not speak above a whisper. "She's got re-fine-ment and in most cases that spells money."

Without meaning to, Miss Jessie caused quite a stir throughout the town. Everyone was especially pleased to see that she attended the First Baptist Church regularly. Zeda Earl and R.B. also worshiped there, "or pretended to," Sue Ella always said. For many years the Goodridges had been members of the Church of Christ, but after Brother Eagleton turned out to be such a dynamic person they became Baptists. Brother Eagleton was a born leader and had, in only a few short months, pursuaded ninety percent of his congregation to tithe. His was the largest church in Splendora; red brick with white columns and a steeple with a front window that was nothing more than a painting. "Everybody thinks that window's real, but it's not," Sue Ella said. "You can't tell them any different, either." To A.P. the whole building, yard, parking lot, and all, looked like it came off a picture calendar. She attended church services there regularly. She believed she had to or God would punish her. Her worst fear was that she would become so fat she would never be able to dance or even move around enough to be able to teach; so every Sunday she went to church and prayed to God not to let her get too big.

Milford Monroe refused to have anything to do with the "Holy of Holies," as he referred to the place, and Lucille went only when she had something new to wear. Snyder Lightfoot had not darkened the door in years. Sunday was his day to wash his clothes, and everyone knew it too, because he always hung them out to dry in front of the icehouse, which he kept open seven days a week. Sue Ella thought Snyder was right in being so out-in-the-open with how he felt. She said she was just like him on that account and let it be known that she did not enjoy being preached to and shouted at. "If you got something to tell me, you can say it in a normal tone of voice, or I don't need to hear it at all," she once told Brother Eagleton, who had been afraid to say much of anything to her since. He had even been noticed to turn around and walk the other way when he saw her coming. "There's no more tranquility there today than there was the last time I went. That was when Prissy walked out," Sue Ella declared. "But the worst disgrace of all is that they shelter their preacher to the point that he don't have idea one what's going on. He don't get in their way so bad tucked off somewhere inside a two-story parsonage, behind a marble-inlaid pulpit, sedated as it were and if you will by the word of God, while every tithe that's collected goes right straight to that bank, and we all know whose pocket that fits inside.

"Now the only way they'll ever get me back inside that church again is to give Leggett more to do besides read the announcements and hold Wednesday-night prayer meeting every other week. The man's got good sense and it's good sense that calls attention to you, and sometimes makes you 'peer to be a fool, especially when you live in a place like Splendora. He's the only preacher I ever met that don't smell like old Bibles left out in the rain, and that's why I think he might be a good match for Jes. He's been here ten years now and ain't never been given nothing important to do and ain't likely to stay much longer unless we find him a reason; and I think I have."

"Only a man of the Christian persuasion will be allowed to enter my door," Miss Jessie said when Brother Leggett made his first visit.

Sue Ella had advised him, "The only way to do something that you're nervous about is to just do it fast and get it over with." And even with her advice echoing inside his head it had taken him all the courage he had to call on her, and at the last moment looked for excuses not to ring her bell. He was determined, however, not to stay long, and refused even to sit down because he had come with the intention of inviting Miss Jessie to attend the Wednesday-night prayer service in his company. He realized if he hesitated too long it would become increasingly difficult, so he asked her at once, almost as soon as she opened the door.

She accepted his invitation graciously, and the following Wednesday he called on her thirty minutes before the service, and they strolled leisurely to the church. He wore his best linen suit and carried a large black Bible under his arm. She wore a white-silk shirtwaist with leg-o'-mutton sleeves and a rather long skirt of right-hand twill. It was navy, slightly fitted below her waist, and pleated thereafter. Over one arm she carried a lightweight shawl, in the event the church was unseasonably cool, and in her belt she tucked a white-lace handkerchief.

After the service he walked her home. And at her door she told him, "Had you pronounced the service yourself, the evening would have been far more meaningful."

"I pray that we will continue to travel the King's highway to eternal happiness, peace, and tranquility," he said formally. It was one of the many statements he often used when he could not think of the proper reply. Then he shook her hand and left.

From her dining-room window, Lucille Monroe saw it all. "Oh, I would give my eyeteeth to know what they just said to each other," she said to herself.

The next day Splendora was buzzing with talk. Everyone approved of the new couple except Maga Dell Spivy, and she told Miss Jessie exactly how she felt. "You ain't gonna get what you're looking for out of somebody's assistant pastor, but if going out with him will help your image, I guess it's O.K."

Lucille heard what Maga Dell had said and told everyone she could find that their sorry excuse for a telephone operator was just plain jealous and had no business showing it, because everyone in town knew that she had a new boyfriend who had just given her a fur coat. "She had to pay for it on her back, of course," Lucille said. "That's where she spends most of her time you know, and in my opinion, she's a disgrace to our sex." Eventually, Maga Dell heard every word of what Lucille had gone around saying, and her only comment was that Lucille was not the kind of woman who had ever wanted or had ever known what pleasure was all about, and that it was really too bad for her because she could have a mink coat too if she would only loosen up and make herself more appealing to the opposite sex. Every word of what Maga Dell said went right straight back to Lucille who called her "a common slut and nothing better." Maga Dell's only comment to that was, "I've been called worse."

"Maga Dell isn't nearly so bad as everyone makes her out to be," Brother Leggett said.

"How it does please me to hear you speak that way," Miss Jessie replied.

Every other week the assistant pastor was allowed to give the Wednesday-evening service. On the weeks he was not behind the pulpit he accompanied Miss Jessie to the church, and on the weeks that he was speaking she saw herself there because he took his evenings seriously and needed every minute to prepare.

Miss Jessie said that she adored his sermons because he delivered them in a normal tone of voice and was never preachy or self-righteous. Brother Leggett said that he enjoyed the company of Splendora's new librarian because she was a woman of many interests, and keen intelligence. So for the rest of the summer he continued to escort her to prayer meeting. Everyone in Splendora watched for them, and Timothy John thought it was quite amusing for them to be seen together.

"Thank goodness they've hooked up," Sue Ella Lightfoot said. "Now let's hope it ain't just one of them summer romances I been reading about lately."

10

The weeks rolled by rapidly and before anyone knew it summer had slipped away. Shadows were beginning to stretch longer and longer over the old Coldridge house and lawn, until some of them, especially the cedars, and at times the shape of the entire house with its many gables and old-rooster weathervane, were reaching all the way beyond the yard and into the street. During the mornings the shadow of the house was in the backyard, but by early afternoon it began easing its way out front, until its many-gabled silhouette fell like a velvet cloak all the way into the street.

Miss Jessie's first few weeks on her new job were spent converting the school bus into a library on wheels. She designed shelves of various sizes and asked the Ag boys to construct them. She sewed gingham curtains with lace trim for all the windows and found space in the back for a small table and three chairs. Then she began stocking the shelves with every title available and ordered more with funds the county provided. She hoped to have the bookmobile in circulation by the first of the year and stayed busy day and night in order to reach her goal.

Esker Dement, who operated the radio station, gave her fifteen minutes of air time each week so the entire county could have a first-hand progress report. She also used the time to solicite donations. "Should you have any stray titles around the house, I would be happy to catalogue them at once and give them a permanent home on *our* new shelves."

From all over the county she began receiving boxes of books. "Most of the volumes," she lamented, "are not suitable, as they contain nothing that will advance the mind." But when she received Brother Leggett's donations she paused a moment and surveyed the titles carefully. There were several obviously used dictionaries, a thesaurus, two books of familiar quotations, as well as *The Varieties of Religious Experience, The Lives of the Saints, The Complete Works of Shakespeare,* and a few well worn children's titles: *The Racketty Packetty House, A Crock of Gold,* and *At the Back of the North Wind.*

"Your contributions pleased me more than you will ever know," Miss Jessie said to Brother Leggett as she showed him into the parlor.

He found her presence stunning, and although he felt somewhat uneasy in her company, he found himself looking forward to every minute he would spend with her.

"I can see by the books you read that I was not wrong about you," Miss Jessie said, inviting him to sit.

Once again he was unable to think of anything to say. Her presence overwhelmed him. Fortunately he had heard piano music as he came up the walk, and asked if she would continue.

"A little recital is just what you need," she said, taking a seat at the baby grand.

Lucille Monroe had watched him arrive. The moment he entered the house her curiosity peaked. She checked her clock. "Eight o'clock. Rather late in the evening for a caller, I would say," she muttered to herself as she made ready to leave. She put on her dark coat, left through the back door, and followed the shadows from her yard over to Miss Jessie's and concealed herself in the evergreens next to the porch, as close to the parlor windows as possible. The curtains in the parlor were drawn and she could not see a thing, but occasionally she could hear voices without being able to understand them. Then came the sound of the piano. "Oh, how adorable. She's entertaining him with music." Lucille decided to stay on in hope of eventually finding a better place for observation. She was just dying to press her ear to the windowpane or creep up onto the porch, but she dared not.

It was a cool autumn evening and not at all good on Lucille's arthritis, but she decided to make the best of it, and stayed out, even though there was a wind blowing up. It was a time of year when cold-air masses from the north blew in fast and collided with the southern sultriness on its way out. It was a time of year that everyone in Splendora dreaded because it could not be predicted. All the elements seemed to act up at once. Miss Jessie did not seem to mind it, though; wearing a woolen shawl thrown over her shoulders and a long brown dress with ruffles falling to her ankles she sat upright, straight as a pine sapling, on a wooden stool that kept wobbling back and forth as though it was about to walk away with her on it.

Outside the wind whipped the shutters against the house in counterpoint to the Chopin while a branch from Lucille Monroe's mimosa reached all the way over into the Coldridge yard, and, like a mad conductor, beat a wild and irregular cadence against the bay windows, against the polonaise Miss Jessie played so well that Timothy John might have been only the day before to the home of the late Pristine Barlow to take a lesson. He could still remember by heart the Chopin, the Bach, the Mozart Pristine had taught him; the musical ability he relinquished to Miss Jessie. Timothy John recalled how Pristine, who for the longest time had been the only piano teacher in Splendora, had always said that that time of year was just like a Bach fugue because two or more of nature's elements were always acting up at once. Most people found the season difficult to live with, but Pristine, who had been one of Esther Ruth's dearest friends, had not; she had always enjoyed not knowing what to expect. She excelled in being able to relate nature to the keyboard, Timothy John remembered as Miss Jessie played on. The clouds were like Chopin, the ripples in Woods Creek like a Mozart concerto, and a little farther downstream the unexpected little waterfall was just like Haydn's "Surprise Symphony"; you were never quite ready for it, no matter how you prepared yourself. Nothing would convince her that Beethoven had not taken his inspiration for his sixth symphony from the East Texas pine forests, and even though she knew perfectly well that Beethoven had never visited the Americas, she insisted that he must have come over at some point, perhaps in his dreams.

In spite of Timothy John's reverie, Miss Jessie finished the piece without missing a note.

When the last chord had died away Brother Leggett paid her many compliments. After a pause he added, "We once had a piano teacher here by the name of Pristine Barlow. She died shortly before Esther Ruth. I think you would have liked her and found her amusing, too."

"Provide me her description," Miss Jessie implored.

Brother Leggett was pleased to see that her interest was keen. "Pristine," he continued in a more relaxed voice, "always insisted that common church hymns were not to be learned in her classes because most of them contained nothing that would advance the pupil artistically. To her face, her effort to improve the idle minds of Splendora was met with approval, but behind her back the irate mothers disapproved mightily, and gradually removed their children from her classes and ushered them off to the church organist, Mr. Treadway, who slowly usurped all her pupils by teaching whatever the parents wanted their children to learn, usually popular songs or hymns. There had been a time when Pristine was the church organist also, but she finally gave up the job because she could no longer bear playing the music she was forced to play. Most hymns, she said, were too shallow. Their phrasing was not challenging to her, yet she played them anyway and believed it was her duty to occasionally incorporate her favorite themes and variations into the offertory music. Needless to say, the pieces she loved most were always met with extreme disapproval."

"Dear heart, it would be senseless for me to offer a contradiction to that," Miss Jessie whispered.

Brother Leggett continued:

"One Sunday she attended services wearing something that everyone said looked like a pink-nylon nightgown. It was actually her last recital dress, but from where she sat at the organ she said that she could hear all the hateful comments so clearly that it made her sick and she dropped her hymnal three times on the keyboard. It was not the first time that had happened, either. She never learned to turn pages without having an accident. She had a mental block against learning the songs by heart because she felt they were not worth the effort it would take. Nothing seemed to help. The pay she received was no compensation, nor would it have been had she been paid something fine. She had her standards. Money was not her worry. The mental decay of the world and especially Splendora was her worry and she didn't know what to do about it."

"I think I would have liked her enormously," Miss Jessie whispered. "Do go on."

"The Sunday Pristine blew up will be remembered a long time," Brother Leggett said with what Timothy John thought was the most endearing smile he had ever seen. "During the singing of the second hymn she pulled all the stops on the organ and raced the choir to the end of Sweet Hour of Prayer. At the finish she stood up screaming that

that was the last time she intended to play that hymn or any other hymn, and she would never again attempt to do anything fine for fools. 'You can have your damn hymnal and all the others like it,' she said, and hurled the book as hard as she could right into the baptismal pool. Then she said that she was sick to death of being forced to play what was not divinely inspired and made her exit up the center aisle with her pink nightgown flapping behind her."

Both Miss Jessie and Brother Leggett burst into uncontrollable laughter. "I adore her," Miss Jessie said. "I thought you would," said Brother Leggett, while outside Lucille Monroe, shivering in the evergreens, heard them laughing and was furious that she had not been able to hear the joke as well.

"May I be so audacious as to ask what occurred after that extremely touching episode?" Miss Jessie said having regained her composure.

"Prayers went up for the Lord to send another organist," Brother Leggett said solemnly. "The deacons of the church waited and waited and prayed and prayed, and when they finally convinced themselves that a musician was not going to materialize on the church steps they selected a committee to go out and entice a minister of music away from another church. They said that they were going out to look for a man, preferably a man with a family, someone who did not have crazy ideas. And somewhere in another town the new musician was found, Mr. Worth Treadway, a husband and a father, who agreed to come and is to this day handsomely paid for his services."

"That angers me beyond belief," said Miss Jessie, bringing her voice as far above a whisper as she dared. "Pristine Barlow had something fine to give and no one wanted it. Those deacons do not amuse me in the least. Don't you find them hard to endure?"

"Frankly, yes," he confessed. "I often wish for Pristine's

courage in dealing with them. In fact, I find everything around here hard to endure, particularly now that Esther Ruth is dead."

"You were close?" 'Miss Jessie asked.

"She was my constant source of information and amusement," Brother Leggett answered. "It's hard for me to be in this house because I expect her still to be here. There are moments when you remind me of her in some way."

"In what way?"

"In the way you inflect certain words. The way you turn phrases," he said. "And also you seem to have some of her perspective on the goings-on around here; her sense of humor too, maybe. Esther Ruth was forever laughing and if she wasn't laughing she was bitterly angry. She was never in between."

God forbid that I should have her perspective on things, Timothy John thought, while Miss Jessie tried changing the subject to a cup of tea. But Brother Leggett declined the offer and returned the conversation to Esther Ruth again, and Timothy John, slightly ruffled by the idea of talking about his grandmother, said, with Miss Jessie's windy voice, "Now I'm ready to hear something about yourself. Why did you enter the ministry?"

"As far back as I can remember I have always heard my name associated with the church," he answered. "Everyone said that I had that look in my eye that went with being a good preacher. I don't dislike the association, you understand, but there are times when I feel that it is rather limiting. Esther Ruth and I used to talk about this all the time."

"And what else did you and Esther Ruth talk about?" Miss Jessie said, as Timothy John relaxed into the conversation.

"We talked about how she wanted to drown R. B. Goodridge in the water tower so she could take over the town and run it her way. She said that she would first make Sue Ella Lightfoot sheriff and then give the town a good facelift. In fact just before she died she left me an envelope and told me not to open it until she was dead at least a year. Naturally I opened it the day she was buried and it contained her plans, feeble as they were, for restoring the town, starting with the courthouse."

"Do please share the letter with me," Miss Jessie begged.

"I am not sure that I feel right about showing it to anyone," said Brother Leggett. "Especially since I was not to have opened it myself."

"I am sure Esther Ruth would want me to know of her plans," Miss Jessie replied. "Especially now that I've come to live in her house, and have also become so fond of you, one of her dearest friends. I feel as though there is a kindred spirit that binds us—the three of us, I mean." She touched him delicately on the cheek as she spoke.

Brother Leggett, moved by her sincerity and charm, agreed to show her the letter. "I'll drive to the office and bring it back in a few minutes," he said.

Lucille Monroe had decided she could not stay in the evergreens much longer. Halfway across the yard, she heard Miss Jessie's front door open and went scurrying for cover behind a trellis. "He's leaving too fast," she said. "Wonder if they had an argument? Bet they did." She hid behind the trellis a few minutes before deciding to leave and was making her way back to her yard again when Brother Leggett returned and sent her running toward a Crepe Myrtle tree.

The envelope contained photographs of the courthouse before and after the remodeling, as well as a letter written in Esther Ruth's ornamental script on lavender stationery and dated the week before her death.

Miss Jessie read it aloud:

"These pictures will say more than I possibly can. They will show, to anyone who is interested, what work of destructive genius R. B. Goodridge rendered to a Texas gothic courthouse. The original building was red brick and had many gables and turrets and gargoyles peering down from every corner. Most of the building is still underneath the plaster. Some of the gargoyles were removed and sold to a Mr. William Ragsdale living over in Honey Island if he's not already dead. The stained-glass windows were taken out and sold to the Baptist church and are to this day gathering dust in the basement and should be taken out of there and returned to where they belong. Start chipping from the top, I think. It will not take long with the help of some good strong men, if you can still find any. R.B. will stand in your way unless you're smart. Bribe him if you have to. Threaten to drag his name through mud unless he rectifies his egregious mistake. I regret not being around to help."

"She certainly was obsessed with it, wasn't she?" Brother Leggett said. "There were days when she would talk of nothing else."

"Well, it is a disgrace to destroy a fine old building," Miss Jessie said. "And I think we might be able to do something about it if we put our heads together."

"Or our pocketbooks," Brother Leggett said.

"That's it," Miss Jessie replied, touching her bodice with the tips of her lacquered fingers. "We'll give him no choice." After a brief pause: "Dear heart, will you permit me to keep this letter for a day or two?" she asked, smiling to him with her whole face. "It would be so sweet of you to trust me with it."

Brother Leggett felt his body disintegrate when she spoke to him tenderly. He agreed that she could keep the letter as long as she needed it, and again he declined tea on account of the late hour. "I've been here too long," he said. "Everyone in town will be talking."

"Perhaps Splendora is not the right place for you, Miss Jessie suggested.

"I have given some thought to leaving," he said, as she saw him to the door and onto the front porch. Before he reached the street she called after him, "My dear, we must never allow anyone to know we've talked this way."

"Talked what way?" Lucille Monroe said to herself. She had taken cover in a prickly holly bush growing close to the porch and was only a few feet from where Miss Jessie was standing. "It sounds too suspicious for words, if you're asking me." When she heard the front door close she slipped through the shadows back to her house. She felt frostbitten from head to toe and still did not know much more than she had when Brother Leggett arrived earlier that evening, but she had the idea that they were planning something and hoped it could be matrimony.

Miss Jessie returned to the parlor and sat once more at the piano. The night had grown still. The house was silent. She began a Bach prelude and played it through twice. Then she stared at the keyboard for a few moments. "I simply can't allow myself to become too fond of him," Timothy John said. "I can see that it's going to be hard expelling him from my thoughts tonight. Perhaps some wine will help settle me down again." Miss Jessie stood up, flounced her skirt, and went to sit on a small love seat. On the side table next to it were a decanter of red wine and one crystal glass with a blue stem.

When she went to bed the decanter was almost empty.

11

∽

Repeatedly Miss Jessie was asked to join every ladies' organization in town, and repeatedly she refused by saying that she had so much to do that she did not believe she had time to take part in regular meetings of any kind. "Why should I bore myself to tears with luncheons, committees, and hen parties," she told Brother Leggett, who was in complete sympathy, but still realized, more acutely than she, that Splendora expected her to take part in some worthwhile cause aside from what she had been hired to do. "It has to be something that will keep you abreast of the happenings in the town, keep you out of everybody's way, and at the same time add to your stature and enjoyment of life," he said. "Now what can that be?" In a few days he came up with a plan which interested Miss Jessie enormously.

Voluntarily, she began telling everyone, once again, that she did not have the time for regular meetings but she did have whirling through her mind an idea for a new club she might very well organize; one that would not take up quite so much time as the others because there would be no formal gatherings, and no informal gatherings either. "In fact," she said, "in the club I'm thinking about there will be no gatherings at all, except, of course, the first one."

"Well, don't keep us in suspense," A.P. howled. "Tell us now what it's all about so we can start deciding if we want to join, if we're invited to join, that is."

"I see no reason why you cannot join," A.P. said Miss Jessie, "just as long as you abide by the governing rules."

"I have always been good at following rules," said A.P. proudly.

"That's good," Miss Jessie said, "because the rules of this club are so strict that only the bravest will be able to follow them."

"It sounds kind of scary," A.P. replied. "Maybe I don't want to join after all."

"Oh, yes you do," Miss Jessie informed her. "I insist upon making you a charter member whether you like it or not. In time you will learn to enjoy the little group I am about to assemble."

Lucille heard of the club Miss Jessie was about to organize and called everyone she knew, starting with Zeda Earl Goodridge, to ask if they had been invited to join yet, or if they knew any details as to what it was all about. How aggravating it was to Lucille that no one knew a thing. Yet she felt somewhat relieved because for days she had had a feeling that something was going on and was terrified that she might be the last to know what it was. Finally Miss Jessie made her announcement, and what a good thing it was, coming when it did, as Lucille was beginning to look haggard from lack of sleep and had also been in the foulest mood anyone had ever witnessed.

Miss Jessie invited five well-known ladies of the town to tea. Lucille Monroe arrived in a tan-rayon blouse and a brown skirt with a ruffle sewn around the hem to make it longer. Zeda Earl Goodridge showed up in a new pinstriped dress with three dozen buttons holding it together, and even though she had always said she would never be caught dead wearing one, she wore a crocheted shawl draped over one shoulder. A.P. arrived straight from her dancing class and was all decked out in a long full dress of polished cotton. She wore her hair balled up, flowers on her wrist, and her little wire-frames sitting crooked on her nose. Sue Ella Lightfoot was dressed in her every day-of-the week shift, and Maga Dell Spivy chose to be seen in her favorite dress of all time, a black polyester with red hearts printed all over it and a hemline that stopped above her knees. Miss Jessie had included her because Timothy John knew that she had always had plenty to say. That was the point of the new club. Neither Zeda Earl nor Lucille could understand why Maga Dell had been invited as she was not part of their social group, nor had she ever cared to be. They had never invited her, either, for that matter, because Zeda Earl felt that Maga Dell was from another class, and Lucille was in complete agreement; "another" meaning "lower" to them both.

"The woman has a different man in her bed every night of the week," Lucille whispered to Zeda Earl. "And that's what I call pure trash."

Miss Jessie was wearing a dress of challis, trimmed in lace and ribbons. After she had served tea and the most delicious cake Lucille Monroe believed she had ever tasted, she said that she had carefully selected them each as charter members of her new club. "We are to call ourselves The Epistolarians, she announced dramatically.

A.P. turned at once to Lucille and asked what that meant, and Lucille, who did not have the faintest clue, but was too ashamed to admit it, told A.P. to be patient and she would find out. "You do not have to know everything at once, A.P., so hush up a minute," Lucille whispered.

Miss Jessie continued. She said that the club was being

created in order to bring letter writing back into popularity. "The Victorians exchanged letters across London, so why can't we exchange our letters across Splendora?"

"But what will they think in the Post Office?" A.P. asked, and Miss Jessie answered that if they were doing their job, they would not notice who was sending what and to whom. "Letter-writing is one of our neglected arts," she said, paraphrasing the speech Brother Leggett had given her to use. "Some of the world's most respected novels have been based on letters coming and going among various people, and it has just occurred to me that we will each get to know one another so very much better if we but sit down and write our innermost thoughts. We will also be able to say in letters what is sometimes difficult to say face-to-face, and, of course, everything will be completely secret. No one should know what is said in the other letters, and no one will. Is that perfectly clear?" All the ladies nodded their heads. Miss Jessie was pleased to see that everyone was eager to begin, and was fully aware that her letters would be the first to be passed around. She explained further that the idea for the club came to her when she realized how little time for socializing she would have in the coming year, and just did not feel able to both attend meetings on a regular basis and organize the library, so she decided that a letter-writing club would suit her time limits just fine. "You can write a letter during just any little scrap of time here or there. Over lunch, or coffee you can jot down a few lines, and pretty soon you've got yourself a letter that someone else will enjoy so very, very much; and may I ask that we not limit our letters to ourselves only, but as often as possible we should address the sick in our hospital and the aged in our nursing home. It will mean so terribly much to them, I'm sure, and will also be of service to the community."

"Oh yes, charming," Zeda Earl said, and Lucille answered her, "Oh yes, ever so."

"You'll just love Lucille's letters, because she writes just like she talks," A.P. said. "I know because I received a vacation letter from her once."

"Oh, it was only a postcard, A.P.," said Lucille, trying to be modest.

"Better than that, it was four postcards," A.P. clarified. "And with writing stretched out over the address space so they had to be mailed all together, locked up in the prettiest envelope with flowers on it I believe I ever saw. I still got it, too, Lucille."

"Oh, how you do go on and on," Lucille said, loving every minute of the attention she was getting.

Poor pitiful Lucille, Sue Ella thought. Way back in her past somewhere nobody ever bragged on her enough, and now all the bragging in the world won't do no good.

"I'm just going to love this new club," A.P. shrieked, "but we've got to have a motto, because all clubs do. We've also got to have a flower and two club colors, some officers, and something to wear that will say who we are."

"Let me make a suggestion," said Lucille. "I think we should each wear white cardigan sweaters on which I will be happy to embroider The Epistolarians across one side."

"How marvelous," Miss Jessie exclaimed. "And on the back, would it be asking too much, Lucille, to have you stitch in the club emblem which is a quill and inkwell with a scroll in the background?"

"I happen to be the fastest needleworker in the county," Lucille testified. "And I will be more than happy to embroider the emblem if someone will draw it off for me."

Sue Ella, holding back her grin, said, "I think more explanation is needed, and since you happen to be so fast, Lucille, I suggest that over or under the emblem you should stitch in: A SMALL-TOWN ORGANIZATION FOR THE PROMOTION AND PRESERVATION OF LETTER-WRITING AND THE CONTINUAL CONFESSION OF INNERMOST THOUGHTS AMONG FRIENDS AND ENEMIES."

"I think that's too long," Lucille said, but before she could protest further, Maga Dell realized what Sue Ella was doing and said that she thought the saying was just the right length. Miss Jessie caught on to their scheming and agreed with them, leaving Zeda Earl feeling as though she had no choice but to take Miss Jessie's side, so she did; and Lucille and A.P. followed her even though they were not sure what was going on.

The turn of events was not what had been planned, but Timothy John was enjoying the ridicule so much he was willing for Miss Jessie to agree to most anything as long as it was at Zeda Earl's and Lucille's expense. He was sure that Miss Jessie could take care of herself somehow.

"Dear hearts, let me see if I've got it all down pat before we go on," Lucille said, sitting up as straight as her back would allow and giving her voice a serious note. "On the front I will embroider The Epistolarians, and on the back a quill, an inkwell, and a scroll, which someone will furnish me with, and over or under that, whichever, I will embroider: A small-town organization for the promotion of thoughts and . . . and deeds . . . and enemies with friendship too . . . Oh, how does it go? Sue Ella, you'll just have to write it down for me, that's all."

"I already have," answered Sue Ella with a smile as she handed a slip of paper to Lucille.

"How sweet of you," Lucille said. "Now, shall I embroider this in all capital letters or shall I use my own judgment?"

"Your judgment is always best, Lucille," said Sue Ella, feigning a serious face with great effort.

Lucille brought her fingertips up to barely cover her mouth, and, hanging her head some, she spoke directly into her collar: "Why, S'wella Lightfoot, thank you so much." And Miss Jessie, looking directly at Sue Ella, said that from everything she knew of Lucille she was inclined to agree wholeheartedly that her judgment was the best around. Sue

Ella noticed a glint in Miss Jessie's eyes and knew exactly what she meant.

"Oh, I just can't believe you mean all that," Lucille said.

"Oh yes, they do, honey," Maga Dell Spivy fabricated. "They both told me lots'a times how much they surely do admire you so much." She thought it was a disgrace that Lucille could be flattered so easily and that Zeda Earl was willing to accept just anything as long as everyone else did.

"I want the Easter lily to be our club flower," A.P. whined.

"God, no! That's too religious, A.P." said Sue Ella, almost shouting.

Maga Dell agreed that they were not, nor should ever be a religious organization. "We've got enough of them already; don't need no more, if you're asking me."

"Well, I wasn't, but I think you're right, for once," Lucille said, adjusting her earring so it would not hurt.

Maga Dell saw what she was doing and said, "If you'd buy the kind of ear-bobs I wear, they wouldn't pinch so bad."

God, how I hate the very sound of her voice, Lucille thought as she said, "How sweet of you to make that suggestion, Maga Dell."

A.P. hung her head low and asked if it would be all right then for the club to adopt the sweet pea because that was her second-favorite flower. Zeda Earl said that she thought it would be awfully sweet to have A.P.'s second choice, and it was agreed upon unanimously.

"Anything's better than a God-awful Easter lily," Maga Dell said, lifting her pompadour and smoothing it down with her fingertips. Her nails were an inch long and lacquered blood red, and on her fingers she wore dimestore rubies, one in the shape of a heart.

How trashy of her, Lucille thought. "Wherever did you acquire those lovely rings, Maga Dell?" she asked.

"Why, down the street in the five-and-dime, Lucille dear.

You know that yourself, for you were there the day I bought them, if you care to remember back," Maga Dell said, having no intention of allowing Lucille to induce embarrassment.

Every time I see that woman I just want to spit, Lucille thought.

Hoping to bring the discussion back to the club, Zeda Earl moved that they select their colors at once.

"Beet red and fuchsia!" Maga Dell screamed.

"And she's got the gall to laugh like a horse for saying it." Lucille was fuming. "I'd be ashamed of myself if I were her. Why, I'd be so ashamed I wouldn't know what to do."

"But my favorite colors are lavender and rose and I think they should be our Epistolarian colors as well," Zeda Earl whined.

"How nauseating!" Maga Dell said, but when it came time to take a vote she went along with Zeda Earl's recommendation anyway. She had her reasons for doing so.

A.P. said that the motto should be: A Letter Makes the Day. But Lucille said that that was not quite right. "Let's change it to: A Letter Makes *My* Day." That, too, was agreed upon, even though Sue Ella thought it made very little sense. "I certainly can't be writing letters to every one of you every day of my life," she said. "I happen to be a telephone person myself, but will manage to drop a post-card, if what I have to say ain't too personal, you know how they are in the Post Office these days, always reading every card they can get their hands on and making no bones about telling off on theirselves, either."

"But with all of us writing, we're bound to get a letter every day or every other day at least," A.P. added.

"Every week or two is more like it, honey," Maga Dell said in her best "Number please" voice. She felt that it was time to suggest what she had been leading up to. Here goes, she thought, folding a stick of Juicy-Fruit until it was no bigger than a lemon drop and popping it into her mouth.

Then she said that as long as they were going the whole hog they each might as well carry a Band-Aid box on a ribbon slung around their necks so they would have a place to keep all their letter-writing equipment as well as a few postage stamps, and would, therefore, never be caught without pen and paper at least. Zeda Earl and Lucille did not think too much of the idea at first. Sue Ella noted their disapproval by the way their eyes and mouths went flying open. But when Miss Jessie said that she thought it a novel idea both Lucille and Zeda Earl agreed readily that it was ever so original, and Maga Dell promised at once to set to work collecting Band-Aid boxes so by the end of the week she could have the neckwear ready. "I intend to work on them while I'm at the telephone company," she said. "Else they might never get done."

With all that on her hands, God only knows who she'll think to connect up, Lucille thought. "How sweet of you to volunteer so much of your time, Maga Dell, dear," she said.

Maga Dell answered, "You don't need to say it as though I've never volunteered for a thing in my life."

"No, I don't," Lucille replied. "And let me say right now how sorry I am for implying such a thing, for we all know how freely you give yourself away."

"It's only because I enjoy it," Maga Dell said. "I'm so sorry for anyone who doesn't."

There was very little Miss Jessie could do, or cared to do, to change the direction of the meeting, the idea of seeing Lucille and Zeda Earl wearing Band-Aid boxes around their necks pleased her so much, even at her own expense. Sue Ella felt the same way, and Maga Dell knew she had very little to lose in the way of reputation because everyone talked about her as if she were dirt anyway.

"Now, is everyone in complete agreement, especially on carrying our supplies with us at all times?" Miss Jessie asked, trying to bring order back to the group.

"Oh, yes," Lucille replied with complete satisfaction.

"How novel it is," and Zeda Earl echoed her: "Oh yes, how completely novel," and Maga Dell, who had suggested the idea just to see how far she could take it, said that she just knew that each and every one of the ladies present would enjoy so much what it was she was going to make for them all to wear.

Lucille was confidentially asking Miss Jessie if they had to wear the Band-Aid boxes everywhere and if she could sometimes keep hers inside her purse if it did not go well with what she was wearing that day. Maga Dell overheard her and spoke up fast. "No, no, no, you may not, Lucy dear. The rules are that you have to plan what you're going to wear around your Band-Aids and then you'll never go wrong."

Well, the very idea, Lucille thought. Just look at the piece of filth sitting there like she's God's gift to man.

"Now, you might think about changing the color of your neck ribbon from time to time," Maga Dell suggested. "I think that will help you to feel better about yourself."

"I think it ought to be a ten-cent fine if we're caught in public without our writing needs around our necks," Sue Ella Lightfoot said. Lucille suggested that church and luncheons should be the exception to that rule. Zeda Earl raised her hand and said ever so solemnly that she thought that funerals, weddings, and garden parties should also be exceptions. Miss Jessie thought it best to declare her agreement and said, "Yes, and I do thank you so much for bringing to our attention that fine point, Zeda Earl." Zeda Earl lowered her hand with pride over her outstanding contribution.

Once again Miss Jessie declaimed her excitement by saying how much she looked forward to writing each lady present, how she would enjoy receiving their letters and innermost thoughts so much, and how she looked forward to carrying her Epistolarian supplies with her at all times. "You just never can tell when a scrap of time will come along and you can sit down and write to a friend. It's so important that we be ready at all times, and this is such a high-minded organization to begin with that carrying our writing supplies in such a way will help us seem all the more down to earth."

"Well, I never thought of it like that," Lucille said.

"You're right, we are very high-minded," Zeda Earl added.

"Extremely, I would say," Lucille rejoined.

"Yes, and because we are, I intend to perfume the insides of each box I string up," Maga Dell said almost in a monotone to keep from laughing.

"I prefer to perfume my own box," said Lucille through her nose. "I have my own secret brand and it's not like the overly sweet fragrance you use."

"You can perfume mine if you want to, Maga Dell, I don't care, because I like anything," Sue Ella declared. A.P. said to go ahead and perfume hers too because she was not hard to please either. When Miss Jessie said it was a wonderful idea and to include her in it also, Zeda Earl thought she had no choice but to say yes for herself as well, and so she did. By then Lucille had warmed up to the idea and said, "Oh, all right then, perfume mine as well, but if I don't like it, I fully intend to wash it out the first thing."

"Now, let's do come back together and elect our officers," Miss Jessie whispered.

"But what about the club song?" A.P. shouted.

"There's no need for one, A.P., because we're not going to hold meetings," Lucille answered.

"Well, you could sing at home when you're all by yourself, if you're the kind of person who happens to be inclined to do such a thing. I would have no way of knowing for sure," Maga Dell snapped.

"I've heard Lucille sing before, and she's got a real pretty voice," A.P. said, taking up for her.

"Do lets come back together and elect our officers," Miss Jessie said again.

"Don't you think we need a mascot?" A.P. said, giggling. "The Lion's Club has one, they say."

"And I'd be willing to bet a new pair of nylons that you can't tell us what kind of mascot they've got," said Maga Dell.

"No I can't, because I ain't never seen it nor heard anybody say, for sure," A.P. said, with a question mark all over her face.

"Well, I'll tell you, honey," said Maga Dell. "It's a lion. The Lion's Club's got them a lion for their mascot; ain't that a roar?"

"It sure is," A.P. said earnestly. "I wonder if it ever gets out?"

"That ain't the point," Maga Dell said, leaning forward, as if what she had to say was a secret. "The point, Agnes Pullens, is this: what kind of animal would you expect the Lion's Club to have for a mascot?"

I tell you, I just hate and despise that nasty-looking woman, Lucille thought.

"Will the meeting please come back to order?" Miss Jessie said, lifting her voice above her whisper. "Yes, that's better, ladies," she said softly. "Now, do let's this minute elect our officers."

How elegantly she said that, Zeda Earl thought as she nominated Miss Jessie for president. Sue Ella moved that they accept her by acclamation. The motion carried. Miss Jessie stood up and thanked all the ladies for their support.

Then Sue Ella nominated Maga Dell for vice-president. Lucille nominated A.P., and the nominations ceased.

All the ladies except Miss Jessie covered their eyes so they could not see who voted for whom. Zeda Earl and Lucille supported A.P. Maga Dell did not. She was saving her vote for herself because she felt sure that A.P. would vote for her as well, which is exactly what happened. As president, Miss Jessie was not allowed to vote unless there was a tie. When she asked to see a showing of hands for Maga Dell, Maga Dell's hand was the first in the air. Sue Ella and A.P. also voted for her, so she won only by voting for herself.

"God, how I hate the maggot," Lucille whispered to herself, peeping between her fingers. "Only the lowest piece of filth on earth would vote for itself."

Lucille was then voted club secretary. Zeda Earl was voted treasurer. A.P. became the social and entertainment chairman, and Sue Ella was elected club reporter both on the local and the regional scene because she had more contacts than anyone inside and outside Splendora.

Miss Jessie adjourned the meeting. Then she served ladyfingers and lime tea, and soon all the ladies went home.

As soon as they left, Miss Jessie phoned Brother Leggett at the church to tell him that the idea for the club had become reality and that the organizational meeting was full of wonderful surprises. "Good," he said. "In my next sermon I'll try to work in some parallel between the Epistles of St. Paul and the Epistles of Splendora."

That evening A.P. telephoned Miss Jessie. "I just want you to know how much Ruthie and Prissy would have enjoyed this new club of ours," she said. "If they had only lived to see it, what joy it would have brought to their hearts. You never knew them, of course, but you would have loved them both, especially Esther Ruth, because in some ways you're so much alike it's pitiful. The Epistolarians sounds just like something Ruthie would have thought of."

12

"I must be ever-mindful of my choice of words," Lucille said, taking her dictionary from the shelf and dusting it off. "Miss Jessie will notice every little thing because, of course, she's a librarian." Then she decided to put the dictionary back as she did not want her wording to seem unnatural. "I will simply be myself," she said, and began.

Dear Miss Jessie,

I was telling someone just the other day how fond of you I have become and in so short a time too, and how glad I am to have you living right next door. I have already told you so much about everybody else, and now I think I would like to tell you a little bit about myself. I was born and raised over in Wishing Well where I still have a sister living. One of the highlights of my life was attending Hillister Baptist College where I also graduated with honors. Bible was my major and I guess I must have read the book a dozen times when I was in school and I don't know how many times since. It did me the world of good too. But what makes me so proud is that my dear Juliet Ann has followed in my footsteps and was a straight-A student just like I was.

She said that she wanted to do things just like her mother. Now isn't that sweet? I also worked in the library, just like Juliet Ann did, so I know all about what you're going through and if I can be of some help I'll be so very happy to lend a hand, or whatever.

As you have probably heard, my Juliet Ann turned out to be a happy well adjusted person. As you know there are so many cases just the opposite around here. There's Zeda Earl's two. One living in sin and the other living in trash with some tramp more than three times her age, calls himself a junk man and is proud he can make a living that way. Well I guess that's all right if you're happy like that but you know they're not. She's not anyway. How could she be? Then there was Esther Ruth's grandson. She was the best thing in the world to him and what did he do but vanish into thin air the first chance he got and Sue Ella said it was all because he went to the other side of the fence, but here you come along and say you saw him in this country, so I guess maybe he went over and came back again. It's so hard to keep up with things. The world is going so fast and all.

What I really wrote to talk to you about is our new club. I do hope that Maga Dell Spivy won't get in our way too much. The way she laughs I sometimes wonder if she's on something. Dope I mean. Her eyes have a funny look in them too. Now she's not exactly our kind do you think? But she'll do of course. My problem is that I can't think of anything to say to her but I guess it will come. I try to be fair in things, don't you? I try to be a good woman, and more important a good Christian in every way, but if you had only come to me first I would have said no, no, no, right out right and would have supported myself with reasons why. But what's done is done. On the other hand, she did make some clever suggestions, the bandaid boxes being the most novel.

Before I forget it, please bring me your sweater the first chance you have. I want to get to work right away or else we might have our neck-wear and not our back-wear, if you know what I mean.

Oh yes, one other thing before I let you go. I'm sure you have heard us all talk about Pristine Barlow, our piano teacher. She's no longer living, poor dear, went a few months before Ruthie. It was cancer. They cut her open here in our hospital and when they saw what it was and how much it had spread they just sewed her right back up again. Poor dear Prissy. When the air got to her she went right like that, and I have said ever since then that if something ever gets the matter with me I will not be cut on because once you are and the outside air gets inside, well, you could just go over night. Prissy did. You would have loved her I think.

Dear heart, write when you can.

Lucille Monroe

Dear Zeda Earl,

I am writing to say please bring me your white sweater at once. I have finished mine. Miss Jessie is next in line and you are after her. I hope that's ok.

The idea of inviting Maga Dell Spivy to join us was nearly too much for me to take, but I'm sure Miss Jessie sees something good in the woman that we cannot see, and for the life of me, I will try to see it too, but it's so hard to look her straight in the eye as she strikes me as so cheap, which of course she is.

I just wanted to write and remind you of the sweater.

Your loving Epistolarian

Lucille

Dear Maga Dell,

Just the other day when I was cleaning out a drawer I found this red silk handkerchief and thought of you, so am enclosing it inside my very first letter to you. Maga Dell I think it will look so sweet folded in points and pinned to your collar or tucked into your belt. I thought of you because it is the reddest red I do believe I've ever seen, and I know how much you do enjoy the color because absolutely everything you own, including your porch light, has some red on it somewhere.

Your Epistolarian and friend

Lucille Monroe

Dear A.P.,

Surprise! Here is your first letter. I am trying to be the first to write everyone. I've even just this minute finished a letter to Maga Dell so I think I'm doing all the good even if I do say so myself.

That's all for now.

Your Epistolarian

Lucille

Dear Miss Jessie Honey,

Girls like us have to stick together around here because this place ain't nothing like the way it is way down in N.O. I know, and I ain't never been there yet. About the way you dress and act and all people don't suspect how you really are, and around here you got to keep it that way or else get talked about like dirt, that's me. You got a real good trick going, but I spotted you right off and knew, you and me, we'd see things eye to eye. It takes one to know one you've always heard them say. I guess it's true.

I want you to know you're gonna hear everything and anything about me around here so just get ready. It's usually Zeda Earl or Lucille that starts it up. They think I listen in on their calls all the time which ain't entirely true and ain't entirely false either. What do they have to lose I keep asking. They think it's just terrible that I entertain certain men friends, most of them married ones they say, and that my porch light burns all night long so they can see to get up and down the steps. Sometimes I get sick of it all and think I ought to be somewhere else like down in N.O. where you've been. I hear it's real French-like and there's plenty going on all the time, and even if it's watered down some it's still plenty good enough for me, and I'd have lots of city to scrub off when I got back, and you can bet your new hairnet on that one too. Maybe you and me ought to take a trip together sometimes. N.O. I mean, as I ain't never been there but would just love to go with somebody who has, and you have and could show me around and all, innerduce me to some real nice types, and if they're married it don't bother me none, got over that a long time ago, and if the Zeda Earl Goodridges and the Lucille Monroes in this world would only do right by their men they would not have to go elsewhere to get what they ought to be able to get right inside their own homes.

Maybe you don't want to take a trip now that you have your new preacher friend, or maybe you do. Let me know.

Maga Dell

Dear dear Lucille,

I adored your long, long letter, and on such lovely stationery. Such unequated elegance! How do you do it?

Do please excuse the brevity of this first letter. I am amidst boxes of books to be shelved and am striving to make a map of the county and a list of all the communities and crossroads to be included on my stops. I am pleased to say that additional funds have been provided for the purchase of new books. Today I sat down and ordered seventy-five titles, mostly for the reference section.

Please write again very soon and keep me abreast of all the happenings in your life. Let it be of comfort to know that my lips will be sealed to whatever you have to impart.

As I am, so are you

Jessie Gatewood

Dear Lucille,

I just wanted to write and tell you how much I'm going

to enjoy writing to you, and how much we missed you in Sunday School last Sunday and the Sunday before that. Everybody was afraid that we made you mad someway, but Zeda Earl said you were staying home because you couldn't afford anything new to wear, and she suggested we take up a collection for you to buy a new dress with. Wanda Lindsey said she'd be happy to let us have something out of her ready-to-wear shop for half price if that was what was keeping you out of God's house, but I said that I thought you would be offended. Did I say right?

Yours in Christ

AP

P.S.
I hope hope Zeda Earl is going to ask me and my girls to dance in the Crepe Myrtle Pageant this year but I hear she told Luta Hickman that I'm too fat. Have you heard anything?

Dear Miss Jessie,

I just wanted to write and find out how you are today. Lucille told me today that she's almost through with our sweaters. Won't it be fun to have them on. I'm teaching tap and acrobatics this afternoon and the parents are coming to watch so I have to go now. Write soon.

Yours in Christ,

AP

PS I'm thinking about going on a diet starting tomorrow.

Zeda Earl

I'm a telephone person for sure but I can't get through to you today to tell you this. Give Leggett and Jes something to do in your pageant coming up. Don't know what it could be yet. That's your worry not mine. Has to be something that will bring them closer together. Know what I mean?

S. E. Lightfoot

Dear Miss Jessie,

I must say how glad I am, we are, to have you in our town. I have grown so fond of you in this oh, so short a time, and I can sense that you have grown fond of me too. I can just tell somehow, and if I ever found out any different I think my feelings would be hurt for life.

I want you to feel free to come over soon for a visit. R.B. said the other day that he wants to get to know you better. Maybe Brother Leggett would like to come too. Just any Thursday is good for us if it's good for you two.

Lucille told me that she wrote to you about herself. Now I don't know what she told you, but if it's like what she goes around telling everybody else you can't put too much faith in it. She feels like she missed out on a lot because she never went to college like her daughter, so she makes up all kinds of tales about her education and none of them are true because I checked up. Sue Ella says she tries to relive her life through Juliet Ann, and what's so sad about that is that Juliet Ann isn't doing very well for herself either. She's a youth director over in Sour Lake at the First Baptist and is awfully highstrung. Has had six different church jobs in eight years and you know that's not a good record. Well all I can say is that it makes me thankful that I don't have that to worry about.

You should not have any trouble with Milford. He's such a dear sweet man who loves children and is generous with the poor in this area. He literally gives his heart away and you can just about always find a crowd of young boys around him on the square each Saturday.

Yesterday I saw Brother Leggett, and I told him to tell you hello. I hope he did. I also told him that I want him to take a big part in my pageant this year. I asked him what he would like to see in the way of a program, and he said that he wasn't good at coming up with such ideas and that I should ask you which is what I'm doing. Just any little

suggestion at all might start my mind working in the right
direction.

Always a friend forever

Zeda Earl

Dear Miss Jessie, A.P., Zeda Earl, Lucille and Sue Ella,

I hope you don't mind getting carbon copies but something's come up in my life and I ain't got time to write you
each a letter personally. I just want you to know that your
necklaces are ready, and I know you each and every one
can't wait to strap them on and smell real good so come on
by the phone company and pick them up.

Here's the perfume code so you can always tell whose
right behind you. A.P. gets *Dancer's Delight*. I found it at
the five and dime. Sue Ella gets *All Spice*. I already had it in
my kitchen. Miss Jessie gets *Wild Wild Rose*. No explanation necessary. Zeda Earl gets a double dose. *Spring Bou-
quet* and *Spanish Victory* and Lucille gets something special and I'm not allowed to say just what it is. A real knock
out I hope.

See you girls round

Maga Dell

Dear Miss Jessie,

I sent Milford to the telephone company to pick up Maga
Dell's contribution to our club. When he came back with it
I want you to know it smelled to high heaven. I have never
been around a worse odor in my life, and I simply refuse to
wear it or anything else the nasty woman has had her hands
on. I also refuse to write her another letter. And while I'm
on the subject, I refuse to write Zeda Earl ever again because she has told everyone that I quit going to Sunday
School because I need a new dress, and that's an out and
out lie. I quit going because Maridel Washmoyer became
my new teacher, and I know the Bible better than she does.
So why should I go? To be completely honest I feel that you

are the only member that I really care for these days. It seems to me that we have an understanding that goes far deeper than the others. So if you don't mind I will take more time with my letters to you and keep my letter to them limited to a note written on the bottom of a card, if that,

I hope this doesn't hurt your feelings.

The sweaters are ready and I'll deliver them real soon.

Do come when you can,

Lucille

Dear Maga Dell,

I am overjoyed with my Band-Aid box. It could not be more charming and I want you to know that you did a superb job assembling it. Such lovely ribbon I have not seen in a long time.

I just saw Zeda Earl wearing hers so proudly and complimented her on it. Sue Ella told me this morning that she carries her chewing gum in hers. That's a good thing to know, isn't it?

Yes, we must plan a trip to New Orleans as soon as possible. I am sure I could assist you in having a good time. The major problem is getting away. I cannot foresee a time in the next eight to twelve months that I will be able to take off, not even for a weekend. Surely I can arrange something, though.

You will forgive me if I don't make this longer, as I am engaged in typing hundreds of file cards. One day soon we must get together for a little breather.

Jessie Gatewood.

Dear Lucille,

You will find me in accord with your decision concerning our club. If you do not wish to write everyone, that is your prerogative, and I will not attempt to persuade you otherwise. However, I would be simply hurt to the core of my existence if you ever stopped writing to me, as I do enjoy your long letters so very much. But please do not feel as though you have to write frequently, as I am well aware that overindulgence may cause one to feel a sense of drudgery, and there is no need in this case for such a negative response.

May I urge you to repair your feelings toward Zeda Earl? I will need to work with the two of you very closely in the coming year, and any animosity whatever will only slow us down. Brother Leggett and I are working on a plan to restore our county courthouse to its original splendor. As you know it was at one time the most beautiful courthouse in all of East Texas and Louisiana combined, and we feel that it should be still and can be with a little effort, and, of course, strong financing. I have agreed to help finance the project and have pledged five thousand to start. I visualize you and Zeda Earl as primary fund-raisers because everyone in the county looks up to the two of you. Should you decide to assist, I trust you will keep all animosity buried or at a minimum. In the meantime, should you care to pledge a donation, I will be happy to add your name to the list.

The bookmobile is going to be a great success when all the problems are ironed out. As you know, I am parked near the highschool until I am completely organized. Please stop in to visit me there.

As ever

Jessie Gatewood.

Dear Jes,

What I'm going to tell you I should of told long before now but you have to understand that I'm a telephone person & not a envelope person. Here's my warning: Don't let Lucille & Zeda Earl know more than they ought. Don't be too much out in the open around here if you've got something to hide & I think you have. We all do you better believe. Maga Dell is ok. Eavesdrops a lot but is still ok. A.P. wouldn't hurt a fly intentionally but sometimes doesn't think ahead of time. And me, I don't hurt nobody that don't hurt me first, & if you do then watch out. That's what they all say anyway.

All for now. Call sometimes.

S. E. Lightfoot

Dear Miss Jessie,

I'm worried to death that Zeda Earl is planning to leave me and my dancing pupils out of the pageant this year. She'll listen to you if you tell her we ought to be in it again. We never get to perform but there. I promise to lose some weight if we can be in it.

I just love my sweater and my bandaid box full of supplies. Dudley Lock told me it looked silly but I told him I didn't think so. I said you didn't think so either.

YIC
AP

Dear Zeda Earl,

The only advice I have about the Crepe Myrtle Pageant is to keep the program short. Historical pageants tend to be too wordy and uninteresting and I trust you are not thinking in that direction. Simplicity is best. After the royal court has been introduced a simple, short, and elegant program of song and dance should follow. Then a fifteen-minute firework display should end the evening. I suggest using local talent all the way. Why not ask The Miss Agnes School of Dance and Expression to perform to three of Dora V. Williford's original hits? Everyone is in love with her new radio program, so I think it would be to your advantage to inlist her talent in combination with A.P.'s fine feeling for movement.

May I take this opportunity to bring up an issue that has been on my mind for some time now? Brother Leggett and I both agree that our courthouse is looking rather shabby these days and could stand a good facelift. Lucille is in complete agreement and so is Albert Posey of *The Splendora Star Reporter*. I have agreed to donate five thousand dollars to the restoration of the building. It is understandable that not everyone will want or be able to pledge that amount. Brother Leggett and Lucille have agreed to give as much as they can. Dorine and Judge Shinn will offer their pledge as soon as possible as will Brother Eagleton, Sonny and Inez Weeks, and others I have spoken to as I have come into contact with them. We are sure you and R.B. will want to give your support. It is so important to uphold our sparkling image, you know. If we allow one building to run down, the whole town will fall on its face before you know it. Sue Ella and A.P. have also said that they will help as much as possible.

Your good friend,

Jessie Gatewood.

Dear Miss Jessie,

Not much doing down here on the switchboard so I decided to write. I hear Lucille won't wear her bandaid box like the rest of us. I never expected her to play the game very long. Not after I used every perfume I have, and that ain't two or three either, to make her necklace smell good and loud. There ain't another in the world like Lucille is. What I'm gonna tell you is at first gonna seem like its made up, but I promise my hine leg it's not. I pieced it together over the years of working down here at the telephone company, and I'm about to give it all out just the way I took it all in. Lucille was married once before, but she don't talk about it to nobody. It seems her first husband wasn't a bit of count. Well they lived with her mother for some time and that was the first mistake. Her father had done already passed on, and the mother, well it was about time for her to be having some kind of close company again so Lucille's first and her mother started getting along pretty good you might say. Seems like he naturally took a liking to mothering and Lucille just was not giving enough of it out so what did he do but run off with her mother, and in the middle of the night at that, and all they left behind was a note saying that they were madly in love and just could not help theirselves either. Beats anything you ever heard of don't it. Now wait there's more and I know you're gonna need to hear this part. Lucille, she waited around in the house for a few days and finally the lovers came back off their trip and stolled into the house like nothing was the matter, and Lucille she put up with it for a few days and couldn't take it a minute longer and divorced the man on the spot, and then moved to Splendora and got hooked up with Milford the first thing and says to this day she married him only because of her poor state of mind at the time. Now this is the good part coming up. The mother died suddenly when they were on a trip to Old Mexico. It was Lucille's sister, her mother and her ex, or first, if you want to call him that, all in the same car together, and it was the mother whose idea it was to go in the first place. She said she just could not see dying without seeing Old Mexico so they got her down there, and she died in the car looking at it. Just this side of Monterrey, I think. Well, there they were, both of them ignert as sin and not knowing what to do, especially when the sister found out it was going to be hard to get her mother's body out of the country without greasing some palms and the ex, he was determined not to shell out a dime to have the body shipped back so instead of doing what was right he wrapped up Lucille's ole mother in a wore out blanket and tied her on top of the car like she was some kind of fancy rug and then started driving out of the country just like nothing was the matter with them. Now you know and I know that that was not such a good idea to start with, but we weren't around to give advice. So then, out they started and got pretty close back to Laredo and stopped for some food. They went inside this place and ate theirselves a dinner and came back out again and what do you know but there was no car waiting for them and no Mamma neither. Well, Lucille's sister she went into hysterics, pure-dee fits you might say, and accused Lucille's first of planning it all, so there was nothing for the man to do but just slap her crazy which he did until she shut up long enough for him to throw her on the next bus and get out of there. So they came on home, just the two of them and left the mother and the car and everything that was in it back there where it was stolen. Then the sister, when she got home, called Lucille and told her all this just like I told you, and when she got to the part about what happened to their mother, Lucille, she just said, and these were her very words—Good, she said, she had it coming to her and I hope to God she rots out on some Mexskin desert and the snakes eat her up bones and all—Now ain't that something for you? Her own mother too. And I promise that every last word of it's the truth and you can just knock me in the head if it's not.

Now by that time Lucille was already married to Milford who was running a little fix-it shop here in Splendora and was doing real good with it too, but nothing was ever good enough for Lucille and never will be either I don't guess, so that's why it don't pay to listen to all her talk. Just let it go in one ear and slide out the other like me.

No more energy to go on so I'll hush and tell you more some other time. Right now let's hear some more out of you. Get down to some real N.O. talk. Don't care what kind. Last letter of yours was real disappointing if you're asking me because I want more descriptions of what you do down there. You'll just have to take me sometimes so I can find out for myself.

See ya round

Maga Dell

Dear Miss Jessie,

R.B. is away on a business trip and will be gone another week or more but I'm sure he will be pleased to make a donation so I am pledging five thousand and five dollars in our name. I am also going to insist that the proceeds from this year's pageant be used for the restoration. Albert Posey has agreed to print the list of doners in the paper each week so we will know where we stand.

I am so pleased to be part of this community effort. We have needed someone like you for a long time now to bring us all together. You have worked miracles in the short time you have been here, and I do hope you will want to stay with us for many many happy years.

Thank you for the suggestions about the pageant. I intend to take them to heart. Your opinions are very important to me and I trust you will allow me to rely on your good judgement in the future.

Your dear friend,

Zeda Earl

Dear Maga Dell,

I am deeply distressed to know that you have found my letters lacking. Perhaps this one will make up for the brevity of my other efforts.

Yes, there are several "friends" of mine in N.O. whom I am sure would meet with your approval. The problem is which one to approach first. The only solution is to allow you to make up your own mind in advance. The choices are enumberated as follows:

Number One: A vegetable salesman in the French Market. Slightly tainted, he prefers to think of his partners of concubitus as victims of unwanted pleasure, and is stimulated to serious copulatory formation through extensive foreplay involving whips, chains, blindfolds, and sometimes tricycles and stick horses, but he is otherwise a perfectly innocuous dinner guest.

Number Two: A gourmet chef known for his cannibalistic tendencies. His appetite consists of peppermint sticks concealed in the carnal cavities of the body.

Number Three: A Protestant missionary whose organ of reproduction is reputed to be quite lengthy and of an admirable diameter, but who unfortunately is prone to various forms of self-pollution and prefers to relax his protuberance within overripe watermelons, warmed to a considerable temperature in the oven. He has been known to fraternize in moderation when melons are not in season.

Number Four: A professor of Ancient History and Mythology. He is recognized by a certain distinguished lubricity and cherishes a predisposition for women with large and pendulous breasts, but insists upon exercising conjugation in bestial positions and demands that his partners wear the head of a cow for effect. Homeric, to say the least.

Number Five: A libidinous oilman and his ever-so agreeable wife. They enjoy entertaining on their yacht, anchored off some remote Gulf Stream island, and their idea of a propitious event consists of at least a dozen uninhibited partisans decked out for the night.

Number Six: A garbage man as well as a participant in coitus interruptus. He houses an extensive collection of Mary Jane slippers which are subjected to periodic acts of repetitious defilement perpetrated in rooms filled with paying guests. On occasions he can be aroused to reciprocal splendor by verbal abuse.

Number Seven: The owner of a small hotel, the top floor of which is reserved for regular patrons who are incapable of reaching normal expression and must resort to various forms of mass ecstasy.

Number Eight: A manufacturer of aphrodisiacs who is himself a regular blister beetle and a notorious promoter of his ample product; is somewhat tribal in instinct.

Number Nine: An elevator boy; prone to sadistic fantasy, criminal conversations, and voyeuristic fulfillment, he will, once challenged, prove to be quite harmless.

Number Ten: An octagenarian resident of a respectable

rest home. He is known for his numerous nocturnal emissions in Audubon Park and is an example for us all to follow in our old age.

Maga Dell, I do hope I've given you enough to choose from. If not, I will send another list. Please do not make a cursory choice as I will be unable to leave Splendora for sometime yet, and between now and then I will undoubtedly think of other tempting opportunities.

Thank you for your interesting letter concerning Lucille's first husband. I find the Mexican episode reminiscent of certain novels, the authors of which delight in forcing their reader into contact with multitudinous vignettes involving pathological behavior of an unbelievable nature.

As ever,

Jessie Gatewood

Dear Miss Jessie,

That letter sure was something. I didn't understand it right at first but after I got my word book down I figured it out real fast. Don't take long with words like that. All mean the same thing. It sure is a good thing you worded it that way too for it never would've gone through the U.S. mail if you had said it in plain talk. Some of the things you mentioned in there I've heard of but I ain't never *really* heard of, if you know what I'm saying. You don't need to bother listing anymore because I've done picked the gourmet chef who hides candy in the cardinal cavities. I'll bet you a new hair net that I got some he'd have a hard time getting it in and out of but sure would be fun to give it a try. I'm ready when you are.

See ya round,

Maga Dell

Dear Maga Dell,

I am wondering if you have ever had to go on a diet.

How did you get that slim and all is what I'm wondering. Did you start out big like me and then shrink, or did you start out your size. I can't remember you ever looking any other way. Dr. Martindale put me on a hard diet is why I'm asking, and I just know there's an easier one to be had somewheres. He won't let me eat anything I like and I got to lose fifty pounds because Zeda Earl said if I did she'd let me and my girls dance in the pageant. Dr. Martindale's got me on some new medicine. I also take a shot once a week. He only lets me have 125 carbohydrates a day. It's hard to figure all that out but I think I've got it down now. One four inch piece of pie with a double crust the way I like it has 55 carbohydrates, that's about half of what I can have in one day, so I got to watch it close and not go over. But just eggs and meat don't satisfy me somehow, seems like I need something sweet ever once in awhile, just to keep me going. You ever feel that way? But Dr. Martindale says that's what puts the pounds on, all the carbohydrates, and I'm way over for my height, five feet, one inch. Am supposed to be around 118 pounds for somebody between 50 and 60, so I guess it's somewhere around 75 to 150 pounds I got to lose fast or I won't get to dance in the Crepe Myrtle Pageant and that would just kill me because I've danced in it for years. Please write right back and let me know how you got to be so slim.

YIC

AP

Dear A.P.,

Thanks for the letter but just one word of advice. You got to have some action to take off weight. Why don't you get yourself a boyfriend and take up bowling together. Or if you're like me you'll choose some other energetic sport that has a little more fun to it. I ain't talking about table tennis either.

Maga Dell

P.S. Do you think you can get me a start of Wandering Jew? The green kind like Lucille's got. I got the purple already. If I ask her she'll say no and if you ask her she'll say yes.

Dear Maga Dell,
Thank you for your advice about losing weight. I'll try to take it if I can. I'm sure I know exactly what you mean though.
I talked to Lucille about the Jew and she said hers all died, but I know she's lying don't you? It's hanging all over her porch.

YIC

AP

Dear Magnolia,
I have organized a letter-writing club in Splendora. I had hoped that it would be an organization that would keep me abreast of things and yet at a distance. Perhaps it is doing just that to some degree, but I have the feeling that it has been nothing short of catastrophic in many ways. I am utterly amazed to find that after fifteen years nothing has changed in Splendora. Everyone has been writing in their letters what they were talking about when I left.
I am trying to take part in some community efforts other than the library, which is coming along smoothly. I should be in circulation by the first of the year or before. Oh yes, Miss Jessie is seeing someone—the assistant pastor of the Baptist church—and to tell the truth, I feel myself becoming attached to him in a way I did not expect.
The annual Spring Pageant is coming up and promises to be quite an occasion. Zeda Earl whom I have told you all about is this year's director and has been making plans already. I have even given her a few suggestions.
Why don't you consider visiting me during the festivities?

It should be a perfect time for you to get to know Splendora.

Love

Miss Jessie Timothy John Coldridge, Gatewood, Esq.

Milford Monroe was determined to write letters also. On some picture postcards that he once bought in Arkansas when Lucille and he were on a short vacation, he wrote the same note to each member of the Epistolarians and sent the cards to his sister in Little Rock to be mailed from there.

Dear Girls,

You don't know what you're missing staying home so much. Here I am in Hot Springs, Arkansas. This trip has done me the world of good. If you'd only step outside Splendora sometimes you'd look a whole lot prettier and when you got back you wouldn't be so hard to get along with. Would take fifty years off each of you just to get away from there. I suggest Alaska in January. You'd love it then.

Be back soon

Your fellow letter writer,

Milford

"And all this time there he sits on the courthouse square and expects us to believe that he's been gone on vacation. Well, the very nerve!" Lucille said. Brother Leggett told her that he was only playing a joke, and she replied, "There's no such thing as a joke like that. Milford has once more embarrassed me in front of all my friends, and I simply don't know how I can face Miss Jessie again after all this. The man has absolutely lost his mind."

Brother Leggett leaned back in his office chair, closed his eyes, and almost went to sleep. Lucille thought that he was praying for her and went on talking a blue streak.

Later that day she wrote to each member of the Epistolarians, including Maga Dell Spivy, and told them not to pay one ounce of attention to Milford because he was old and crazy and there was nothing she could do about it.

Miss Jessie called Lucille and said that she should not take Milford's pranks so seriously, but Lucille could not be pacified so easily. "If you had to live with him, you'd take it seriously too," she said. "To think that ignert fool is my Juliet Ann's father. Well, it just about makes me sick every-time I think about it."

After a few days Milford went to the high-school English teacher, Mrs. Whitehead, and asked to borrow a book of social correspondence. All the way to the drugstore Milford thumbed through the book. Johnnie Mitchell sold him some pastel stationery, and then he returned to the courthouse square to copy letters.

Dear A.P.,

Yesterday afternoon the ding-a-ling of my front door bell brought me out of my backyard flower garden and around the side of my house to find the delivery man standing there with the flowers you sent. Oh, those lovely violets! Fresh with dew on their faces, they looked as though they had just been plucked by a fairy from a magical garden.

Thank you for thinking of me on my birthday. Because of you it has been the best one ever.

Love,
Zapora

"But I don't know anyone by the name of Zapora," A.P. said. "Do you think it could be a mistake?"

"Only Milford's mistake," Lucille said, as though she could care less. Inside she was actually burning alive.

Two days later Zeda Earl received a letter on some of the prettiest stationery she believed she had ever seen.

Dear, dear Zeda Earl:

I returned home exhausted but refreshed from our good

visit. What joy it brought to my heart to spend three whole days in your beautiful house and to meet your husband and your lovely children. We should never have allowed these years to pass without staying in contact with each other. I do hope you will come to Springville soon so I may be able to show you the same good time that I have just enjoyed. Richard and the children are hoping so too. Won't you please say "Yes" and bring the whole family during the last week of June. That is the time of our annual Turkey Shoot and I cannot think of anyone else I'd rather have visit us except you and your family. The children are already making plans, and Richard and I are as excited as we can be. We look forward to seeing you then.

Your friend,

Susan Rose Bush

After Zeda Earl received Milford's letter she wrote Miss Jessie at once.

Dear Miss Jessie,

I am writing to tell you that I do not think I can go on with this letter writing club much longer. I am sorry to have to say this but Lucille Monroe makes me sick, A.P. makes me sick, Sue Ella makes me sick and Maga Dell Spivy makes me deathly ill. Even Milford is getting on my nerves because he has no right to invite himself to join. I like wearing my sweater but can't stand that bandaid box that Maga Dell made. It stinks just like she does and makes me sick. You are the only one in the club that makes me feel good so I'm going to write only to you until I feel better about everybody else. I hope you don't mind.

I have planned the pageant just as you suggested and I think you will be very very pleased. I have reserved a very large part for you but I am not at liberty to say what it is right now.

Love,

Zeda Earl

Dear Zeda Earl,

I am sorry to hear you are not getting along well with the members of our club. I am always respectful of your wishes and will be pleased to continue receiving your letters which mean the world to me.

Recently I have received many complaints about our organization, not only from our own members but also from non-members who aren't quite sure of our intentions. I think it is best that we not call attention to ourselves, and since we are experiencing internal strife, we are likely to do just that; more than what we have already, that is. Perhaps we should bring this chapter of our lives to a close this very moment. We will, of course, be able to go on writing each other, not as the Epistolarians, but as Friends. Sue Ella agrees with me. If the rest of you are in agreement, then I will ask Sue Ella to publicly announce our decision.

Your friend,

Jessie Gatewood

The next week in the front page of *The Splendora Star Reporter*, Albert Posey, who elected himself chairman of the courthouse restoration project, announced the list of donors and the amounts donated. The list began with two matching contributions of two dollars and fifty cents, each given by Bertha and Beth Miller. A.P.'s pledge of three dollars and fifteen cents was next, followed by dozens of citizens in the five- and ten-dollar category and a few in the twenty-five-dollar range, Brother Leggett and Maga Dell among them. "I don't have to wonder very long to figure out what she had to do to earn that twenty-five dollars," Lucille says when she read the paper. After Maga Dell's name Albert and Inez Weeks were listed with a thirty-five-dollar contribution. Sue Ella and Snyder managed to scrape up forty-one dollars between them, while Judge Shinn and Dorine were proud to donate one hundred. Following much discussion and earnest prayer Brother Eagleton and wife Eloise gave one hundred as well, and from there the contributions leaped to Miss Jessie, third from the last, with five thousand dollars beside her name, followed by Zeda Earl with five thousand and five, and ending with Lucille Monroe's pledge of five thousand and six dollars and sixty-five cents. "Oh my god, what's run away with my mind?" Lucille screamed when she saw her name and contribution in print. "How on earth did I think I was going to come up with that kind of money without going into debt for the rest of my life?" The thought that she might be recognized as the most generous woman in the county gave her comfort, but not for long. Finally she phoned Albert Posey and told him that he had made a terrible mistake because her contribution was for fifty-six dollars and sixty-five cents. "I accuse you of printing a lie and embarrassing me in front of all my good friends," she screamed.

"But I really thought I heard you say five thousand, Lucille," said Albert apologetically.

"You should have waited to receive my check," replied Lucille. Then you wouldn't have been wrong."

In the same edition of the weekly paper, but on another page Sue Ella had written a brief statement to the effect that The Epistolarians was no longer an active organization serving Splendora and Splendora county, because the members already had too much to do. Lucille was furious over the wording. "You made it sound like we weren't much to start with," she said, and Sue Ella answered her, "Well, maybe we weren't."

"But we did last for almost two months, and that's saying something for us, for sure," Maga Dell said. "As much fussing as I 'magine was going on in everybody's letters, it's a wonder we didn't bust it up before now."

Timothy John was the most relieved of all, and A.P. was the most disappointed. But to Sue Ella Lightfoot it did not matter much whether the club lived or died. "We've still got our telephones," she said. "And they're much better anyway, because you don't have to use no paper, nor do no writing, just talk."

13

After the Epistolarians announced their demise, Brother Leggett took it upon himself to find Miss Jessie something else to do with her spare time. He had hoped she would consent to become a Sunday-school teacher, but she refused adamantly. "I must decline," she said, "not because my mind freezes at the thought, but because I do not feel the calling to become a teacher just yet. I am certain, however, that you can help me find an outlet for my talents."

On Brother Leggett's urging she became a member of the First Baptist Church choir, but she stated at the very beginning that she would not sing solos. "I simply haven't the voice for it," she told Mr. Worth Treadway, the Minister of Music. Dora V. Williford, who sat next to her in the choir loft each Sunday, said that Miss Jessie had the tiniest voice she had ever heard. "In fact," she said, "it's so small that I'm not sure I've ever heard it at all."

"But it's her presence that's felt," Mr. Treadway said, "and in this case that's the most important thing."

The first Sunday she appeared with the choir the congregation almost broke into applause. Everyone began chattering the moment they saw her.

"It's such an inspiration to see her face shining out at us. Isn't that what you say?" Bertha Miller said to her twin sister, Beth. They were both dressed in navy blue with white polka dots and pillbox hats to match.

"She's done more for the general morale of this town in the short time she's been here than anybody I know of," said Hortense Gladly to Dudley Lock, who was hard of hearing.

"Come again?" Dudley shouted. But instead of speaking into his ear, Hortense wrote what she had just said on her church bulletin and gave it to him.

Unfortunately Dudley had left his glasses at home.

Oh, how I do admire everything that woman does, Lucille thought.

"She can do no wrong, if you're asking me," Opel Flowers said to Esker Dement and his wife, Ethel, who had just sat down.

"Next to Dora V. Williford's hour of song, Miss Jessie's library news is the best radio program I've got on the air today," Esker verified.

"I just love the tone of her voice," replied Ernestine Martin.

"I'd do absolutely anything she said do," said A.P.

"I've never known her to be wrong about anything," declared Inez Weeks.

"She's the Lord's gift of the year," cried Daphne Hightower at the top of her voice.

Brother Eagleton announced to the congregation that they were truly blessed to have Miss Jessie as a new member of the choir and that she had agreed to be the pianist for the Christmas cantata in order to relieve Mr. Treadway of some of his burden.

"I'd walk a million miles out of my way just for that woman," Mr. Treadway told the deacon of the day, Jiggs Overstreet.

"She's a saint and nothing but, if you're asking me," said Henrietta Lamb to her husband, Buddy. They had locked up their drive-in grocery that Sunday and attended church together for the first time in months because they had heard that Miss Jessie was going to be singing in the choir. Buddy thought she was the most beautiful woman he had ever seen. Henrietta warned him not to get any funny ideas in his head. "She's a lady from the word *go*. Besides, you're already spoken for. Remember?"

If only we had found her years ago, Zeda Earl wished. R.B., sullen faced, was sitting next to her, but they were not speaking that day. He had just arrived home from his business trip and was still not too happy about Zeda Earl's participation in the courthouse project. After the service, when everyone was shaking hands with the preacher and visiting on the churchyard, R.B. cornered Albert Posey. "It was my idea long ago to have a modern courthouse, and it's going to stay modern, do you hear?" Albert said that there was nothing wrong with a modern building as long as it looked like something. R.B. wanted to know if Albert was trying to tell him that the courthouse was an eyesore and Albert said that he certainly was.

"We're all telling you the same thing, Mr. Goodridge," said Miss Jessie. She had rushed from the choir loft to meet Brother Leggett out front and had overheard most of the conversation. "The fact is, the building, as it now stands, ruins the appearance of the whole town."

"I differ with you Miss Gatewood, and I do not beg to do so," R.B. said firmly. "Furthermore, you can remove the contribution my wife has made in our name, for we have no intention of supporting your foolish project."

Zeda Earl, nearly dead with embarrassment, slipped away

to the other side of the street to greet Geneva Handly, who had not been to church in weeks.

Brother Leggett joined the group just as R.B. called Miss Jessie a meddlesome woman. "She is anything but meddlesome, Mr. Goodridge," said the assistant pastor.

"Brother Leggett is right," replied Miss Jessie. "I am not meddlesome, but I am troublesome. If you're in doubt, put me to test. I'll be so happy to prove myself."

"I don't know why you're making such a thing over a building," R.B. shouted. Everyone on the church steps heard him and turned his way. Zeda Earl, still pretending that she did not know what was going on, continued talking to Geneva Handly about her bursitis.

"We are making such a thing over a building because it has been disgraced by a disgraceful person," replied Brother Leggett. "Furthermore, we are giving that person a chance to rectify his egregious mistake and to restore something of his lost integrity as well." After he had finished he realized that everyone coming out of the church had heard him, and he wondered if he had been too forthright, but Miss Jessie gave him a look of reassurance and his confidence was suddenly restored.

"Should your obstinancy continue," she whispered, "I will be forced to become troublesome. By that I mean I will elicit the help of everyone in the county who will be more than willing to stand on my side.—Troublesome: to perturb, inconvenience, or bother. A state of distress, danger, affliction, or need.—I am more than willing to contribute to such a state, Mr. Goodridge. Now, good day."

She took Brother Leggett by the arm and they strolled off in the direction of Sonny Week's hotel where they planned to enjoy lunch with Sonny and Inez, who employed the best cooks in town.

"Makes me feel right good to see somebody stand up to R.B. like that," said Lem Williford, Dora V.'s father, as everyone on the churchyard watched the couple stroll away.

"Leave it to R.B. to start a row in front of the church," said Daphne Hightower.

"I'd just as soon it be here as anywhere else," said Maga Dell, who had surprised the world by attending church that day. Everyone said that they were so glad to see her in God's house, even if she did come in halfway through the sermon.

"Yes, but all she did was twist her hair and smack her gum," said Lucille. "You know the woman didn't listen to a word, and if she did, it didn't sink in." She was talking to Esker Dement, but her eyes were on Brother Leggett and Miss Jessie strolling leisurely up the street. In front of the Post Office they stopped for a moment, and she whispered something to him. Lucille's curiosity peaked. "Now I just wonder what she could be telling him that's so important she has to get right up in his ear to say it?" she said out loud.

When the next issue of *The Splendora Star Reporter* went on sale the town and the county alike went into an uproar over the removal of R.B.'s contribution.

Over the radio Miss Jessie apologized for him. Zeda Earl went into hiding and did not show her face for a week. The Goodridge residence was flooded with telephone calls, and their mailbox was overflowing with hateful letters. Both Sue Ella and Lucille persuaded Zeda Earl to come out of hiding and take a stand for Miss Jessie, which she did. It was the first time Brother Leggett or anyone in Splendora or Splendora County had ever known her to take issue with her husband, and it was all they could find to talk about for days to come.

"She's really gotten on her soapbox, that's for sure," Dorine Shinn said.

"Absolutely everywhere you go there she is sounding off

just like that revival preacher we had here last spring," replied Laura Lou Handcock. "I surely do hope we get him back again this coming year."

"Well, if we don't, Zeda Earl can just step right up there behind that pulpit and take his place, because I think she's doing all the good," stated Esker Dement without blinking an eye.

"I'm for her all the way," said Sonny Weeks.

"It's the best thing the woman's ever done in her whole and entire life," said Geneva Handly to Maridel Washmoyer, who was carrying a Christmas wreath made out of cut-up egg cartons to the hospital.

"What she's doing must agree with her, because she looks ten years younger, and that's no lie," said Maridel, terrified that she was not going to make it to the reception room with her latest creation.

"I think for once in her life Zeda Earl knows what she's doing," said Milford Monroe, talking only to himself.

When Zeda Earl felt as though she had sufficiently talked up the project in Splendora, she drove to every neighboring community and spoke on the importance of keeping the county looking its best. At every stop she circulated a petition, and urged everyone to sign up in support of a countywide restoration, beautification, and cleanup. After she had been all over the county she called Miss Jessie to give her a report. "I tell you," she said, "it makes me feel myself all over again just to be doing something on my own."

Before she went much further, however, R.B. reconsidered. He said that it had all been a misunderstanding and agreed to make an even more generous donation to the restoration committee. He also announced, just as though it had been his idea all along, that the proceeds from the Crepe Myrtle Pageant would also be used for the project.

Albert Posey promised that work on the courthouse would start as soon as the weather warmed up that spring, and Milford said that that might be a long time coming because the winter was going to be one of the worst on record.

If only we can have a snowfall before Christmas it will enhance my yard display so very very much, Zeda Earl thought, and consulted Milford on the possibility.

"No snow, just ice. And it's all coming after Christmas," was his answer, but Zeda Earl was convinced that he was wrong, and whether it snowed or not she was determined to win the yard prize that year, even if it killed her.

Christmas was just around the corner. As part-time Youth Director, it was Brother Leggett's duty to organize weekly caroling parties. Miss Jessie always attended as one of the two chaperones. She insisted that they all wear colorful scarves, hats, and carry candles and musical instruments.

"Every Friday night they sing like angels standing right out in front of my house," A.P. said.

"They make me so happy, I just don't know what to do," replied Lucille Monroe.

The only night they went outside the city limits they rode in a wagon piled high with hay and pulled by Chester Galloway's old plowhorse. Snyder Lightfoot agreed to be the driver. Sue Ella said that it was an awful mistake to ask Snyder to do such a thing, but she agreed with Brother Leggett that he did need to get away from the icehouse and have some fun for a change. Miss Jessie said that it would be a pleasure to have him along, and told him to remember to wear lots of warm clothing.

They left from the church just after sundown and headed toward Sawdust Road, which was unpaved and mostly clay all the way through the next county. Miss Jessie chose to wear a dress of bright-red wool set off with a challis scarf tied loosely around her neck. In her hair she arranged sprigs of mistletoe and holly with bright-red berries.

"You're a Christmas vision," Brother Leggett said as they approached the first community.

Marybeth Faircloth heard him and told her boyfriend, Bobby Shinn, what he had said. Together they started giggling and buried themselves in the hay.

"What's all that giggling about, I wonder?" said Snyder to his old dog, Popsicle, who was sitting beside him on the driver's seat and getting ready to howl at the moon.

When the first row of houses came into sight, only five of the carolers were visible above the hay. Brother Leggett pretended not to notice the absence of voices as they burst into song. Popsicle began to howl with the singers, and Miss Jessie said that he provided a most unusual accompaniment, but Snyder said, "It just sounds like racket to me."

After they left the first community Miss Jessie reclined on the hay, and after some deliberation Brother Leggett joined her. They watched the stars pass slowly overhead and listened to the horse's hooves clopping against the red clay road.

If only I could tell him everything, Timothy John thought. Someone behind them began singing "Silent Night," and the assistant pastor was moved to tears. Miss Jessie, swooning from the excitement of it all, rested her head on his shoulders.

When she did someone on the other side of the wagon said, "Look at them now."

Hearing the comment, Brother Leggett pretended to see a falling star and sat up fast. "Did you see that?" he said. Miss Jessie confessed that her eyes had been closed. When she sat up her dress was covered with hay. The sprigs of mistletoe and holly were falling from her hair, and the moon was shining brightly in her eyes.

It's the most beautiful moon I've ever seen, Timothy John thought. Miss Jessie said so, and Brother Leggett agreed with her. "I'm so glad I know you," he said, squeezing her hand tenderly in the hay. The moon went behind a cloud; the wagon passed under a low-hanging live oak, and they were surrounded by almost total darkness. Without thinking about what he was doing, Brother Leggett lifted Miss Jessie's hand to his lips and kissed her fingers.

"How dear of you," Miss Jessie said, almost in Timothy John's voice, for he was on verge of breaking through. The wagon left the canopy of branches and the moon came back out again. Somewhere in the distance an owl was hooting, and from the nearby swamp a bobwhite could be heard singing his heart out.

"It's unusual to hear one this time of year," Snyder said over his shoulder, but no one heard him.

Brother Leggett gathered the mistletoe and holly falling from Miss Jessie's hair and arranged it in a crown around her head.

Sometimes I wish I had stayed in New Orleans, Timothy John thought. It would have been so much easier there.

At each community there were fewer and fewer singers as the teenagers disappeared two by two under the hay. Brother Leggett sang as loud as he could, not only to make up for the shortage of voices, but also because he was not quite sure how to handle the pairing-off situation and was afraid that it was going too far, but wanted to avoid the problem as long as possible. At Point-blank, the last community before the next county line, Miss Jessie and the assistant pastor suddenly found themselves singing a duet. Everybody in the row of the houses came out on their porches to see what was going on as Miss Jessie and Brother Leggett, struggling to keep the song going, uncovered their chorus members and insisted that they sit up and sing at once. Brother Leggett was seized with fear and trembling each time he uncovered another couple.

Finally everyone was once again visible and lifting their voices in unison. What a relief, Brother Leggett thought as they finished the carol and shouted, "Merry Christmas!" to everyone standing on the porches of Point-blank.

One community followed another in rapid succession after that until Snyder looked around and discovered that he could not recognize one familiar landmark. He did not get alarmed, though. He took a moonpie out of his coat pocket and began eating it without allowing anyone to see what he was doing. Because he only had one, he was not about to share it unless he was forced to. After he had finished the last crumb he admitted to himself that he was lost as a goose, but still he did not say anything to the carolers. "The road's bound to come out at a highway somewhere," he said to Popsicle, who was sleeping with his head hanging off the seat.

It was nearly twelve o'clock but no one on the hayride realized it was that late. Back in Splendora, however, Sue Ella was getting anxious for them to return. She could imagine all sorts of bad things happening, but her worst fear was that Snyder had driven off a bridge. Then she remembered that the road they were supposed to take circled around through three counties and passed some of the roughest backwoods beer joints in East Texas. At a quarter past midnight she tried to call Sheriff Fred Polston, but he was nowhere to be found, so she cranked up her car and went out looking for them herself. The road was narrow and full of holes. "It ain't never seen a road grader in over a year, at least," she said. "No wonder these people who live way out here can't never get to town without tearing up their cars. Something ought to be done about it and if I had a say in anything around here something would be done about it."

She drove for two hours before she caught up with them a mile into the next county where they were parked in front of a beer joint.

By that time everyone in the wagon realized that they were lost. Some of the girls began to cry and the boys made them cry louder by saying that they would never find their way home. Snyder was trying to ask two drunk loggers how to get to the nearest highway; Miss Jessie was trying to calm the crying girls; Brother Leggett was wondering if he should go inside the beer joint and ask to use the telephone; and Sue Ella was just standing there watching them with amusement. When they looked around and saw her a sigh of relief passed through all of them. Even the boys who were pretending not to be afraid were glad she was there.

"Pore ole Snyder," Sue Ella said to Miss Jessie and Brother Leggett only. "He don't never know how to turn around and go back the way he came. Sometimes I feel so sorry for him I don't know what to do because he's always getting penned in between a rock and a hard place and can't get out by himself to save his neck. So then I have to come along. But that's what I'm here for, I guess."

Then she walked over to Snyder who was still trying to get a straight answer out of the drunk men, and when he saw her, his face lit up like the Christmas tree that could barely be seen through the door of the beer joint. "You follow me on back, Snyder," she said. "I know the nearest way out of these parts. I'm from this county and you ain't, remember?"

She guided them back to Splendora, and when they arrived, some of the parents, sitting on the church steps, were hysterically begging to know where their children had been. But Sue Ella managed to calm them down by saying that the roads look different at night and they got lost before they knew it. Then she took Brother Leggett and Miss Jessie off to one side and said, "Now, I suggest you keep your songfests inside the city limits from now on, but if you find yourselves just itching to get outside of town again, you better call on me to drive you, because I don't never forget where I am."

Both the assistant pastor and the county librarian agreed to stick to the streets of Splendora. The next Friday night they added a flute and a trombone and sounded better than ever, so said Sonny Weeks.

"Oh, I just wish they would come out every night of the year," Bertha Miller said.

"They look like one big happy family, if you're asking me," said sister Beth.

"Pretty soon they just might be, you never know," said Hortense Gladly.

"Wouldn't it be nice to have a Christmas wedding," squealed A.P., turning around and around on her toes.

The week before Christmas the yard displays went up, and everyone drove around at night to pass judgment on the colorful lights and decorations. Zeda Earl had come up with the idea back in June to create a yard full of wrapped presents. All summer long she had collected every household appliance box she could find, and come December first she began wrapping them in colored paper. "What a stupid idea," Lucille said when she saw the Goodridge lawn filled with giant presents with ribbons and bows. "It's so pretentious, if you're asking me, and will never take the prize." Lucille had decorated every tree in her yard with ornaments she had spent the whole year making herself. "It's so old-fashioned, just like Christmas is supposed to be," she told Miss Jessie the day she was hanging a simple holly wreath on the Coldridge house. "It's going to be hard to choose between your yard and Zeda Earl's," Miss Jessie said, and Lucille replied, "There's no question in my mind whose yard is the best."

Maridel Washmoyer thought her styrofoam igloos made the best-looking display of all, but A.P. said that to her way of thinking igloos had nothing whatever to do with Christmas. A.P. had resorted to her usual covered wagon with Santa Claus sitting on the driver's seat. Maga Dell Spivy outlined her porch with blinking red lights, and Lem Williford wrote "Happy Birthday, Jesus" in big blue letters all over his white roof. "I don't know what he wanted to do such a thing for, because he's too lazy to wash it off, and you know the rain's not going to," said Inez Weeks. Her husband, Sonny, decorated the front porch of their hotel with the Christian flag on one side and the American flag on the other. Esker and Ethel Dement hired some small boys to climb the oak in front of their house and hang dozens of blown-up balloons from the branches. "I declare to goodness, it looks just like a giant gumdrop tree," said Ethel. She was so proud of it she could have died. Wanda Lindsey took home all the department-store dummies from her dress shop and with them created a manger scene in modern-day dress under her carport. Eloise Eagleton said that it was sacrilegious. On top of a six-foot pole out in front of her house Eloise displayed a giant star she made out of crushed-up aluminum cans and pieces of cellophane to add a little color. "It looks so cheap, I'd be ashamed of it if I was her!" said Lucille. "She should have done like Daphne Hightower who couldn't think of one original idea this year so she didn't do anything at all."

The night of the judging was also the night of the christmas cantata. That year the choir was singing *Peace of Mind* which had been composed by Trenda Clayton and Waverly Powell, who wrote exclusively for Southern Baptist churches. At the last moment Dr. Martindale was called to the hospital and Mr. Treadway had to sing his part. Dora V. Williford came in six measures late on her solo and did not realize it until the music stopped and she still had another line to sing. Bubba Wiggley, refusing to observe the decrescendos, sang at the top of his voice, and, according to Lucille, who was sitting in the back row, he sounded like a bullfrog. Only Miss Jessie seemed calm. After it was over, Mr. Treadway said that it was a joy to look over and see her smiling and that he would not have made it through the program had she not been sitting at the keyboard.

A brief reception was held in Fellowship Hall, and afterward Zeda Earl and R.B. returned home to find all the giant presents opened and the wrappings scattered all over their block. The next day it was announced that Lucille had won the yard prize, and Zeda Earl was certain that she had lost only because her yard had been vandalized. She told Sheriff Fred Polston that it had to have been the work of the mean Birdwell boy who was seen lurking about town all day long, and the sheriff said that he had been wanting to find some good reason to get his hands on that boy for years.

That afternoon Lucille gladly assisted Zeda Earl in putting her display back together. "It's the very least I can do," she said. "After all, it is Christmas and we're supposed to lend a helping and where ever possible. I have always believed that to be true."

14

Winter had fully arrived and the land was barren of green but for the holly, the cedar, the pine, and the wax-leafed magnolia and live oak. "Thank God for evergreens," Esther Ruth Coldridge always said, and would have again, had she lived. "Without them I guess we'd altogether stop breathing in the wintertime." Christmas had already come and gone and the first big freeze had just struck. "Something mighty unusual is going on this year," Milford Monroe said, "for we usually begin warm and end cold, but this year it's started up early. Must be in for a long hard one." Everyone in Splendora listened to him for the local weather changes, but not everyone believed him. He had watched the skies all his life, had felt his joints ache before a blue norther, had listened to his jaw crack before a heavy rain. Migraines set in just before autumn, arthritis before winter, and usually he went into a lazy slump the day before spring. Summer always brought on hay fever running into sinus, and then it was back to the migraines of autumn. It happened that way every year. He swore to it. More than half of Splendora county laughed at his predictions, but there were those who heeded his every word and seldom knew him to be wrong.

Synder Lightfoot swore by him, as did Sue Ella. They both had listened to Milford and therefore had been ready for the freeze that just had struck, bowing the trees over to the ground, freezing the water pipes to bursting, breaking telephone lines, and causing the electricity to go off for hours. Lucille had not believed it would freeze. And, because her maid was home sick, she had done a late-afternoon wash, hung her sheets out to dry overnight, and the next morning they were stiff as boards.

Milford said that she should have listened to him. "I told you it will either hit next Monday or Tuesday." He had told everybody; had embarrassed Lucille to death because she could not shut him up. She was forever telling her friends not to pay any attention to him because he was partially out of his mind. Only Sue Ella challenged her by saying, "If he is, and I don't believe so, just look, I wish you would, at who put him there."

Before the current freeze not only had his joints ached, he had also been able to smell cold air moving in. "There's no other smell in the world like it," he said. And the fact that the storm did blow in, and as early as he had predicted, made some of his disbelievers finally sit up and take notice.

Overnight everything was covered with ice. Trees blew over or broke off at their main trunks. Branches split and hung in icy suspension like broken appendages dangling, "just ready to fall on a head or roof, and I hope to goodness it's not mine," A.P. worried. "Let it be the other fellow's."

Esker Dement was out trying to unthaw his water pipes with his wife's hairdryer and gallons of boiling water when a giant icicle fell on his head and knocked him unconscious for hours.

Sheets of ice coated porches, sidewalks, and streets. Lucille Monroe would not dare leave home for fear she would slip and fall. Milford said he preferred to take his chances.

Sue Ella did not mind going out either because she kept a pair of track shoes with cleats for just such bad weather. She bragged that she could stand up on anything. Milford said she was just like a mountain goat going down the hill to the depot. "Her ole car can't make it over the ice, but that Sue Ella ain't never been known to slip or fall yet," he said to himself, for there was no one else to talk to. He was the only one in town willing to brave the courthouse square on such a cold day.

Miss Jessie Gatewood—her hair all in a frizz, unwashed, uncombed, already late for the bookmobile—could not move fast enough in the cold. Timothy John tried to hurry her along, but the house was freezing and Miss Jessie was taking longer than usual because of it. The house had always been difficult to heat, but never had it been so slow to warm up as it was that morning. He could hear Esther Ruth's voice coming from the ice-covered windows, the cold walls, the thin air. "Cool places are much better for you than hot, stuffy places, so we'll just turn the heat down and put on our coats."

"No, we will not turn the heat down and put on our coats," Timothy John said.

"I simply will not have the temperature above sixty degrees," came Esther Ruth's voice through the creaking floor.

Timothy John did not answer. Carefully he shaved his face with lukewarm water and then, sitting at his vanity table, he examined himself for cuts. Before him were dozens of tubes and bottles of color, boxes of facepowder and an assortment of pencils, eyelashes, and brushes, everything that Miss Jessie required to look her best. Slowly, he began transforming his freckled complexion to the smoothness of satin, slowly the cheeks were tinted, the eyes were highlighted, and the excess powder was brushed away. Then the dress came on, and then the shoes, laced and tied, and next the buttons, fifteen to be exact, running all the way down the bodice and into the skirt. The buttonholes were not big enough, or had shrunk in the cold; something had happened; what was it? something was wrong; the routine of getting ready was not what it had been. It was no longer systematic. At first it had hardly taken any time at all to complete, but now one thing no longer followed another. The shoes were on, but not the stockings, the dress, but not the slip; the face was set, but the wild slept-on hair neglected. Everything seemed to be slipping again. Facing Splendora had become a hypocrisy, and the cold morning did not make it any easier. He tried to hurry but could not. Slowly the dress came off; the slip went on; the shoes came off; the dress went on; the stockings stretched, the garters fastened, the shoes slipped into and laced up again and again the buttons; so many to fasten once more. Then around her neck he hung a small pocket watch on a gold chain, pinned a cameo below her left shoulder, tucked a handkerchief in her pocket, dangled a purse on her arm; and next the rings, diamonds and opals, cold as frost, were forced onto long frozen fingers.

"Finished," she whispered.

Miss Jessie Gatewood, a frostbitten apparition, floating across the room to the closet for her coat, noticed in the wall mirror that her hair had not yet been done. She rushed back to the dresser, brushed it, combed it, twisted it loosely into a bun, pinned it down and smoothed the hairline with her fingertips. Her nails, she noticed, were chipped again; one had been completely bitten off. I will do them in the bookmobile, she thought, slipping a bottle of polish into her dress pocket. She stood up and looked at herself; the hair, the shoes, the dress, the slip, the stockings, yes, everything was there; the metamorphosis completed. Yet he realized that she was not completely put together; the powder had been spilled on her shoulders, the hair fastened off-center, the cheeks rouged unevenly, the lips left pale, like alabaster, and her stance: rigid, as though the blood in her veins had turned into ice. The coat! She almost forgot it again. Like a somnambulist she glided toward the closet to select one; chose a cape instead. It had belonged to Magnolia.

She descended the stairs slowly, like a wraith, remembered the keys to the bookmobile, went back for them, and checked herself in the mirror once more. "I feel as cold as the back of a dead cat," came Timothy John's boyish voice, but the image standing there was Miss Jessie's slightly disheveled, pale in that light, the color on her cheeks subdued like the face of one of Esther Ruth's antique dolls whose features had faded into a tint, giving only a vague idea of what perfection there once had been. He stood there, Miss Jessie Gatewood, tired from the ruse he daily performed, tired that morning from working against the cold, and thought of returning to himself, but the moment the thought struck him, he said that it was impossible. It had been too difficult being Timothy John. His unearthly beauty had placed him in the center of attention and he had been unable to walk down a street without attracting stares and painful comments.

"Will you look at *that*!"

"What is it?"

"It ain't got no idea what it is; don't know if it's coming or going."

"I ain't never seen anything looked like that in my life."

Those painful memories were still fresh in his mind. Closing his eyes he could see long hot southern streets filled with men clicking their tongues at him, calling him one of those "funny boys" and whistling as he walked by. "No," he said, "I can't go back to that, not ever."

"Just stay with me, and you won't need to," replied Miss Jessie Gatewood.

In spite of the bad weather Miss Jessie was able to keep the bookmobile in full operation. Everyone in the county began watching for the old yellow school bus she drove herself. Overnight she was a success with the young and the old alike and was able to recommend just the right book for each person. On Mondays and Tuesdays she was parked in Splendora. On Wednesdays she divided her time between Lovelady and Point-blank. On Thursdays she visited the Fred river bottom, Paradise and Pluck, and on Fridays she made four stops before sundown: Mid-way, Wishing Well, Egypt, and Moss Hill.

Along the way she delivered flower-making materials to the various ladies involved in the Crepe Myrtle Pageant. Every spring the outdoor theater in Splendora was decorated with thousands of paper flowers, each handmade and hand-tied onto the trees. "Last year we had far too many white flowers, so the stage looked washed out," Zeda Earl said, deciding that the coming pageant would be one of brilliant color. "There will be a predominance of yellow cape jessamine and purple wisteria, fewer dogwoods and magnolias than ever before, and, of course, more red crepe myrtle."

Milford was the fastest flower-maker in the county. He could sit all day on the courthouse square, even in the worst weather, and make several hundred blossoms in just a few hours.

"Milford's blossoms are not too pretty, though, when you get right up close to them, Lucille said. "He twists their petals around until they every one look like they're deformed, and I say he does it on purpose, too."

Sue Ella Lightfoot said that she had never given a nickel for the Crepe Myrtle Pageant, and refused to have anything to do with it except for a few words of advice here and there. She was sitting in her ticket booth on one of the cold icy days and thinking about the year Esther Ruth first organized the Crepe Myrtle Pageant and Parade. "She would have to choose a Crepe Myrtle," Sue Ella said to Duffy who was crowded into the ticket booth with her. "And if you want the truth, here it is: A Crepe Myrtle is the ugliest flowering tree God ever created, and the only thing it's good for is to be planted in cemeteries, because you don't have to look after it. But you couldn't tell Ruthie that. She thought it was the most beautiful thing she'd ever seen back then, and I always told her that a Crepe Myrtle looked like nothing in this world but a chewed-up, spit-out watermelon."

"That woman won't never be forgot around here," said Duffy.

"She went to a terrible expense to have that outdoor theater built and then wasn't satisfied with it," Sue Ella said. "I'll never forget that first pageant. There we were in the middle of the spring and colder than the North Pole and Ruthie would not for the life of her put on a coat because she said it would mess up the sleeves on her new spring dress. Way back then she always wore puffy sleeves and long skirts and never was seen without her stockings on."

A vivid picture of Esther Ruth came to Sue Ella's mind. When it did, she tore out of the ticket booth so fast Duffy was afraid it would fall down on top of him. "I gotta go home," she said, running to her car. "Something just came to me, and I don't know when I'll be back, because my house is a mess like always, and I ain't got no idea how long it's going to take me to find what I need. Just hold things down til you see me again."

Duffy stood out in the cold and watched her drive straight up the hill. Even though it was iced over it did not take her long to make it to the top, and before she knew it she was home again.

In spite of the fact that the week before she had given away hundreds of old magazines, her house was still overrun with them. Stacks of *True Detective* climbed the walls while *Police Gazettes* were scattered all over every table and chair. Old newspapers were stacked in her bathroom and the hall was filled with the overflow. When she arrived, two tomcats were sleeping on top of the dining-room table which was also covered with weeklies and magazines as well as coupons, boxtops and a ball of tinfoil the size of a four-gallon bucket. All the foil had come from chewing-gum wrappers and it was an amazement even to Sue Ella that she had saved as much as she had because she never chewed more than a half a stick at any one time. A cat rubbed up against her legs. Another cat was drinking water from the kitchen sink, and still another one leaped from the top of a pile of newspapers where he had been sleeping and begged for food.

"You got food," Sue Ella said. She went from room to room routing through chests, trunks and dresser drawers before finding her way to the back screened-in porch over-crowded with two wringer-type washing machines, both broken, a deep freezer full of old clothes and an old icebox that belonged to Snyder's mother. "That's where they are," she said, opening the icebox and taking out a brown paper bag filled with photographs.

She sorted them out carefully, until she found the one she was looking for, a picture of Esther Ruth when she was young. "Just as I thought," she said. "Jes girl, I got you covered from all sides."

She left the house in a hurry and headed straight for the bookmobile. Miss Jessie was busy with some schoolchildren, but when they left, Sue Ella wasted no time in approaching her. "Don't ask me how I figured it out," she said. "I just did. Ever work crossword puzzles? I do sometimes and the words commence coming to me in flashes, and there's no explaining it. What I'm saying is, the joke's on me, not you, because I should have figured it out a long time ago and didn't. Jes, I got your number, and am here to tell you that you don't have to worry none, because I'm betting that your number and Leggett's number is the exact same number. Thought it about him for a long time now, but didn't have nobody to say it to around here. They'd jump ten feet if I did. What I'm trying to tell you is this: he needs you bad. And who knows? It might work out after all. Just like in some story I read somewheres."

"I had a feeling that it was only a matter of time," whispered Miss Jessie. "If the discovery had to be made, I'm glad you are the one who made it, Sue Ella. In a strange sort of way I am relieved that you know who I am. Looking back on things, it is possible for me to believe that you have known about Miss Jessie Gatewood far longer than anyone else including Timothy John. Years ago she drifted into his life as a last resort, and even though he's tried many times to forget about her, she refuses to be forgotten. Most of the time she makes things easier for him. She has always been more readily accepted than he, you understand."

"I understand all kinds of things, even things I ain't never been around," said Sue Ella. "I've read about people in your kind of shoes lots of times. Some need to trade clothes worse than others, you know. That's what I think is real inner-resting, but I'm the only one around here, besides yourself, who'd take the time to put my mind on things like this. What I'm trying to say is that you don't need to worry about me. I ain't about to go home and tell everybody in Splendora who you are. They'd be after me as well as you if I did."

Then she pulled an old folded-up piece of paper out of her pocket. "I thought since I was the first to know about you, you ought to be the first to know about me," she said, slowly unfolding the paper and handing it over to Miss Jessie.

It was a flyer announcing her candidacy for sheriff. "I think this is the best news ever," said Miss Jessie even though Timothy John was eager to burst through and speak for himself.

"I had hundreds printed up ten years ago, but I never went through with it. Cold feet, I guess. Or maybe I was just scared then. But this time I think I'm going through with it because I got the feeling that it's now or never. I always wanted to be sheriff, and I still do. I want it bad, and besides that, nobody else is as qualified as I am, but that don't mean nothing. You know as good as I do that it ain't always quality that brings in the votes. Esther Ruth, you might remember, always tried to get me to run, but I always told her it would take a miracle to put me in office, either that or a good death, R.B.'s, and that ain't too likely to happen. Some people's too mean to die, you know."

"I intend to give you my full support," Miss Jessie whispered. "I will do anything I possibly can to see you elected."

"In that case my mind is completely made up," said Sue Ella. "Somehow I needed to know what you thought about it before I threw myself in the ring." She looked at her watch, said good-bye, and then turned suddenly and squashed Miss Jessie in a hug that left her gasping. "Gotta go, Jes," she said gruffly. "Time to meet the train." But, as she hurried off, her real intention was to call Zeda Earl Goodridge right away.

Zeda Earl had just painted her fingernails when the phone rang and she was not about to pick it up herself because she knew that the polish was not yet dry. She called for her maid to hold the receiver to her ear, and while she spoke to Sue Ella she blew on each fingernail.

"I just called to talk to you about your Crepe Myrtle party," said Sue Ella.

"It's a pageant, not a party," replied Zeda Earl as though talking to a child.

"Pageant, then," said Sue Ella. "Have it your way. But since you're the one planning it this year, I thought I'd give you this idea. As you know, Jes and Leggett's getting along pretty good, but I think they could be getting along a lot better, so you ought to give them something important to do in the pageant. Something that will draw them closer together, if you know what I mean, and I guess you do, and if you don't by now, I don't know how come."

"I'll ask them to serve as assistant directors," said Zeda Earl exuberantly.

"That ain't good enough, and that ain't exactly what I had in mind," Sue Ella replied. "It's got to be something in front of the scenes, not behind the scenes, something that will show them off, but not make fools out of them. I think they ought to come out all dressed up and holding hands, give the crowd a fine speech, and then both of them together could crown Miss Myrtle."

"Miss *Crepe* Myrtle," Zeda Earl corrected.

"Call her what you will, I don't care," said Sue Ella. "The only thing I care about is helping Jes and Leggett get to know each other just a little bit better."

"That's the only thing I care about too," said Zeda Earl. "And I just might take your suggestion after all."

That evening when Sue Ella went home she had the feeling that everything was falling into place. She carried all her campaign posters down from the attic and dusted them off. "I see we're going to have to go through all this again," said Snyder with an exhausted look on his face.

"You sure are. But this time it's for real," Sue Ella said. "I ain't backing out no more."

"Well, I hope you mean it," said Snyder. "Now I'll go make us some coffee, if I can find the kitchen."

"You'll find it in there somewhere," Sue Ella said and began looking over the speeches she had written ten years before. "All the issues are still the same," she said. "Nothing around here ever changes too much." She was sitting on her chenille-covered couch. There was a megaphone at her feet as well as a box of campaign buttons, bumper stickers, and flags, all announcing her candidacy.

A few minutes later Snyder poured her a half cup of coffee, sugared the way she liked it. Then he returned to the kitchen and began making soup from scratch. "Make it the way you did last night," Sue Ella said. "It was the turnips that made it taste good; bitter, kind of." Snyder made it to suit her but she did not stop her work long enough to eat.

Late that night when everything got still and Snyder had already gone to bed she was still sitting there studying her speeches. "I got a good feeling about this race," she said, drinking her cold soup. "The kind of feeling I didn't have last time."

The next morning Snyder found her sitting up on the couch and sound asleep. Four tomcats had curled up around her and two were fighting to sit in her lap.

15

Another spring slowly arrived. Scaffolding had already been built around the courthouse, and the plaster was being slowly removed starting from the top. The stained-glass windows had been found, as had some of the decorative ironwork and drainpipes. Here and there the gables were beginning to emerge, patches of red brick were gleaming in the sun, and the clock, like a diadem, was once again announcing the correct time in four directions.

So far the original building seemed to be unharmed. The workers said that they had never seen anything like it. "Whoever covered it up like this went to some thought to do it. Looks like a lot of work has been done, but it's just frame work and plaster. A real cheap way to remodel a building."

Milford said that he enjoyed watching the plaster being chipped away because it reminded him of a woman letting her dress slowly drop to the floor.

"Shut up," Lucille said. "I'm tired of your vulgar talk."

Miss Jessie and Brother Leggett spent a great deal of time on the courthouse square. It gave her an intense thrill to see the old building slowly emerge. "It's just like a renaissance," she went around saying.

During the warm weather Brother Leggett and she were seen together more often than ever. On a Sunday afternoon after church, Billy Daily saw them picnicking on the banks of Woods Creek, and later that afternoon Luta Hickman caught sight of them wading up to their knees in the cold water. On another day Sonny Weeks spotted them strolling in Galloway's pasture back behind the sawmill, and Inez went there to see if she could see them too, but they had already left, probably for the picture show. Lucille thought it was too beautiful for words when she looked out her window and there they were playing croquet on the front lawn, and Zeda Earl was deeply impressed, because no matter where they were or what they were doing, they always got dressed up to do it.

"Oh, how glad I am to know that you were brought up on a farm," Miss Jessie whispered one sunny afternoon while they were lolling on a quilt on the shady side of Galloway's pasture. "I have heard such fascinating stories about farm-boys. Life in the country, I have been told, develops one's instincts, is that not true? I understand that observing the animals can teach one a great deal."

"Certain instincts were developed in me, I suppose," he said. "But others were thwarted."

"Which ones were thwarted, for goodness' sake?" Miss Jessie asked, and Brother Leggett, blushing, replied, "I'd rather not say."

From his back porch Chester Galloway saw them in his pasture and said that he did not think it looked too good for the assistant pastor and the town librarian to be entertaining themselves on the ground. His main concern was what the young people would think. But his wife, Verna, said that it looked perfectly all right as long as they were carrying the Bible with them. Chester got out his spy glasses and brought the recumbent couple into backyard range. "They're turning our pasture into a park is what they're doing," he said. "But I guess there's nothing we can do about it because he's got his Bible with him. I can see it big as day. Holding down one corner of the blanket is what it's doing."

"You see, I told you there was nothing to worry about," said Verna.

While Miss Jessie dozed off on the quilt, Brother Leggett took the notion to kiss her. It required all his courage just to arrive at the decision, and although he was not too sure how and where to start, he had the idea that it would be much easier if her eyes were closed—part of the time, anyway. He thought about what he was going to do until he made himself uncomfortable, so he decided to put the idea out of his mind. The moment he attempted to forget it, however, he found himself going through with his plans. Almost unaware of what he was doing he leaned over and kissed her, lightly, carefully, upon the lips. Her eyes flew wide open, and during those few seconds in which they stared at each other, he found himself more relaxed in her company than ever before. She was the first woman he had ever given his heart to, and still he was not sure he had given it, not completely, that is.

"I simply adore the way you kiss," Miss Jessie stated emphatically. "So succulent and sensible and not the least bit out of control. Should you care to please me again and again, you will find me receptive. And should you care to give me far greater satisfaction, you could hold each future kiss just a little longer—the longer, the better, is best."

He kissed her again, that time a little longer, and then,

feeling as though he had become too intimate, he pulled away without seeming abrupt.

"That's better. They're sitting up now," said Chester.

"That's sometimes a safe position to be in," said his wife. "But I'd feel a lot better about them if they were standing straight up; wouldn't you?"

They folded the quilt and started walking back to town. On the way he remembered that the following weekend he was scheduled to take some teenage boys and girls on a youth retreat at Camp Mystic Hangover. He said that they would study all topics pertinent to the Christian experience as well as enjoy many hours of recreation.

"Will you attempt to inhibit their participation in physical conjugation?" Miss Jessie asked with the utmost seriousness.

"I do not believe in encouraging nor discouraging cohabitation," he replied. "By the same token I do not ignore the fact that it exists. But, as for myself, I find it quite unnecessary."

"How fascinating," Miss Jessie whispered.

Tragic, Timothy John thought.

And Brother Leggett wondered if he really believed himself or not.

The dogwood and the redbud began to bloom. The grancy-greybeard burst forth with fringelike blossoms as though clouds had settled low over the earth. Spring had fully arrived, and with it came Magnolia for her first visit to Splendora. It was the day before the Crepe Myrtle Pageant.

Miss Jessie had told Sue Ella to expect her. "Please give her the door keys, and if it's not asking too much, could you see that she's met with transportation up the hill? I will be in the bookmobile most of the day and will not be able to meet her; and it is my concern that her appearance might seem startling to some of the townspeople. She's just become a widow and will be dressed in mourning."

"Mourning clothes is often a cover up for something else, you know," Sue Ella said.

"Yes I know," Miss Jessie answered, "but in this case there's a great deal to be covered up."

Magnolia arrived wearing a black tailored suit of lightweight wool. She wore a black hat with a purple veil, carried a black purse and umbrella, wore black gloves, stockings, and shoes. Her corsage was a black silk orchid with a ruby throat.

"How suspicious-looking can a body get?" Sue Ella said when she saw the dark figure stepping off the train. "We gotta get this one up the hill fast before somebody spots her." Duffy said that the passenger was one fine-looking lady. "That's neither here nor there," Sue Ella told him. "We all know or ought to know by now that appearance is the most deceiving thing there is." She walked straight up to the visitor and said, "I'm so sorry to hear you lost him. Jes told me all about it and my only advice for you at this time is not to get so close to your next one, and he won't be so hard to give up, maybe."

"There will never be another one as long as I live," Magnolia said, trying to cry a little.

"You've come to the right place," Sue Ella assured her. "Jes is good at consoling the bereaved, but I ain't, so I'll get you to her fast. You can't go running around town looking like that anyway. People'll pay too much 'tention to you if you do. Jes goes around dressed up fit to die all the time, but she can get away with it and does, because of who she is. Jes is just plain Jes, when you get to know her, but people around here ain't apt to know that about you. Have to give them time to get used to your looks, and I ain't referring to your complexion either."

She insisted that Magnolia wait inside the ticket booth until they could get the suitcases loaded. Then she took Duffy off to one side and whispered in his ear, "In these cases you're never supposed to let on you know as much as you do. You gotta keep your mouth shut or else get buried up to your you-know-what with more involvements than you know what to do with. In other language, you gotta make out like the woman is exactly who she looks like and says she is, even though you know she ain't." Duffy gave her a puzzled look and went to get the bags. Sue Ella started the car. And Magnolia, tucked away inside the ticket booth, remembered Miss Jessie having said that Sue Ella was the only woman in town with a grain of sense; she was beginning to think that it was indeed only a grain.

Sue Ella motioned her out of the ticket booth and toward the car. No sooner than she had gotten off the platform did Hortense Gladly drive past the depot and honk her horn. Magnolia waved passionately. "Sit down on that horn, honey, because Magnolyum has come to town."

"She just wants you to know you've come to a friendly town," said Sue Ella. "But I wouldn't count on it if I were you, because Hortense, she just wants you to turn your head so she can get a good look at you, wants to know who you are and what you're doing here. Town's full of them just like her. Smile you in the face and stab you in the back is what they'll do, and if you don't believe me, just stick around and see for yourself."

Hortense stopped at Clyde's service station and telephoned Lucille. "Keep your eye out," she said, "because it looks like Miss Jessie is about to have her first out-of-town visitor, and I think you ought to be the first to know she's the most dressed-up Negro woman I've ever laid eyes on."

"Any friend of Miss Jessie's is a friend of mine," Lucille said. She hung up without saying good-bye and rushed out to her porch to wait for the visitor. She had just returned from the Beauty Cottage with a clean head of hair and a fresh face of makeup, and how good it made her feel to be able to look her best on the day Miss Jessie was receiving.

When Sue Ella and Magnolia arrived at the Coldridge house, Lucille shouted from her porch, "Hello, hello, hello. I'm Lucille Monroe, and Miss Jessie is off doing her good work, so you just go right inside her beautiful house and make yourself right at home. I'm sure she would want you to."

"She's already been given that set of instructions, Lucy!" Sue Ella said.

"S'wella Lightfoot how many times have I told you not to call me Lucy?" Lucille vociferated.

"Nine hundred and ninety-nine times in one year alone. I counted!" said Sue Ella without a trace of concern.

"Now just how and why did she get herelf so involved in all this is what I'd like to know?" Lucille said, going back inside her house. "I would have been more than happy to meet the train and show the woman around town, but no one asked me, and there she is stuck with that awful S'wella Lightfoot who is no more entertaining than a groundhog.

After Lucille had her coffee and settled down some, she passed the time by gazing out her dining-room window and thinking of the interesting friends Miss Jessie must have, and how good it made her feel to list herself as one of them.

Meanwhile Magnolia was trying to relax in Miss Jessie's parlor. She put herself in the most comfortable chair she could find and unscrewed her flask of Scotch. "God in heaven! I ain't never seen anything like it," she said, drinking as fast as she could. "First there's that Lightfoot woman and her sidekick trying to slip me into town without anybody getting to look at me, and then there's old blue-hair next door screaming her head off to let the whole world know that I finally arrived."

That morning Miss Jessie had been on the Fred river bottom recommending reading for young and old, and that afternoon she had done the same thing in Paradise and

Pluck. At four-thirty she prepared to leave, and, knowing that Magnolia's train had already arrived, she took all the shortcuts back to Splendora and approached the town on the sawmill side. As she neared the courthouse she noticed that a third of the original building had been exposed. Sue Ella had cornered the workers leaving for the day and looked like she was giving them instructions. Milford was listening attentively. She parked the bookmobile near the school, and Zeda Earl happened to see her hurrying home and gave her a ride the rest of the way.

She found Magnolia still sitting in the parlor and drinking Scotch from a hand-painted tea cup.

"Honey, here's your black Magnolyum, and just as rare as they come too, believe you me," she said, trying to embrace her friend without falling down.

"You're the only person I've seen since I left who can really understand all I've been going through," said Miss Jessie. "At times I question my sanity for even thinking of returning," came Timothy John's voice.

"Magnolyum wants to hear all about it, but first let's go into this pretty parlor-music room of yours and have us some tea in your oh-so-pretty cups. Only ladies like us would know that tea always tastes better in pretty cups."

"That doesn't look like tea to me," said the county librarian, but Magnolia, trying to sit down without losing her balance, swore that it was.

When Miss Jessie confessed that, in spite of anything she could do to discourage herself, she had given her heart to the assistant pastor of the Baptist church, all Magnolia could say was, "Honey, you ain't planning on going backwards or nothing like that are you?"

"I have considered it many times," said Miss Jessie.

"You don't seem to be remembering how Timothy John was all the time being laughed at and pushed around," replied Magnolia.

"But Miss Jessie has become a travesty," came Timothy John's voice. "She's cumbersome and suffocating, and I just want to be myself again, if I can remember who that is."

"I never thought I'd live to hear you say you'd wanna go backwards, but I guess I just have," Magnolia said, hoping the same thing was not expected of her. "I think the problem is you're getting stale just like some old maid stuck off in a back bedroom somewhere where no fresh air can get to her. What you need is some new blood around you, something to revitalize your insides, but falling in love with some country preacher who ain't got sense enough to realize who you are ain't gonna revitalize nothing. Magnolyum raised you to know better than that, and here you've come off to the country and proceeded to forget Magnolyum's teachings, proceeded to take things into your own two hands just like you know what you're doing, and it's obvious to anybody who has any brains left that somewhere along the line yours has spilled out. Now you get that Baptist preacher here and let Magnolyum take a good look at him for you."

"He's coming over tomorrow afternoon along with some ladies of the town, and we're going to watch the parade from the front porch," Miss Jessie said. "But you must promise me that you will not interrogate him."

"I halfway promise," Magnolia said. "And that's the best I can do."

All of Splendora was buzzing with the news of the Negro woman that Miss Jessie was entertaining. "Her name is Magnolia," Zeda Earl told everyone whether she was asked or not. "And for your information, she's a dress designer and makes a lot of money as well as all of Miss Jessie's clothes, and I'm going to ask her to take my measurements and create something for me as well."

"I intend to do the same thing," Lucille said, and Zeda Earl answered through her nose, "It's going to take more yardage than you can find in this entire county to cover you up.

The next afternoon Brother Leggett was the first to arrive. Miss Jessie introduced him to Magnolia, and not for a second did she leave them alone.

"I have heard so much about you already," Magnolia said suggestively. "But what I don't know is how and why such a good-looking man like you got involved with sinners and saints, outdoor singings, and dinner-on-the-ground."

Magnolia's approach put Brother Leggett on the defensive, but he tried not to show it. Timothy John could see him pulling away. "She makes him nervous like I did when we first met," he thought. The assistant pastor was determined not to give Magnolia more information than necessary, so he said that he had always been involved in the church and that the involvement just happened, and Magnolia asked, "Why and how and when did it just happen?"

Annoyed by her manner, he decided to tell her something, anything that might make her stop questioning him, so he said that one day, while sitting in his car over in Imagination, he turned on the radio and heard God's voice telling him to drive to Splendora and preach to the lost, so he did.

On the other side of the porch where she was watering her begonias, Miss Jessie heard his story and laughed out loud; Brother Leggett joined her. And Magnolia, feeling as though she had just been the object of a joke that she did not quite understand, refrained from asking her next question.

Miss Jessie requested Magnolia's assistance in the kitchen. "Honey, he's the best looking thing I ever laid eyes on," she said when they were alone. "But something's wrong somewhere, because you know and I know that the radio voice came from inside the preacher's head."

"He was merely discouraging your little interview," Miss Jessie said, preparing the iced tea. "You were asking too many questions, you know."

"What's questions for if they can't be asked?" Magnolia screamed. "It looks like to me he's hiding something."

"Hiding behind something is what Sue Ella thinks," said Miss Jessie arranging the glasses on a silver tray. "I haven't been able to form an opinion myself."

"And you never will, either," replied Magnolia, carrying the tray of glasses toward the porch. "You'll just keep going on like this until you drive yourself crazy. You've come off here and forgotten how to play by the rules, and the major one you can't seem to remember is that you don't fall in love with somebody who can't fall in love with you, all of you, I mean. Magnolyum knows all about it, because she's had more experience, because she's been there before, and because she knows a whole lot. And therefore, you must listen to Magnolyum when she says it's the man's body that you covet and not his mind."

"It's both," Miss Jessie whispered. "Now lower your voice."

The two smiling ladies reappeared on the front porch. Lucille had just arrived, as had A.P. and Sue Ella. "I do believe we must partake of some reviving liquid before Zeda Earl joins us," Miss Jessie whispered, filling the glasses with crushed ice.

The parade was scheduled for two o'clock and the pageant was to take place that evening under the stars. All morning long Zeda Earl and her workers had decorated the stage with paper flowers, and, come parade time, she was exhausted and ready to sit on Miss Jessie's porch and relax. She arrived with the news that Milford had just that day agreed to dress up like the devil and march at the end of the parade.

"His costume is a sight to this world," she said. "I tell you, it's going to make my afternoon to see him."

"Milford wouldn't need a costume to appear as the devil," Lucille said, sipping her drink.

The parade consisted of the usual array of marching bands, commercial floats, and young ladies in evening dresses sprawled over convertibles driven by pimply-faced young men with broad, vacuous smiles. The Honey Island High School Band opened the parade, and behind them marched Missy Hemphill twirling two fire batons at once. Ernestine Martin's nursery school, called The Toddle House, was represented with a Mother Goose Float. The goose was made out of chicken wire and kleenex and was structured around Billy Daily's four-wheel-drive jeep. The tiny toddlers, singing "America the Beautiful," marched alongside the float, and everyone thought they looked so cute until Mother Goose lost her head on the only traffic light in town and all the children started to cry. The East Texas Bareback Devils were the next in line. They came galloping down the street, and then made their horses dance and jump. Behind them the Old Folks' Home of Happiness was represented by five of its senior members riding on the back of a pick-up truck fixed up to look like a pink cloud. "Oh my God!" screamed Hortense Gladly when the float passed by. "There's old Uncle Jumpy Ogletree up there, and somebody told me he was already dead and buried." Behind the old folks' home came a low flatbed trailer pulled by a tractor. The tractor was not decorated, but the trailer was covered with artificial grass, and from the middle of it sprang a flowering tree carrying a banner in its branches. The banner read: The Tree of Life. Across the back of the trailer was a sign: The Hickman Funeral Home Phone 283–3430. Behind the Tree of Life were several floats from out of town. No one paid too much attention to them, but Wanda Lindsey's entry brought applause up and down the street. She had rented a lumber truck and turned the bed of it into a western dance hall complete with square dancers and fiddlers. The Hospital Volunteers were next.

They created a float to represent an operating room. Opel Flowers was the patient and everybody else was dressed up like nurses and doctors about to perform surgery. Maga Dell Spivy, wearing a magenta formal with a tight skirt and a bodice sprinkled with blue sequins, rode inside a papier-mâché telephone, and directly in front of the judges' stand she came bursting out of it and scared everyone to death. The Splendora High School Band with six rhinestone twirlers (three of whom had gone to All-State) and the only boy drum-major anybody had ever heard of, was the last official entry in the parade, and behind it came Milford Monroe on red roller skates. He was wearing Lucille's best Sunday dress of rose-pink satin embellished with dozens of necklaces, cameos, and bracelets. He had powdered his face but not his neck, had painted his lips and cheeks crimson and his eyelids a glossy green. His wig, straight from Zeda Earl's dressing table was bright-sky blue and fashioned into a bubble. Although it had been his idea all along, Zeda Earl had been more than willing to assist. She had stayed up late the night before to style the wig, and that morning Milford had colored it with a can of spray paint. "I'll never be able to use it again now," said Zeda Earl, "but I guess it's worth it just to see Lucille's face."

Sitting on new porch furniture, Miss Jessie and her friends were enjoying iced mint tea with lemon swizzles and discussing the dress designs that Magnolia had agreed to create for Zeda Earl and Lucille, when all at once Milford skated by on one foot and attempted to do some fancy turns. "Anybody seen Milford lately?" he shouted. "If you have, tell him to stay away from me, because I sure ain't got no more use for a man as crazy as that."

When Lucille saw him, two ice cubes slipped down her throat, and she coughed herself into a dead faint. A.P. attempted to revive her by splashing cologne all over her face. Miss Jessie telephoned the hospital to send a physician as well as an ambulance, and Brother Leggett fanned her with *The Saturday Evening Post,* while Sue Ella tried but could not control her laughter, and Zeda Earl swore all over herself that she had had nothing to do with Milford's trick. Lucille was about to come around and A.P. was trying to help her sit up when Zeda Earl got close to her face and said, "Can I help it if Milford thinks the devil looks like you?" At that Lucille broke into another coughing fit and did not stop until Dr. Martindale arrived.

Magnolia stood horrified at the sight of him; a general practitioner, Dr. Martindale had spent almost all of his seventy-five years in Splendora. He was short, slightly on the heavy side, had a red face, and rather large ears with tufts of white hair billowing out over them. He arrived out of breath from a delivery, took one look at Lucille, and, in what Magnolia could best describe as a hysterical falsetto, said, "And now for your injection."

"Dr. Martindale is very famous for his injections," A.P. explained to Magnolia, who was wondering where her flask was and whether or not there was anything in it.

From his medical bag the doctor brought forth a hypodermic needle that looked to Zeda Earl as though it should be used only on large animals. Before he could go any further, however, Sue Ella stopped him. "We don't need no shots around here, Martindale," she said, pushing him out of the way and routing through his bag for smelling salts, with which she revived Lucille long enough for them to get her onto a stretcher and into the ambulance. "What she needs is a little rest in the hospital and one or two of Dr. Martindale's famous little injections," Dr. Martindale said with a smile on his face that looked as though it had been drawn there with a blunt pencil.

"I prescribe rest without shots," Sue Ella said, overpowering him in volume. "And I'm going with her to the hospital to see that she gets what she needs, else God only knows what'll happen to her if she's left by herself a minute."

With that, Dr. Martindale spun himself around and went scurrying off to visit another patient. Brother Leggett and Sue Ella rode in the ambulance with Lucille, and just before they arrived at the hospital she came to her senses long enough to say that Zeda Earl Goodridge was responsible and that Milford Monroe should have been divorced years ago.

Every year the pageant began immediately after sundown. The outdoor theater seated fifteen-hundred people, and the crowd was beginning to gather when Brother Leggett returned from the hospital with the report that Lucille was going to be all right. Then Miss Jessie and he assumed their responsibility of organizing and instructing the spring beauties and their escorts representing thirty-five surrounding towns and communities.

Wearing strapless evening gowns, the four princesses from the senior class at Splendora High, one of whom was to be the new Miss Crepe Myrtle, were sitting on a bench behind a clump of paper azaleas and making eyes at their escorts dressed in rented tuxedos, who were on the other side of the stage. Zeda Earl was giving The Miss Agnes' School of Dance and Expression some last-minute instructions and was about to go over the order of songs with Dora V. Williford. Dora V.'s dress was a midnight-blue formal, taffeta, with a full skirt and narrow straps cutting into her shoulders. Her hair was a mass of spitcurls with long waves falling almost to her thighs.

"That Dora V. has the longest, and the blackest, and the thickest, and the most beautiful head of hair I do believe I have ever seen on any one human," said Maridel Washmoyer when she arrived backstage with the wrist corsages.

Out front the audience was chattering away.

"I just know Jancy Overstreet's going to be the new Miss Crepe Myrtle, because she's the prettiest one of all," said

Gladys Odom to Laura Lou Handcock, who was betting on Marybeth Faircloth instead.

"After what we saw today, I wouldn't be surprised if it was Milford Monroe," said Billy Daily, as the lights went up on the stage and the audience gave a huge round of applause for Zeda Earl's colorful decorations.

The theater was a variation on the traditional Greek style, and had been designed by Esther Ruth without anyone else to help her. The audience sat on long cement benches and looked down at a rectangular stage, also cement, behind which was a forest of tall trees. With the help of some boys who could climb, Zeda Earl had draped the branches with hundreds of paper flowers: purple wisteria, yellow cape jessamine, and dogwood. On the smaller trees she had hung paper Crepe Myrtle blossoms, and all around them she had covered the ground with tulips, daffodils, and azaleas. Milford had made all the tulips himself and had opened them up to look like stars. Zeda Earl thought they looked disgraceful and said that Milford should never be permitted to make another flower as long as he lived.

When the applause died down Sonny Weeks took his place at the microphone. He was the master of ceremonies. The honor usually went to R.B., but because Zeda Earl was in charge of things, she decided to use someone else, just to be different. After days of deliberation she fixed upon Sonny because she liked the way he smiled, and besides that, she had never heard anyone say a bad word against him.

Sonny opened up the pageant with a prayer, after which he announced the winners of the float competition. In spite of the fact that she fell apart under the red light, Mother Goose took first prize; the hospital volunteers came in second; then the old folks' home, third; and Milford Monroe was awarded an honorable mention for being the most talked-about citizen of the day. Next Sonny introduced the thirty-five young ladies and their escorts. The couples were supposed to slowly stroll to center stage, stand facing the audience a few moments, and then take their seats under the rose arbor Zeda Earl had designed herself. She had insisted on a strict code of dress that year. The escorts had been asked to wear white dinner-jackets with green pants, while the young ladies could wear any color at all as long as their gowns had full ballerina-length skirts.

While Zeda Earl was watching the spring beauties being introduced, she noticed that backstage there was one girl wearing a long dress. "Young woman, what's your name?" Zeda Earl asked, marching herself up to the girl, who happened to have been from Sour Lake.

"My name's Joy Precious," said the blond, with a faint lisp.

"Well, little Miss Precious," said Zeda Earl, "you are not about to walk out on my stage wearing the only long dress in sight, and there's only one thing to do about it, so hold still." Zeda Earl got down on her knees, took a pair of manicure scissors out of her purse, and began shortening the skirt to ballerina length. When the beauty from Sour Lake realized what was happening, she tried to get away fast, but Zeda Earl grabbed her by one leg and said, "If you don't come here and stand still and let me do this, I'm going to rip that ugly dress clear off you, do you hear me?"

At that, Joy Precious tuned up and cried, but at least she stood still until Zeda Earl had finished.

When Sonny Weeks called her name, however, Miss Joy Precious was still crying and did not want to walk across the stage, but Zeda Earl informed her that she had no choice.

"You either get out there or you get every hair on your head cut off," she said waving her miniature scissors in front of the girl's face. Joy Precious immediately started crying louder than ever, but off she flew across the stage so fast her escort had to run to catch up with her, and not once during the whole evening did she turn her face to the audience.

"Serves her right for going against the rules," Zeda Earl said under her breath.

After the thirty-five spring beauties and their escorts had been introduced, Sonny announced the time everyone had been waiting for. "This year, for the first time in the history of the pageant, Miss Crepe Myrtle and her Crepe Myrtle Cavalier have not been chosen from the senior class," he said. The audience interrupted him with hisses, boos, and shouts of protest. The Splendora High stage band played a short but loud fanfare to drown out the resentment, and after Sonny could hear himself again, he continued, "It is with great pleasure that I present to you your new Miss Crepe Myrtle—Miss Jessica Gatewood."

The audience broke into thunderous applause.

"Zeda Earl Goodridge!" Miss Jessie screamed, more in Timothy John's voice than in her own. "I refuse to take part in any of this."

"Smile, honey. You're Miss Crepe Myrtle and everybody wants you to look happy," Zeda Earl shouted above the audience, gone wild with exuberance. The four princesses, who had known all along what was going to happen, rushed to Miss Jessie's side and forced her into a long velvet robe with a ten-foot train.

Magnolia was summoned backstage at the last moment. Zeda Earl dressed her in another robe and told her that she was the royal flower girl. "I'll be so happy to do my part," she said through a smile that showed off every tooth in her mouth. The audience broke into cadenced applause, shouts, and foot-stomping. Sonny Weeks made excuses for the delay until, with much relief, he saw Magnolia coming onto the stage as though she owned it. She acknowledged the audience with a low curtsy, and then, hurling rose petals left and right, she continued her walk toward center-stage. Behind her came Miss Jessie. Two of the princesses were leading her by the arm, and the other two were holding up her train. The audience rose to the occasion. Timothy John swore that he would seek revenge on Zeda Earl if it was the last thing he ever did, while Miss Jessie attempted a smile, but could not hold it for very long. From the wings, Zeda Earl was still shouting, "Smile and look happy!" And Magnolia, enjoying every moment of the pageantry, was telling Miss Jessie to show some appreciation to the audience. "Honey, you'll never get another chance like this in your whole life, so give them the biggest curtsy you know how to give; Magnolyum did."

But Miss Jessie did not hear her. By the time she made it to center-stage, she was wearing a fixed and uncomfortable smile the likes of which Magnolia had never seen. "I'm wondering if that child's at herself, is what I'm wondering," she said to Sonny Weeks, who did not appear to be in command of the situation at all. When he asked Miss Jessie to name her cavalier, she just stood there in a state of paralysis and continued baring her teeth as though seized with an excruciating pain she was trying to ignore. Finally Magnolia whispered over to her, "Honey, tell him who your man is so we can sit down and get comfortable again." Still Miss Crepe Myrtle did not utter a word. But from the wings Zeda Earl shouted, "It's Brother Leggett. She told me so earlier." Sonny Weeks repeated the choice in the microphone, and again the audience cheered as though they were at a football game. Zeda Earl hurled a cape over Brother Leggett's shoulders, and pushed the assistant pastor, who had a horrified and stricken look on his face onto the stage to take his place beside Miss Jessie.

"Did you know this was going to happen?" she said to Brother Leggett, trembling at her side.

"I wouldn't be here if I had known," he answered. "I suppose we have no choice but to make the best of it."

"Relax and be natural," Timothy John told Miss Jessie, and she passed the word along to Brother Leggett. "Just relax and be natural, dear heart. There's nothing else we can do."

Sonny placed crowns of Crepe Myrtle blossoms on their heads and garlands of the same around their necks. Then A.P., dressed in watermelon red from neck to knees, came toe-tapping across the stage. Her costume was solid ruffles and made her appear to be a giant Crepe Myrtle blossom with two feet, two arms, and a sparkler in one hand. The audience gasped when they saw her, not only because of her outstanding costume, but also because she was tap-dancing on her toes, and fast, too.

"She lost fifteen pounds just to be able to do that," said Wanda Lindsey to Bubba Wiggley and his wife, Willie.

"I swear I can't tell that she's lost an ounce," said Bubba.

A.P. presented Miss Crepe Myrtle with what was left of the sparkler. She held it in both hands as though she could not imagine what it was, and to Magnolia's way of thinking, she looked like nothing more than a cardboard cutout. "You got to pep up, honey," she said, taking Miss Jessie's right hand, sparkler and all, and lifting it above her head as though she were the Statue of Liberty. At that moment, Sissy Jane Wiggley, a member of The Miss Agnes' School of Dance and Expression came cartwheeling across the stage. She was dressed like Uncle Sam, hat and all, and was carrying a small American flag which meant that she had to turn cartwheels with one hand all the way to center stage, where she stopped just long enough to present the flag to the new Miss Crepe Myrtle. Then she made her exit doing backward somersaults. The audience went wild.

"It makes me dizzier than a duck just to watch her," said Esker Dement.

"Put your head down in your lap and you'll feel better," said his wife.

Sonny Weeks told Miss Jessie and Brother Leggett that they could take their seats, but they did not move. He waited and waited, but they just kept standing there, staring off into space. Finally he turned them around as though they were windup dolls, and they walked mechanically to their thrones under the rose arbor.

The audience clapped and cheered. The sparkler went out. The lights dimmed. Dora V. Williford took her place and began to yodel. Her first song, which she had written herself, was called "Springtime in Splendora," and she sang it more to Miss Jessie and Brother Leggett than to the audience. During the second verse A.P., followed by her dancing girls all costumed to look like Crepe Myrtle blossoms, tap-danced across the stage, and, working their way into drill-team formation, they began forming the letters S P L E N D O R A. Unfortunately there were not enough members to spell the word all at once, so they resorted to one letter at a time and were nearly finished before anyone realized what they were doing. Dora V. could not be heard over the tapping feet.

I knew we should have rehearsed this, she kept thinking, but not once did she stop her medley. As she drifted into her second song, "I Knew You When I Saw You By the Look in Your Eyes," two of A.P.'s dancing girls performed a slow waltz around the stage. One was dressed in a man's tuxedo and the other in an evening gown of pink tulle.

"How pretty," cried Daphne Hightower. "Don't they look grownified?"

"I wish I could dance like that," said Gitsy Hawkins.

"You could, if you'd try," answered Hortense Gladly.

For the last number, Dora V. sang, "The Yellow Rose of Texas," while upstage the spotlight came up on A.P. in her Crepe Myrtle costume garnished with garlands of blue-bonnets, the state flower. As Dora V. sang on, A.P. performed a toe dance which she made up as she went along, and was delighted that she was able to end it with a leap into the wings just as Dora V. sang the last note.

Next, the firework display evoked wild shouts of excitement from the audience, and everyone left agreeing that it had been the best pageant in the history of the Crepe Myrtle Festival.

"I don't even mind that our Marybeth didn't win the Miss Crepe Myrtle title," said Arlene Faircloth to her husband, Barney, "because the look that came over Miss Jessie's face when her name was called was sheer joy and not to be missed."

Sue Ella was the first backstage. "You done good, Zeda Earl," she said, and then headed for the couple of the hour. "Jes, the only thing that would have made this better is for Esther Ruth to have been here too," she said confidentially.

"I never felt for a moment that she wasn't," Timothy John whispered in her ear.

A barbecue celebration then took place in the high-school gymnasium. Miss Jessie and Brother Leggett, still clad in their robes, crepe myrtle crowns, and garlands, held hands during the entire evening.

For their official photographs, Junie Woods touched up Miss Jessie's hair, and A.P. put a fresh sparkler in her hand.

"Oh, they look so beautiful together; don't they?" cried Laura Lou Handcock.

"It's as though they need each other to lean on," said Inez Weeks.

"They do," answered Sue Ella.

Bertha and Beth Miller, both in the same paisley print, were convinced that they made the perfect young couple, and Gitsy Hawkins said that just thinking of them together made her so excited she simply could not stand it.

"Well you'll just have to get hold of yourself this minute, Gitsy," Zeda Earl told her. "There's no use going to pieces over what may be the most wonderful romance this town has ever seen."

Shortly before midnight, cheers and shouts went up for the reigning couple. The walls of the old gymnasium rocked with excitement. Milford blew long blasts on his cow-horn, and Maridel Washmoyer ran to the top of the bleachers and threw confetti as far out over the crowd as she could. The Birdwell boy found a ball and began shooting some baskets, while the School of Dance and Expression played tag in and out of the crowd, and Zeda Earl went around accepting praise for her good work and was often heard to say that it was such a shame that Lucille could not take a joke. Magnolia and Sonny Weeks danced a jig; Maga Dell and her new boyfriend joined them; and Sue Ella Lightfoot told everyone that it was the closest thing to a wedding reception she had ever been to without it really being one. Daphne Hightower thought it was the most beautiful evening she had ever lived through, and when the four Crepe Myrtle princesses led everyone in singing "Dear Hearts and Gentle People," Luta Hickman wept for joy.

As the town clock began striking midnight, a silence came over the crowd. "Oh, how good it is to have our clock in running order once again," Verna Galloway said. "We can hear it clear to the other end of our pasture, it's so loud." On the last stroke, Brother Leggett told Miss Jessie that he hated to see the day end. "I never thought anything like this would happen to me," he said. "And I'm not just talking about the pageant, either. It's something else. And I don't quite know how to say what I feel, but I think . . . that is, if you are agreeable . . . I would like to spend my life with you. Will you . . ."

"Yes I will," Miss Jessie answered, without considering Timothy John, without even so much as listening to his voice. "Yes, Anthony. My answer has always been yes."

A.P. overheard his proposal, and, without waiting to hear Miss Jessie's answer, she told three people that Brother Leggett and their reigning librarian were engaged to be married and that the wedding was to take place in June.

The news floated like pollen around the gym. Miss Jessie and Brother Leggett were besieged with best wishes, handshakes, hugs, and kisses. Zeda Earl was the most exuberant of all, and Sue Ella, with a broad toothless grin, told Zeda that she had good reason to be happy because it was her pageant and her idea that made it all possible. "Oh, I'm so happy you said that, S'wella," exclaimed Zeda Earl. "I am always ready to do whatever good I can."

A.P. broke forth in dance and did not stop until she had circled the gymnasium three times on her toes and landed in a heap next to brother Leggett.

"You've never danced better in your life," he told her.

"That's what shedding over fifteen pounds will do for you," A.P. informed him.

Zeda Earl overheard her and said, "I'm responsible for that, too."

"Well, I'd be ashamed to admit such a thing," stated Geneva Handly. "I think A.P.'s fallen off something awful."

But everyone else thought she was as fat as ever.

At three a.m., when they returned to the Coldridge house, Magnolia, who was not too pleased over the proposal, went straight to bed while Miss Jessie and Brother Leggett lingered on the front porch. His heart was full, but he could not find the words to express how he felt, so he kissed her good-night, even though it still made him nervous to do so, and they parted without exchanging a word.

The moment she was inside again, Timothy John surfaced. "You can't go on with this. You must stop seeing him altogether," he said. "Not yet," Miss Jessie answered. "Not just yet."

On the way back to his garage apartment Brother Leggett kept thinking that he was not the kind of man she needed, that he was not, nor would he ever be capable of fulfilling her every desire, and that it was a mistake to even consider entering into matrimony with anyone. He had his work to think about. That was enough. And there was always that church in Mississippi. He had been asked again to pastor it. The offer to leave Splendora was even more tempting. He saw it as his way out. But before he went to bed he was once again in favor of his decision to marry Miss Jessie and went to sleep vowing that he would go through with it.

The next day Magnolia left on the morning train, and she could not be happier to be leaving. "Honey, I can't be party to this small-town role-playing you got yourself mixed up with. Magnolyum is heading back to the city where she belongs, where she is loved and understood, and if you had any sense at all, you'd stop fooling around with this minister friend and come back too. You've had your fun. That's what you came after, so now you better leave before you get yourself all twisted up with somebody you don't need to get twisted up with. I guess you've forgotten already how hard it is to untwist yourself again."

"Maybe I won't have to," Miss Jessie replied.

"You has gone stir crazy in your head, honey," said Magnolia with grave disappointment. And then, without saying good-bye, she boarded the train, took her seat, and pulled down the shade. She had no intention of ever returning to Splendora and told herself that she hoped never to see Miss Jessie Gatewood, or Timothy John Coldridge, one or the other, or both, ever again.

Miss Jessie watched the train until it was out of sight. "Maybe I *am* being a fool," she said, turning around to find Sue Ella Lightfoot standing directly behind her.

"Jes girl, you better dry them eyes quick, because that friend of yours don't know what she's talking about," Sue Ella said. "She ain't investigated this case like we have. And I tell you right now, it's far from being closed, because the solution ain't nowhere in sight. The problem, of course, is how you're going to get through to Leggett without shocking the man out of his wits. What I suggest is for you to sit down and be calm for a few minutes, and somehow the answer will come to you. It always does."

"I couldn't be calm now if I had to," said Timothy John. "I feel like ten miles of dirt roads."

The town was filled with spring fragrance, chirping birds, butterflies, and warm breezes, but Miss Jessie took no notice. She left the depot and started walking up the hill. That day it seemed steeper than ever before.

16

~

"Zeda Earl, I hesitated to respond during pageant day," Miss Jessie said, "but today I will not hesitate. You and Lucille must stop all this bickering at once before you go too far, which I think you already have. Lucille is in the hospital, and she thinks you put her there. Surely you must know that I do not think what has happened is humorous, and if you are the creator of Milford's little prank, you have no right to be proud of yourself for thinking of it. Both of you have acted ugly, evil, hateful, and base, and I insist that you stop it right now. If not for yourselves, then for me, for I cannot tolerate this foolishness another moment. Now, I suggest that you come with me to visit Lucille, and if you are indeed guilty, then you should apologize to her."

"I most certainly will not do anything of the kind," Zeda Earl said, throwing back her shoulders. "For your information, Milford was in on it too."

"Milford is not my concern, but you are," Miss Jessie replied. "And if you value my friendship, then you will come with me."

When they arrived at the hospital Lucille screamed, "Let me get my hands on that ugly, wrinkled throat of hers." It took two nurses, Miss Jessie, and the patient from the next bed to hold her down.

Zeda Earl left the room on Miss Jessie's advice. Lucille settled down some. Miss Jessie told her that Zeda Earl had come to apologize, and Lucille said that an apology would not restore her beauty and cheerful personality.

"You're just being dramatic," Miss Jessie said. "Now either you both apologize and determine once and for all that you will be friends, or I will have to withdraw my friendship from you both. I would certainly hate to do that, but you have both acted ugly, evil hateful, and base, and there is no other way of putting it."

Zeda Earl came crying her way back into the room. "Please forgive me," she sobbed. "I only did it because I didn't think it would make you sick."

"My health is ruined for life," Lucille cried.

"Oh, I'm so sorry," Zeda Earl said. Big tears fell down her cheeks. "I have acted ugly, evil, hateful, and base toward you and I hope you can find it in your heart to forgive me."

They embraced like long-lost friends.

"Oh, I'm so sorry I made you sick," Zeda Earl said, squeezing Lucille's hand.

"I've done bad things to you too," Lucille confessed. "I was the one who knocked down your yard display last Christmas so you wouldn't win the prize, and I'm so sorry I did it now, because you deserved to win more than I did."

"I forgive you, Lucille, because I didn't deserve to win, not after the way I've treated you all this time. You did the right thing by tearing up my display. If I had only thought of it I'd have torn yours up too."

"You should have," Lucille sobbed. "I didn't deserve to win."

Toy Phillips, the head nurse, entered the room and announced that visiting hours were over. Zeda Earl promised to visit Lucille the very next day. They both said cheerful good-byes and hugged each other again.

"So she's the one who knocked down my beautiful display," Zeda Earl said on their way out. "And here I had that dear sweet Birdwell boy arrested and thrown in jail because I thought I saw him fooling around in my yard, and it was Lucille Monroe all along. Just wait until I get even with her."

"You have already gotten even, and now you must stop and start all over again, and once and for all stop all this fighting," Miss Jessie said firmly. "Hateful words are one thing and somewhat tolerable, but malicious practical jokes are outright cruel, vicious, and mean. Besides that, we've probably got enough evidence on the two of you to have you jailed for life."

"Oh, my husband, R.B., would never stand for such a thing," Zeda Earl said smugly.

"Dear heart," Miss Jessie replied in her best barroom voice, "I'm sure your R.B. has hung up a lot of things in his life, but the moon sure ain't one of them."

"You scare me talking in that tone of voice," Zeda Earl said. "It's so unlike you."

"Well you're going to hear it plenty often if you don't promise me right now, or I'll never speak to you again, promise me right now that you will not do anything harmful to Lucille."

Zeda Earl reluctantly promised, and when she did, Miss Jessie left her standing on the sidewalk out in front of The Charity Fountain and went back inside the hospital. "Lucille," she said. "You must promise me that you will never say a nasty word about Zeda Earl as long as you live."

"How can you ask such a thing of me when it's plain to see that I'm drawing my last breath?" Lucille said faintly. "I'm dying and I can't wait to get up there to the Good Place because I know I'll be safe from that monkeyfied moron who was just in here. Let me die, because I want to so bad."

"You must promise me that you will not say another bad word against Zeda Earl before you die," said Miss Jessie sternly. "No telling what will happen to you if you die with such hate on your mind."

"Oh, all right, all right, I promise not to say a nasty word against Zeda Earl ever again," said Lucille, groaning and gasping. "Now leave me alone to die in peace."

"Thank you, Lucille," said Miss Jessie. "Dr. Martindale just told me you'll be able to come home this week, and I'll be glad to have you back. Remember though, deathbed promises are binding."

17

Maga Dell Spivy, wearing puce pedal pushers and spike heels, came into the drugstore at exactly eleven forty-five, fifteen minutes before she usually took her lunch hour, and still Johnnie Mitchell was able to prepare her ham sandwich on white bread with no pickles and have it ready almost before she sat down. "I cannot take another minute of what I'm having to put up with," she said, lighting a cigarette to have with her sandwich. "All everybody's talking about these days is Miss Jessie's wedding, and I'm sick to death to have to sit there and listen to how this whole town is going to pieces over a silly proposal. I'll be the happiest one of all when he marries her and we can get back to normal."

Johnnie said that there had been a sudden rush on love magazines and that Wanda Lindsey had just bought the last one left. "She said she was going to chew her fingernails off if she didn't have something like that to read."

"Well, if Wanda had somebody special in her life, she wouldn't be falling apart the way she is," said Maga Dell, slapping her sandwich against her plate so hard the potato chips went flying into the sundae Johnnie was making for

Bertha Miller, who was sitting on the other end of the counter and trying to pretend that she was not listening by studying her Sunday-school lesson that just had arrived in the morning mail. Finally she spoke up.

"I just heard that Gitsy Hawkins has got herself so worked up over it all, she's had to go to bed with her nerves," she said, tearing the pages of her Sunday-school book into little pieces before she knew what she was doing.

"Well, I know somebody else who'd better take hers to bed too, honey, and it ain't Gitsy, either," Maga Dell said, rolling her eyes at Johnnie, who was looking on the other end of the counter at the mess he was going to have to clean up. Johnnie served the sundae to Bertha. Sister Beth stepped out of the prescription department and asked for another spoon. Then she said that Maridel Washmoyer was scared to death that she was not going to be asked to do the floral arrangements.

"What's she got to worry about?" Maga Dell said. "She runs the only florist in this town. That ought to be assurance enough, but no, everybody's got to have something to get nervous over."

Bertha said that she always fed her nerves; found that that was the very best way to live with them. "So do I, Sister B.," said Beth, digging the spoon into her side of the sundae. "But now take A.P., for example, she gardens for hers. Very wise, I think."

Maga Dell finished brushing her hair right there at the counter and twisted herself around to face the comment Beth Miller had just made. "Yes," she shouted, "but A.P. has been known to transplant every bush in her yard twice in one month, summer at that; even had it in mind to dig up that big cedar tree in her backyard and move it up front until somebody told her it would take a bull-doozer to come and dooze it up, and even then, with lots of dirt around the roots, it probably would not live, because you cannot transplant a fifty-year-old tree, a bush maybe, but not a tree."

From across the store, Esker Dement said, "Only the day before yesterday, A.P. hoed up her entire yard and half of mine before I could stop her."

"Well, how wise of her, Beth honey; isn't that what you say?" said Maga Dell with a wavy smile, and commenced cleaning her teeth with her right index finger. Then she reached down and straightened her fishnet stockings, twirled her way off the revolving stool, and said that she had to go back to work because she did not care to sit around and listen to how everyone was going to pieces over a wedding that might not ever happen.

"Oh, don't say it might not happen!" Bertha and Beth shouted simultaneously.

With a devilish grin on her face, Maga Dell said, "It might not happen," and then left the drugstore fast.

Lucille was just about to die to get out of the hospital so she could plan Miss Jessie's bridal shower. When Dr. Martindale finally released her, she went straight home and, in the space of an hour, she chose the date, time, and place (her house), and sent out shower invitations to every lady living within the city limits, with the exception of Maga Dell Spivy. On the bottom of each card she wrote, "Only practical gifts for a practical bride." Miss Jessie tried to persuade her to postpone the event until the wedding date had been set, but Lucille would not hear of such a thing.

"This ain't too serious yet, Jes," said Sue Ella. "Let them buy you all the presents they want to. If it was me, I'd make a list of all the things I need most."

"As long as I've got to go through with it, I might as well make the time useful," said Miss Jessie. "I think I'll take the opportunity to endorse you for sheriff and see what happens."

"That suits me just fine, Jes," said Sue Ella. "Now that the pageant's over, people need something else to think about besides your wedding, so I'm going to start campaigning every day."

A few days before the shower Lucille got on the telephone, spoke to each lady invited, and urged them again to select only practical gifts because they were not honoring an ordinary bride-to-be, but someone a little older who had already set up her life style and clearly did not appreciate anything that was not utilitarian. "We don't want this to be your common everyday towel-sheet-and-pillowcase shower, but something different, something special," she instructed. "And if you find that you cannot come up with something useful and original, just don't you come at all. Now, it will be a slightly difficult task, for some of you are not accustomed to this kind of thinking. Some will have to think harder than others, because we are not dealing with an ordinary person, but with someone special and dear to most of our hearts even though we have known her so short a time; so, I urge you again to arrive with something special and useful other than what I intend to give, which is rhinestone-studded hairpins and tortoise-shell barrettes. She does have long hair, you know, so you must think along these lines: What would be useful to you if you were her?"

A.P. said that the whole thing was most confusing because she was unable to put herself in Miss Jessie's place or anybody's place for that matter. Finally she settled upon some shoelaces as she had noticed that Miss Jessie's were looking a little frayed.

"I never knew you sold shoestrings before till now," A.P. said to Henrietta Lamb, who was cashiering at her drive-in-grocery. "My Mamma used to wear lace-ups too, long time ago, that was."

Henrietta smiled.

A.P. paid for the strings and then asked to have them gift-wrapped.

Henrietta's smile went away.

A.P. just stood there waiting.

Henrietta said that she had better go to the dry goods if she wanted a gift-wrap done.

A.P. asked why Henrietta could not do it herself.

"Because this is a grocery store!" Henrietta screamed. "Grocery stores do not do gift wrappings. But if you want them sacked up I can take care of that."

A.P. said that she could sack them up herself, but she could not wrap them up because her packages never turned out looking pretty.

"Well, for crying out loud," Henrietta Lamb replied, as if she could care less.

"You don't have to be so hateful about it," A.P. said, and walked out and went over to the drugstore where she had Johnnie Mitchell do the gift wrapping for her. She insisted that he wrap each shoestring separately so it would look like Miss Jessie was getting more than what she was.

"I only paid thirteen cents in all for them, and I think that's real good. Don't you?"

Johnnie said that that beat drugstore prices.

A.P. asked him to put a bow on each wrapped-up string and then tie something around them so they would stay together until she could get them to the shower. Johnnie did it all just as she said and refused to charge her a cent.

Feeling as though she had received a double bargain that day, A.P. left the store and started walking home. On her way she wondered what everyone else would bring to the shower.

Zeda Earl did not have so much trouble with her gift selection. In the space of two afternoons, she had her maid sit down and crochet a dozen doilies of various sizes, plus a pair of booties, and the tiniest mittens anyone had ever seen. Inez Weeks came with a fine writing pen, complimentary to the gift Sue Ella brought: a one-hundred-page, leather-bound diary given to her years back. In ten years' time she had not made a single entry in it. She had no use for keeping records but thought that Miss Jessie might. Zeda Earl coveted the thought behind the diary and fountain pen. Inez could tell by the way her eyebrows went flying up her forehead and her eyes stretched out like two thin pencil lines. Eloise Eagleton, the preacher's wife, thought her gift was the best of all: a set of six bookmarkers with illustrated Bible scriptures on each. Bertha Miller gave a pound of coffee, and Sister Beth gave an old-fashioned coffee-pot that had been in their family for years. It was galvanized. Gitsy Hawkins, who worked part-time at the hospital, thought a dozen glass straws would be the most appropriate gift ever, but broke two of them before they were wrapped up, and arrived with only the ten. Hortense Gladly, sick with a sunburn, was unable to make it, but sent her best along with a box of wooden clothespins and twenty feet of clothesline. She had painted the clothespins pink and dyed the clothesline a bright purple. Maga Dell Spivy gave a black negligee and confessed that she had slept in it once, but did not see that it mattered very much. "Guess you're surprised as hell to see that it ain't a blood-red one I picked out," she said to Lucille, who got up from where she was sitting and moved across the room. "You know," she said to Ohma Lee Carlson, "I did not invite the woman to my house. She just showed up and came right on in."

Henrietta Lamb arrived late carrying a bright-blue kitchen apron with orange storks and blue eggs appliquéd all over it. Toy Phillips handed over a jar of pickled okra; Gladys Odom, a string of pinecones frosted for Christmas. Ernestine Martin covered some coathangers with satin and hung sachet balls from each, making Timothy John think of Esther Ruth and how she would have done the exact same thing. Mildred King potted a fern. Sara Sue Hamilton knitted a hat. Lois Ann Beech hooked a rug. Maureen Kelly baked a pineapple-upside-down cake, and Mable Brown churned some butter. Dixie Calling copied down all her family recipes and handed them over neatly collected in a little black notebook. Daphne Hightower could not think of a thing other than six one hundred-watt lightbulbs and a new calendar with pictures of wild birds representing each month of the coming year. A glass paperweight with a country scene and falling snow inside it was given by Maridel Washmoyer, and a pincushion shaped like a heart was the best thing Wanda Lindsey could do. She did not have much money to spend. Holly Wilson thought a year's subscription to *The Splendora Star Reporter* was the best gift ever, but Lucille thought it was awfully common. Opel Flowers showed up with a jar of picked-out pecans and a broom she had just bought from some blind people who were selling on the courthouse square. How they ever found their way there she could not imagine. Much to everybody's surprise, Laura Lou Handcock latched on to the idea of giving away her old brass birdcage. "I can't believe she's actually going to part with it," gasped Daphne Hightower, her neighbor. It had once been the home of Laura Lou's beloved Sweetie, a singing canary that died with a song in his heart. She had spray-painted it flat black, entwined artificial flowers in the bars and placed a plastic canary on the perch, and was terrified that somebody else would think to do the same thing. "It's practical because it looks real, and yet you don't have to take care of it at all," Laura Lou explained. Lucille Monroe threw up her shoulders and said it was the best thing on earth to catch all your house dust, and the very hardest thing she could think of to keep clean.

Junie Woods was not present. She had washed and set six heads of hair, combed out two wigs, painted three faces, and manicured fifty fingernails for the occasion, and still no one thought to invite her.

After all the gifts had been opened and put away, A.P. asked Miss Jessie what she thought of her husband-to-be.

"He's the most assiduous man I've ever known," she answered.

A.P. asked just what she meant by that, and Miss Jessie said that he was most high-minded and diligent in his profession, and A.P., innocent of how she sounded, replied, "Oh, just like you. Well I sure hope you won't get bored or nothing."

Lucille shot A.P. an insolent glance, and she wilted like a flower into the dense vegetation upholstered upon the grandfather's chair she had raced Geneva Handley to sit in and had won only by a hair.

"I just know you're going to have lots of children," Lucille chirped.

"Five is such a good number," Gitsy Hawkins suggested.

"We were thinking more like three," Miss Jessie said.

Across the room Sue Ella laughed out loud. A.P. wanted to know what was so funny, and Sue Ella said she was only trying to cough. To that A.P. replied, "You see, that's what you get for having your teeth pulled out. Can't cough no more, can you?"

"We know so much about Brother Leggett already," said Lucille, trying to change the subject fast. "But I don't recall ever hearing you say much about your background."

Giving her voice an exaggerated and feigned solemnity, Miss Jessie bowed her head and whispered as if it were painful for her to talk about it. "I was reared in an orphange in Opalousa. Later on I was able to locate my only known relative, a great aunt, who died a few years ago and left me a small source of income. The rest is rather bleak, I'm afraid."

Sympathetic sighs could be heard around the room. "Oh, I'm deeply sorry," Lucille said, feeling as though she had pried too deeply.

"You're going to have a family, Jes, I just know you are," Sue Ella said with a half-smile on her face. "And when you get one, it'll mean more to you than it would to most people, because you never had one to start with."

"What a sweet thing to say, S'wella," Lucille said.

"I hope you're right," Miss Jessie replied, bringing her handkerchief to her eyes.

Then there was a spell of silence into which everyone suddenly leaped to interject their best wishes or condolences, and after all had taken their turn Miss Jessie said a brief word of thanks to each lady present and took the opportunity to turn the subject toward Sue Ella. "As you know it's election year again, and Sue Ella is running for sheriff against Fred Polston. It is my opinion that Sue Ella would serve us admirably. She stays on top of local issues and is always around when she's needed."

"That's the most important thing," interrupted Daphne Hightower. "I've worked in the courthouse for years now and can't remember when I last saw the sheriff's office open."

"But Sheriff Polston's been our sheriff for over twenty years," A.P. said. "Wouldn't it be rude to make somebody run against him?"

"Nobody is making Sue Ella run for anything, A.P.," said Maga Dell. "What we need is somebody we can count on to keep the doors open, and we got us a candidate who's willing to sleep in the sheriff's department if that's what it takes, and I say let's help her move right on in there."

All around the room the ladies nodded their heads, if not energetically, at least because they felt they had to keep up an appearance.

"I'll do the best I can," Sue Ella said. "I'll at least tell the truth, which is more than has been done around here in the last twenty years." Then she passed out pamphlets with a list of her qualifications and objectives. Albert Posey had designed and printed them and was also taking charge of all her campaign publicity.

"I give you my total support," Lucille said lifting Sue Ella's arm into the air just as though she had won a prizefight. "Furthermore, I intend to do everything I can to see that you're elected to office."

The ladies broke into applause, and when all was quiet again Lucille announced that pineapple punch would be served in the next room.

"Oh goody," A.P. said, clapping her hands. "My favorite."

18

∽

The week after the pageant Brother Leggett and Miss Jessie saw each other only twice, once at choir practice, and once at prayer meeting, and both times they exchanged very few words. After the shower she saw even less of him, and when he was not present for Wednesday-night prayer meeting, Timothy John became concerned. He overheard Brother Eagleton say that the assistant pastor had taken a few days off to prepare his next sermons, but Timothy John felt that there was more to the absence than just that.

When Miss Jessie returned from her Friday schedule she found Brother Leggett sitting on her porch. He asked her to take a stroll, and, to the enjoyment of everyone who saw them, they ended up walking all over town. Brother Leggett was wearing his white linen suit; and Miss Jessie, a vision in pink, shouldering a parasol, was dressed in dotted swiss with puffy sleeves and a gathered skirt.

They hardly spoke a word until they came to the courthouse square. There they stopped and watched the work in progress. With great difficulty Brother Leggett began telling her what was on his mind. "The situation has gone too far," he said. "I have spent many days and nights in prayer and supplication and have been lead to believe that it is not in God's plan for me to seek a marital relationship. I should have spoken to you before now, but I have not been able to find the words to express how I feel."

"I will attempt to understand and accept your decision," Miss Jessie said. Timothy John felt a mixture of disappointment and relief. "But it will be very difficult for me because, you see, I have come to love you more than I thought possible."

"I sometimes find it impossible to love as I ought," Brother Leggett confessed. They did not look at each other as they spoke but kept their eyes on the courthouse, and the workers, and the falling plaster.

"Clarify your statement, please," she said.

Lowering his voice to a quivering whisper, he told her that it was not impossible for him to love, but that it was impossible for him to demonstrate his love to a woman, especially a woman such as herself. "I have never said this to anyone before," he said, his voice still almost inaudible, "but I feel that I must say it to you. It is not that I do not find you lovable. On the contrary, I find you to be the most lovable person I have ever known. But . . ." He looked around for something to lean on. Miss Jessie, sensing his need, led him over to a sycamore against which he rested the weight of his confession. "The fault lies within me," he continued, still almost unable to speak. "I would like to think that I am capable of pleasing you in every way, but I am not. My heart resides in another place, where I am told it should not be, but there is very little I can do about it, except to sublimate my desires as a man of God."

Timothy John's feeling of disappointment was beginning to vanish like the last traces of plaster clinging to the old bricks high above his head. "How long have you carried this knowledge of yourself?" Miss Jessie asked with perfect equanimity.

"For as long as I have had memory," he said. "I have

lived with myself only by dedicating my life to Christian service."

Miss Jessie spoke up with an authority that Timothy John suddenly invested in her. "May I say that I am not in the least disconcerted by what you have just implied. In fact, because of what you have told me, I am able to love you more than ever before, and would be deeply fulfilled to continue seeing you just as I have been these last few months."

Brother Leggett said that he found himself most unworthy of such goodness and that he had decided to leave Splendora as soon as possible.

"It would be a mistake for you to leave on my account," she said. "I see no reason why we should force matrimony upon ourselves even though everyone else is trying to."

Timothy John wanted to stand alone without Miss Jessie. He wanted to strip away her mask and expose himself to all of Splendora, and especially to Brother Leggett, but he was afraid that the truth revealed too suddenly might cause the assistant pastor to leave town that day. "Somehow I must tell him," he thought. "But I need to find the right way."

Milford walked over to them and pointed to the top of the courthouse. "She's been up there all afternoon," he said. "Telling them what to do, I guess." The clock struck five o'clock and the workers began scrambling down the scaffolding. Sue Ella Lightfoot was among them. She was wearing her every-day-of-the-week shift, a pair of green goggles, sneakers, and white dust from head to toe. "Don't nobody know how to do nothing no more, Jes," Sue Ella said, her eyes flashing behind the dusty goggles. "You ought'a be glad to see that you ain't the only woman around here who knows how to assert herself."

"I'm pleased to see you taking such strong initiative, Sue Ella," Miss Jessie replied.

They left the men alone and went over to a bench and sat down. While Miss Jessie reiterated her conversation with

Brother Leggett, Sue Ella pushed her goggles to the top of her head. Her face was completely white except for two circles around her eyes.

"That's just what I thought, Jes," she said. "Leggett, he just needs a little help, that's all. Maybe it's high time you showed him a thing or two, but if you do, you got to be careful, or you'll scare the living daylights out of the man. He ain't never been around like you have, and would probably make all his hair fall out to realize right fast just how far around you've been. Can't pull it on him all at once. You got to be easy like. Some have to crawl over the fence, you know, whereas others take it in one leap. I always thought if I was faced with the situation, I'd be a leaper myself."

Miss Jessie looked around to find Milford still standing there, but the workers had already departed, and so had Brother Leggett. "One minute he's there, and the next minute he's gone," she said. "I just don't know how much more of this I can take."

During the next week when it seemed that he was avoiding her more than ever before, Timothy John became aware of something shifting inside him. Miss Jessie was losing her footing, slipping somehow. Again he was out of patience with her as he had been back in the winter. When she had first been conceived he was aware of thinking for two people. Then, gradually, it had seemed that the two thought processes had blended into one; now he was becoming acutely aware of thinking for two again, but this time he felt Miss Jessie's voice getting weaker.

The weather had suddenly become hot and humid, and it was once again difficult to keep her looking her best. To Timothy John everything seemed to be swimming under boiling water. The world was slightly elevated, higher on one side than the other and lighter in weight. Nothing seemed real anymore. Miss Jessie could not balance her coffee cup in its saucer. She was unable to paint her fingernails without her hands shaking. At times her legs wobbled when she crossed a room, and every piece of furniture seemed to be walking away by itself. "Must everything be bolted down?" he said. "Must everything be anchored firmly to keep the world still again?"

He was constantly distracted, yet Miss Jessie managed to appear in control whenever in public. It was at home alone, or when driving the bookmobile that the world seemed distorted. "And how much longer will it be until the same thing starts happening everywhere?" he worried. To compensate for how he felt inside, he labored to keep Miss Jessie looking her best. Wisps of lace about her neck and sleeves, cameos pinned here and there, a freshly powdered face, a beaded reticule, a pleasant smile, and she was the most interesting person Splendora had seen in many a year. Lucille Monroe said so.

Oh, if she only knew the all of it! Timothy John could not help thinking as Miss Jessie struggled to keep the bus on the narrowest dirt road in the county. On either side the forest seemed to close in on her. Little sunlight penetrated that neck of the woods, so the road with its canopy of trees was more like a long dark tunnel. Timothy John's vision blurred. Miss Jessie was unable to keep the bus in the deep ruts. It was as though the road was changing its course, and the trees alongside it were crowding in closer. "Oh, how tired I am of all this," she whispered, weaving from side to side.

Just ahead of her where the road forked there was a sign, hand-lettered on a piece of weathered plyboard. One arrow pointed toward Point-blank and the other toward Paradise. Timothy John could not remember who he was, where he was going, or what he was supposed to do when he got there. Miss Jessie squeezed the steering wheel, crashed into the sign, and sideswiped a pine tree before she managed to stop the bus in the middle of the road. She rested her head on the steering wheel for a few minutes.

"I should have told you before now," she heard Brother Leggett saying. "It's not meant to be. . . . The situation is out of hand. . . . It has all been my fault, not yours . . . my fault not yours . . . my fault . . ." Over and over she heard him until his voice turned into Timothy John's. He tried not to cry but could not hold back the tears. "I've got to get out of here," he said. He started the motor, raced the engine, and drove slowly down the road. A few miles later when the bus finally emerged into a clearing he was able to regain Miss Jessie's surface composure, but inside he felt like a priceless vase that was slowly cracking with age and wear. "I've got to get out of here, somehow," he kept saying as he brought the bus to a slow stop in front of the pump station that marked the only visible landmark in the community of Point-blank.

Miss Jessie Gatewood, with almost perfect control, stepped out of the bookmobile. "I guess everyone wants to be someone else. Only for some of us it's much easier to be someone else than who we really are, or at least we think it's easier until we try," she whispered to Cecil Faircloth, who ran the store and Post Office.

"How you feeling today?" he asked.

"Vertiginous," Miss Jessie answered, leaning on his arm.

"Well, I sure hope it ain't catching," Cecil said.

Nadine, his wife, came from out back where she had been washing and remarked that Miss Jessie looked a little peaked, and ought to have a short rest.

She had a cup of coffee, repowdered her face and said that she was then ready to receive the Point-blank readers.

Only three people visited the bookmobile that afternoon, and Cecil thought it was a good thing when he saw her driving away early. "She's caught some bug that's going around," he said. "Good that she has sense enough to get out of here before we all come down with it."

Miss Jessie drove straight as she could to Junie Woods' Beauty Cottage. Junie, between customers, was pinching her face blue and smoking up the room. Lucille Monroe, reading the latest issue of *The Baptist Standard*, was under the dryer and did not hear Miss Jessie when she arrived and asked for a haircut that very afternoon. "A bob will do me just fine," she said. "I'm tired of all this hair and all this makeup, and I intend to go natural for awhile because I'm exhausted and unhappy with the way I look."

"A change is always good," Junie whined, hoping that Miss Jessie's new look would bring her more business, because she had already decided she wanted to open a barbecue pit on the side and needed more cash in a hurry.

Miss Jessie took a seat, and soon the hair began to fly. Lucille Monroe looked up from her magazine, saw what was going on, and screamed as if she had been stabbed. "You have no right to do me this way and you know it, too!" Then she came out from under the hood dryer like something had stung her and attempted to stop the cutting by snatching the scissors from Junie's hand. "You don't know what you're doing," Lucille cried, as if the world depended on what she was about to say. "My hair is just now getting long enough to wear it in a bun. I've been waiting all these months to ball it up, and you're not going to stop me by changing things around before I get there."

Miss Jessie assured Lucille that it had been her decision all along. Unable to believe what she was hearing, Lucille slowly backed away and watched the curls fall to the floor. "Leave her some ears, for God's sake!" she cried. Junie said she intended to even the hair off at earlobe level, and she did not stop until she had done just that. Miss Jessie stood up and modeled her new hair style. Lucille was flabbergasted over the transformation. Finally she managed to say that she just might like to have hers cut in a similar fashion after all, but she would have to think it over a few days.

Miss Jessie went home, removed her layers of makeup, and reapplied a light base of powder through which Timothy

John's freckles could faintly be seen. Then she made an appearance on the courthouse square.

The news of her new look took the town by storm.

"Oh, I'm so sorry she did it, I just don't know what to do," said Wanda Lindsey. "I don't know what she wanted to go and ruin her good looks for, do you?"

"She said she did it because she didn't have time to take care of her hair and the library too, so she just cut it off," said Dorine Shinn. "But if you want my opinion, I just can't stand to look at her any more. She looks so mannish, if you know what I mean. I never thought I'd be saying that about Miss Jessie, but it's the truth."

"Stop, I don't want to hear any more!"

"She's lost some of her femininity, that's for sure."

"Oh, I can barely draw my breath!"

"Something's come over her. Wonder what it is?"

"Well, it stands to reason that women change completely after they take on a career, you know. They become more like men and that's the danger of it."

"Yes, I know just what you're saying. When I saw her without a drop of makeup on I thought I'd fall down on the spot."

"I have never seen the like of freckles on any one face in my whole life."

"She better keep them covered at all times is what she better do."

"Let me sit down and tell you something: She just isn't herself anymore. She just doesn't know what's good for her, and that's all there is to it."

"Oh, I'm so sorry to hear that."

"Well, not as sorry as I am to have to say it," said Hortense Gladly. "But I have always said, and I'll say it again: Brother Leggett's a much better man than she is a woman; and after it's all over and done with, you'll look back on it and see that I'm right, too."

Lucille and Zeda Earl came at once to Miss Jessie's rescue. Although the shock of seeing her without her long hair was, at first, more than they could cope with, they quickly adjusted to it and had theirs bobbed off as well.

"Oh, how good you look, Lucille," Miss Jessie said. "And may I make one more suggestion. I think you should also allow your hair to return to it's natural silvery grey and refrain from using so much makeup. We must allow our faces to breathe more freely, you know. And besides that, we don't look quite so artificial."

Lucille said that she intended to make those improvements on herself, and Zeda Earl said that she was right behind her.

Before long the new look had caught on. Junie Woods was booked up for weeks in advance and was already making plans to open up her second business, The Smack 'n' Chew Barbecue.

For awhile Timothy John felt more comfortable with Miss Jessie. Brother Leggett said that the new hairstyle was most becoming, but he did not make any move to call on her. He intended to give his resignation at the church one day and leave the next. He told her he would be gone by the following Sunday. "I still think it's a mistake," she told him, but he refused to listen.

Unable to sleep, Timothy John prowled the house that night. He wandered from room to room in the dark and ended up at the piano until dawn slowly drifted in, filling his life with the misery of another day spent with Miss Jessie Gatewood and without Brother Leggett.

After three sleepless nights he decided, for better or for worse, to take matters into his own hands. In the middle of the night Miss Jessie telephoned the assistant pastor. "My spirit is dwindling," she said. "Fever is the word."

In a matter of minutes Timothy John heard a car drive up and stop. On the front door Brother Leggett found a note telling him to come to the upstairs bedroom. He had never been upstairs before and did not know one room from the next. Timothy John counted the footsteps as the pastor advanced up the stairs and then down the long hallway. He could hear him knocking at all the bedrooms one by one; he could hear the doors being carefully opened and closed and could hear footsteps leading from one room to the next until there was only one left.

His knock was timid. Neither Timothy John *nor* Miss Jessie answered it. Slowly the door swung open and Brother Leggett stepped into the half-dark room. Sitting on the edge of the bed, he saw a man with short blond hair. He was dressed in a three-piece suit, his grandfather's, and was staring at the floor. Gradually he lifted his head. Their eyes met. Brother Leggett had fully expected to see Miss Jessie and had the feeling that he still might be seeing her, yet the figure was that of a man. Or was it? Angels, he had been told, were neither men nor women. For an instant he considered the possibility. Then he heard the voice, a combination of Miss Jessie Gatewood and someone else, someone he did not recognize, but felt as though he should.

"I wanted to tell you long before now," said Timothy John. "Esther Ruth, as you must realize, was my grandmother, and Miss Jessie Gatewood is no more."

Timothy John watched Brother Leggett's face pale, his arms shake, and for a moment wished he had not exposed himself. The assistant pastor tried to speak, but he could not; tried to step forward, but his legs would only take him backward. Suddenly he was gone. He left the room so rapidly it was as though he had vanished into the walls. Only his footsteps on the stairs gave him away. With perfect control Timothy John walked to the window and watched him get into his car and drive off. "How glad I am to know that it's all over," he said stoically, but before he made it across the room he realized that it was not over. He collapsed on the bed, and broke into uncontrollable weeping.

Trying to regain his composure, he began reliving his life

as though watching a film running backward inside his head. His desire was to rest in the memories of happier days, but he did not find those memories, even his first years in New Orleans, as comforting as he had hoped. Nothing he could think of was calming. He beat the mattress with his fist, tore feathers from his pillow, and rolled himself up in his comforter as though it were a straightjacket and cried himself to sleep; he thought it was sleep. And he thought it merely a dream when he looked up and saw Brother Leggett standing again in the doorway. He was dressed in his black Sunday suit and carried his open Bible balanced in both hands. Slowly the figure came into sharp focus. Timothy John realized that he was not dreaming, freed himself from the comforter, and sat bolt upright on the bed.

The assistant pastor began to recite. " 'When I was a child I spake as a child, but when I became a man I put away childish things.' "

Then, in pious tones, he began to preach on the sins and iniquities of the false prophets. "Verily I say unto you, the kingdom of heaven shall not be opened unto them who bed up with treachery, deceit and misrepresentation. Let it be known that all men who profess one thing when in their hearts know they are another, live their lives in danger of everlasting damnation."

"Don't come in here dressed like a saint and ready to preach to me," Timothy John screamed, leaping to his feet. "Preach to yourself. You need it just as much and maybe more than I do. At least I've managed to live with myself one way or another. All you've ever done is hide behind the pulpit, and your clerical costume, and your pious friends, and that solid foundation of a church, which, for you, is nothing more than a garage to park your poor, tender, guilt-ridden soul. Now you get the hell out of here, because Timothy John can do just fine without you."

Brother Leggett, ready to do battle, stood firm and refused to leave until he had finished his say. "You stand in need of religion," he said, bracing himself against the door-facing. "I have come to lead you down the pathway of righteousness."

"I could kill you for saying that," said Timothy John vehemently. "And if I had something to do it with, I would."

"'The Lord is my light and my salvation; whom then shall I fear? The Lord is the strength of my life; of whom then shall I be afraid?'" the pastor replied with a labored seriousness.

"I'll teach you who to be afraid of," Timothy John said. His eyes scanned the room for a suitable weapon. There was a flatiron on the mantle, a Civil War saber over the door, and a branding iron hanging on the far wall; the only knives were in the kitchen; and the hammer had been left on the back porch; there was some rope somewhere, a large bottle, a gun hidden in the attic, and a hand-saw in the hall closet as well as a hatchet and perhaps a few other things. But nothing he could think of appealed to him as much as the French bed doll whose seductively crossed legs seemed to be taunting him. "God, how I hate you," he shouted, hurling the doll at Brother Leggett. Its head smashed against the wall behind him. He did not flinch, nor did he even move to take a step.

"'Though there rose up war against me, yet will I put my trust in Him,'" he said prayerfully.

"You'll think war when I get through with you," said Timothy John going for the American Bride standing on the windowsill. He took the doll by its legs, and, like some demon escaped from an attic, he used it to beat Brother Leggett out of the room.

"'The Lord is my shepherd, I shall not want," the pastor said, running to the far end of the hall.

"You want plenty, you just don't admit it," Timothy John answered, catching up with him, and applying the doll to the preacher's head and shoulders.

"'The Lord is my strength and my shield, my heart has

trusted in Him, and I am helped,'" said Brother Leggett, falling to his knees. Convinced that Timothy John was possessed by the devil, he formed a cross with his two index fingers and, trembling while he spoke, said, "Get thee behind me, Satan."

"Get thee out of here," said Timothy John, swinging the doll violently. "I have no use for anybody like you."

Brother Leggett stumbled down the stairs, while Timothy John raced to the front balcony, and, as the pastor was running down the sidewalk, he hurled the bride after him. Her arms and legs came off in mid-flight, and her head smashed on the lamppost.

"Next time that will be your head broken in half," Timothy John said, and then pronounced his benediction. "You take your revival meetings, and your memory verses, and your tithes, and baptisms, and silly prayers along with your holy spirit and go straight to hell for me, will you please?"

It was all Brother Leggett could do to find his keys and start the motor. Vowing he would leave town before sunrise, he drove away fast, wishing he had never come to Splendora and that he had never heard of Miss Jessie Gatewood, while all the time wondering what he would do without her.

Timothy John returned to the upstairs hall. The house was silent, yet as soon as he closed the door behind him, it seemed filled with activity. From his bedroom he thought he heard laughter, then voices faintly chattering against the sound of chairs being shifted, spoons striking against china cups, and pairs of tiny feet scurrying all about.

"He's the sweetest little thing I've ever seen," came Esther Ruth's voice wafting on the scent of lilac.

"If you're asking me, he's just too pretty to have a name like Timothy John, and we're going to have to think of something else to call him," said Pristine Barlow. Her voice came to him through the closed door.

Timothy John walked straight to the hall closet, armed himself with the hatchet and cautiously reentered the bedroom. From every sitting place, from every corner, from the tops of every table and bureau, there were dolls laughing at him. Their voices sounded like Lucille, and A.P., Zeda Earl, Pristine, and Esther Ruth. "I'm ready for you now," he said. "Soon I won't ever have to listen to you again."

"I wish I had his complexion is what I wish," came a voice behind him that sounded like Lucille. Timothy John swung around and saw his first victim, a Southern belle in antebellum dress. Refusing to take pity on her, he advanced slowly, and with one swing of the hatchet he lopped off her head.

"And that's only the beginning," he said, pointing the hatchet at every face surrounding him as though he felt it necessary to issue a warning.

"He's so gentle and sweet. There's not a mean bone in his body," he heard Zeda Earl saying.

"If I only had his hair, I'd be so happy I wouldn't know what to do," replied A.P.

Then, swinging at anything that resembled a human body, he raced madly around the room. Heads and arms flew left and right. He hacked the stuffing from their bodies, tore their wigs off, chopped their legs into small pieces and piled all the broken appendages and torsos on the bed. "Now we'll see who has the last laugh," he said, dropping a match onto their mutilated bodies.

In the adjacent bedroom he performed the same slaughter on every doll in sight, piled them onto the bed, set fire to them, and hurried to the next chamber. Finally he came to the small room he had occupied as a child. The Irish doll with the green skirt was sitting on the bed. "I never want to see you again as long as I live," he said, throwing her onto the floor. He ripped off her arms and legs, tore the skirt to shreds, and chopped her porcelain face and hands until there was nothing but small pieces and fine dust. What was left of her he set blazing.

He stood back and watched the flames spread to the curtains, the mattress, the overstuffed chair in the corner. Again he heard Esther Ruth. "He's the sweetest little angel that God ever created, and the very prettiest one as well."

Looking up, he saw the angel doll hanging over the bed. The flames were beginning to curl around her feet and wings. He felt Esther Ruth's presence in the fire, in the angel, and in himself. "I don't want to destroy you," he said, tears rolling down his face. "And I don't want to destroy everything you love, but I can't go on listening to you. And I won't. All of my life I've felt like something living inside a handpainted vase, something that couldn't get out, or wouldn't let itself out, because it was too afraid of being hurt. You've got to go away now and let me be Timothy John."

For a few moments he stood listening, but could hear nothing. Not even the flames crawling across the ceiling made a sound. Before it was too late, he plucked the angel from the fire, carried her downstairs, out the front door, and onto the street. Side by side they sat on the curb. "This is as good a place as any for them to find us," he said. "It won't take long for the whole town to come running." Behind them the fire had reached the roof and the old house was beginning to collapse as if made of cardboard.

Sue Ella Lightfoot, up late as usual, was writing another campaign speech when she happened to look out the window and spot the flames. Right away she called the Fire Department, but after twenty-five rings, no one answered. "I should have known nobody would answer," she said, shouldering an ax and racing to the Coldridge house by herself.

Timothy John watched her running down the street. When she was less than half a block away, he called out to her. "It's all over, Sue Ella. Leggett knows who I am. When I told him, he preached a pious sermon and I ran him off. I don't need anybody like that. And I don't need the memory of Esther Ruth telling me what to wear, what to say, and what to do, so I set fire to everything that was hers."

Sue Ella put down her ax and thought for a moment. "You can't burn Ruthie all the way out of you, I hope you know," she said. "And it would be a shame if you did, because there were some good things about her, too. I don't think she ever realized how much pain she caused herself and everybody else, because all she ever looked at were her good intentions." Sue Ella stared into the fire before she spoke again. "I feel like she's dead now, and it's the first time I felt this way since we buried her. The only thing is, I hope we don't let her die completely, because when she felt like it she could be the most entertaining human who ever walked the earth. She told some of the funniest stories I ever listened to and found the craziest things to complain about."

"Like hummingbirds," Timothy John said. "And Uncle Raymond's famous funeral, and how she wanted to drown R.B. in the water tower."

"And that father of hers who lived in the attic," Sue Ella said. "And those paper flowers she tried to pass off as the real thing."

"And the time she elected herself dogcatcher," Timothy John added. "And the way she carried those dolls piggyback all over town, and even read stories to them at night."

"The sad part is," Sue Ella said, "she was always too serious to laugh at herself. Never found herself as entertaining as the rest of us did. So you see, you got to hang on to part of her, but only the good part. The rest you can let burn plum up right now. The trick is to keep her more on the inside than on the outside, and you'll get along just fine. You ain't as pretty as you used to be, you know."

"I sure am glad to hear that for a change," Timothy John said.

A car came to a screeching halt and stopped in the middle of the street. There were suitcases strapped on the top and boxes of belongings in the back seat. Brother Leggett, the driver, jumped out almost before he had stopped.

"I saw the flames," he shouted. "Thank God you're all right. I was afraid you had burned to death." They embraced. "I love you," Brother Leggett confessed. "I can't live without you, and I don't care who you are or what you want to be as long as I can be with you." They kissed gently as Sue Ella and the angel in her arms looked on. Behind them the flames raged; before them, Splendora was turning on her lights.

Sue Ella realized that they had very little time left. "Kids," she said, "this ain't Hollywood on fire here, you know, so you better cut this scene in a hurry. Lots of people'll be coming quick, and you can't live around here no way, so you better get going and let me take care of all this."

She led them toward the car. "You get out of here and go find someplace where you can live, and when you get there, let me know where you are so I can have a place to take me a vacation to." They exchanged good-byes. Sue Ella, still holding the angel, stood in the middle of the street and waved until they were around the corner.

Under a full moon the car slipped silently through the town. At the courthouse square Brother Leggett stopped for a moment. They looked up at the old building in all its restored glory. Esther Ruth seemed to emanate from every brick and window. "I'm glad to be leaving it this way," said Timothy John. "I feel as though I'm released from something that's been hanging around my neck for years."

"So do I," said Brother Leggett. "I have spent so much of my life hiding, and I never want to do it again."

Their car left the curb and proceeded down the street past Wanda's Ready-to-Wear with sale signs still in the windows, past the local hardware, the grocery, the Post Office, the bookmobile and the First Baptist Church. At Clyde Gingham's service station they caught the green light and coasted down the bluff past the laundry, the florist, the lumberyard, the depot, R.B.'s sawmill, and the Splendora city limits.

While the town was scrambling to get to the fire, Sue Ella Lightfoot, still standing out in the street, was preparing herself for action. Milford Monroe, who had been sleeping on the courthouse square, was the first to arrive, and behind him came scores of people in cars and on foot.

"She's dead! She's dead!" Sue Ella screamed as everyone arrived. "I seen her burn plum up, seen her frying just like a chicken wing," she said, flinging her arms around and enjoying every minute of her act. "There she was sitting at the piano all covered with fire and playing something sounded like 'Jesus, My Precious Redeemer,' and then all of a sudden she went up in smoke before I could get in there to her, but the worst part of all is that she could've been saved if the Fire Department had answered the phone when I called, but no, they were either not in or not answering, just like always, and if you want to know what I think, it's a sin and a disgrace to this world, bordering on murder, and if you put me in office, you'll see some changes made around here. We'll have us a dependable Fire Department, and a dependable Department of Public Safety, and a good ole down-to-earth dogcatcher, and there won't be no sorriness going on like what's gone on here tonight, you can be sure of that."

Then she realized that she was still holding the angel by one of its arms and had been slinging it around ever since she started talking. "You see this," she said, holding the doll high above her head. "One of the last things Jes did was throw it through the flames and tell me to keep it always as something to remember her by, and I'm aiming to do just that, and you better not let me catch you forgetting her and all the good things she did around here, and I mean it, too."

The crowd began weeping and wailing as if on cue.

Geneva Handly, wearing her nightgown and a ruffled sleeping cap said that she would never get over it if she lived to be a hundred, and Daphne Hightower, clutching her housecoat around her, said that it should have happened to anyone else, but not to Miss Jessie. "It's the will of God, I tell you," screamed Eloise Eagleton. "Don't ask me to explain it, but I know it is. It just has to be." At that moment Zeda Earl, screaming to see Miss Jessie alive and well, came running down the street in her duster. Brother Eagleton told her the bad news and she said she intended to throw herself into the fire as well because she simply could not live without her dear friend. Brother Eagleton and Sonny Weeks forced her into Lem Williford's ford pickup and took her home at once. R.B. remained at the scene of the fire, and although on the surface he appeared to be upset, Esker Dement overheard him saying to Fred Polston that the woman had it coming to her for stirring up things the way she did. A.P. absolutely refused to believe that Miss Jessie had burned to death and walked around in hopes of seeing her in the crowd, but Dudley Lock, who fortunately thought to wear his glasses, hearing aid, and nightshirt, assured A.P. that it was true and that he could never have dreamed such a thing so horrible as it was. Milford Monroe stood to one side, calmly surveyed the scene, and told Inez Weeks, who was crying her eyes out, that he somehow found it hard to believe, even though Sue Ella said it was so. Before long everyone within the city limits had gathered at the scene of the fire. Sue Ella repeated her speech to the latecomers, and finally, when it was obvious that she would lose her voice if she said another word, she walked through the crowd and went home.

At that moment the fire truck arrived.

The next morning Lucille woke up refreshed and tried to telephone Miss Jessie to let her know that she had dreamed of her all night. After several busy signals Lucille got out of bed and went to her dining-room window. When she threw back the curtains she saw nothing but a pile of smoking ashes and two walls still standing. "Oh my God!" she screamed. "Tell me I'm crazy. Tell me I'm imagining things. But don't tell me what I'm seeing is true. I just can't live if it is." While staring blankly out her window, one of the two walls collapsed, and when it did, she fell over backward on her dining-room table and was out of commission for days. All that week she lay in her bed taking Dr. Martindale's famous injections and watching the workers search for Miss Jessie's body in the debris. Every day Sue Ella Lightfoot joined the search party, but the only thing they found in four days were the charred remains of a hairbrush.

"Oh, give it to me. I want it. I loved her too!" cried A.P. Handling the brush reverently in both hands, she carried it straight home and put it on top of her dresser. The next day she sent it off to be bronzed.

The ashes and what was left of the house were carried away to the city dump. Milford raked the yard a half-dozen times but could not remove the traces of fire, and Maridel Washmoyer planted a Crepe Myrtle where the parlor had been.

The front page of that week's edition of *The Splendora Star Reporter* was completely blank except for the official photograph of Miss Crepe Mrytle holding her sparkler and baring her teeth. The headlines read:

TIME CANNOT DULL THE ACHE AND GREAT SORROW
OF SUCH AN UNTIMELY PASSING

"What an awful way to go," Lucille cried when she saw the paper. "She was too young and innocent and beautiful to meet such a death, and besides that, we needed her so much. Ruthie one year and Miss Jessie the next. Well, it's just too much for me, that's all, it's just too much, and I can't help thinking that I might be the next one to go." She turned the page quickly to put her mind on something else and read an announcement there that Sue Ella had written herself and told Albert Posey that Brother Leggett had given it to her to have it printed. It stated that the Lord had called him to a church in Mississippi and that he would forever remember his good friends in Splendora. She also sent Brother Eagleton a similar message all typed out without errors, and during Miss Jessie's memorial service the pastor said that Brother Leggett just could not live in Splendora without her. Sue Ella, forcing back a grin, turned to Lucille Monroe and said, "He's about to find out, if he ain't a'ready, that he just can't live nowheres without her; and that's the truth, if I ever in my life told it."

EPILOGUE

∾

The town of Splendora, the Splendora county seat, had always been known for its outward charm and jewellike effulgence that no other little town in the area could boast. The streets were always suspiciously clean, storefronts anything but shabby, and the old nineteenth-century houses with their picket fences and trellised gates seemed starched and ironed, even in summer's blistering heat. From beyond the city limits, the steeple of the Baptist church could be seen glistening above sycamores, cedars, sweetgum, and pine. And off to one side, the newly restored courthouse made the place seem too perfect to be real. To the traveler passing through, the town was impeccable, and to the family anxious to get away from the city, it was a good place to rear their children. There was an uphill section and a downhill section. In Little Splendor, on the downhill side, the streets were unpaved, unnamed, unplanned, and were likely to come to a sudden dead end most anywhere: in front of Sweet Dreams Cafe, Fletcher's Funeral Parlor, or Duffy Jones's front porch.

"Streets come and go in my part of town," Duffy had

been known to say. "If a house was to burn plum down tonight, it might not ever be put back up. The folks would move in with other folks, and soon enough there might be a path where that house once was, and after that a little bigger path, and the next thing you know, cars is using it for a cutoff to get somewhere else fast. Nobody minds much though; don't give much thought to it; not like it is up in the big part. People up there looks like are always shifting back and forth, first one way and then another way. Always dissatisfied about something, like it is with their court building. Everybody's acting like all at once they got something brand new, when all it is is the same old thing before the plaster got put on. Back then though, they thought they had to have something new-looking, and now they think they've got to have something old-looking, but just between you and me, I hope they stay with it the way it is, because the old-looking is better-looking, to my knowledge, which ain't much. People up there, they sure act funny sometimes. Now, take that Miss Jessie woman for you; done been dead a week now and already they're carrying on about her like she was some kind of saint or something. Well, they can say what they want to, I guess, and maybe she was a good woman and all, but as far as I'm concerned, there ain't nobody in this world that's got it over Su'zella Lightfoot.

Duffy took charge of things in Little Splendor. He saw to it that Sue Ella's political posters were hanging on every tree, house, and fence post. He made sure everyone had registered to vote, and on the two election days he ran a car service from porch to polling place.

Uphill it was much the same. Snyder had turned the icehouse over to Barney Faircloth so he could campaign for his wife. "It's the best thing she's ever done, this running for sheriff business," he said. "She's read my mind for years now, and I'm ready to turn her loose on everybody else. Not one thing slips by her, and if it does it don't slip by her for very long. I know. I've lived with her thirty-five years, and it ain't been easy. But, come to think of it, I wouldn't have her no other way."

Sheriff Fred Polston did not seem to be too worried about his opponent winning the election. He said that it was impossible for her to do so. All he did was walk around with his hand on his pistol, and was occasionally heard to say, "I 'preciate all the support you give me." He had never had to do much campaigning in the past, and did not see why he had to start with that election.

All day Friday and half a day Saturday were election days. On Saturday afternoon the newly restored courthouse was to be dedicated in an official ceremony, and after that, the election results would be announced. At the dedication R.B. spoke on city pride. Not once did he mention Esther Ruth and how she would have enjoyed living to see the building put back in shape, and not once did he mention Miss Jessie and all the effort she made to accomplish the goal. A.P. thought it was a disgrace that he overlooked her. Sue Ella said that it was no oversight.

After his speech the crowd applauded. The national anthem was sung by the high-school glee club, and the American flag went flying up the pole. Lucille Monroe then hurried to the microphone with her special announcement. She said that the county library had at last found a permanent home. "There are four vacant rooms on the top floor of the courthouse and we intend to move the library there and still keep the bookmobile in circulation as soon as we can find someone to take it over. Meanwhile the new location in the new courthouse will lend itself gracefully to bookshelves and reading tables. Miss Jessie would have wanted it that way. She would have wanted her good work to continue." With that she signaled for the unveiling, and Milford took the sheet off a large sign posted on the lawn. It read:

THE SPLENDORA COUNTY COURTHOUSE

HOME OF

THE JESSICA GATEWOOD MEMORIAL LIBRARY

The crowd could be heard expelling one deep breath together.

"Oh, I'm so proud to have known her, even if it was for such a short time," Zeda Earl said.

"She didn't have a mean bone in her body," cried A.P.

"I'm going to miss her most of all," weeped Lucille, "because, as you know, she was my closest neighbor and friend."

"I just love her since I met her; I'm so glad I did," sang Hibiscus Bee Sims.

"Me too," Sue Ella said with a smile she could not hold back growing all the way across her face.

Then Albert Posey stepped up to the platform to announce the election results. There had been a rumor of a plot to steal the ballot box, so he had guarded it himself for over twenty-four hours. Bubba Wiggley had stayed with him most of the time and Maridel Washmoyer said that they both looked tired and worn out just like a pair of old droopy-eyed hound dogs that had spent the whole night treeing coons.

"Four offices are up for reelection this year," Albert announced. He was so sleepy he could barely talk. "Daphne Hightower has retained her position as county clerk. Lem Williford is our new county treasurer. Dudley Lock is the next tax collector, and Sue Ella Lightfoot, you will all be proud to know, has won the sheriff's election by a landslide."

Everyone cheered until Sue Ella came forward to give a speech. Just as she was about to utter the first word, Fred Polston, sitting in his pickup truck, started the motor and raced the engine.

"Shut that motor off," Snyder shouted. "You've had your chance. Now let somebody else have theirs."

But the outgoing sheriff refused. He just sat there shaking his head. "I ain't gonna be beat out by no woman," he said.

"You done been beat by one whether you like it or not," said Snyder, sauntering up to the pickup as though he were about to have a friendly conversation, but he was not. Just as Fred Polston was backing out of his parking place, Snyder reached through the window and snatched off the sheriff's badge. "This don't belong to you no more," he said. "Now you can clear out of here."

Everybody on the courthouse square watched as Fred Polston drove off, gunning the motor all the way.

"When his wife finally gave birth to a boy is when he loaded that truck up with long loud tail-pipes," said Milford. "He just wanted the whole county to know that he was man enough to have a son to go along with them eight daughters."

After the noise had died down everyone turned their attention to Sue Ella standing on the platform.

"Thanks for electing me," she said with her toothless grin. "I'll do the very best I can, but you know that a'ready. I always try my best. There's a few things you better know right off though and here they are: I ain't about to wear no silly hat. I ain't about to wear no funny uniform. I ain't about to carry no six-shooters, but that don't mean I don't know how to use them, because I do. But now, I *am* going to wear me a badge, and I *am* going to keep my eyes open and my office unlocked, and you're going to mind me, too, because when I get started, you'll want to more than anything."

Before Sue Ella left the platform Snyder stepped up to the microphone and told the crowd that he had the sheriff's badge in his hand. "I think I'd like to ask the mayor of our town to step up here and pin it on her right now," he said.

Everyone waited for the mayor to step forward, and when he did not, Snyder asked again. "Will the mayor please come forward and pin the badge on our new sheriff?"

Still there was no mayor in sight.

"Who is the mayor?" cried Daphne Hightower. "I've

been working in the courthouse for going on twenty-eight years now and I don't think I've ever met the man."

"Come to think of it, I've never met him either," said Esker Dement.

"We ain't got no mayor," Sue Ella said. "I've said so for years and nobody has ever listened, so I guess tonight when you go home you better wash your ears out and think about who you might like to have in that office too. Now Snyder, you come pin that badge on me and don't put it on the right, and don't put it on the left, because I want it right square in the middle."

With a big smile on his face, Snyder pinned the badge on her every-day-of-the-week shift. Then she stepped down from the platform and shook hands through the crowd until she was out on the street again.

Everyone was preparing to linger on the courthouse lawn and visit awhile, but Sue Ella was not. It was ten minutes till the next train. It was still her job to meet it, and nothing was going to make her late, either. As she left the square she thought of Esther Ruth and how she always said that the courthouse was like somebody hiding something that he had no business hiding, but was made to feel like he had business hiding it, so he did; that the courthouse was in disguise, like somebody who was ashamed of what he looked like so he let everybody else make him over to look like what they wanted him to look like, whether he wanted it or not.

"But that's all over now, and we've managed to live through it one way or the other," Sue Ella said as she started walking down the hill. Again it was July-near-August; heat was steaming off the pavement; even the trees were beginning to wilt. "It's cold washrag weather for sure," she muttered. "I got mine with me today and I pity the poor devil who don't." The washrag, wrapped up in wax paper, was tucked into the side pocket of her shift. She unwrapped the wet cloth and wiped her face all over. "That sure feels good," she said, and kept on walking. Halfway down something sped past her so fast she thought it was going to knock her off her feet. She stopped for a moment and tried to focus on what it was. She saw roller skates, blond curls flying, and something green disappearing into the heat. For a few moments she stood there fingering her badge, and then, wondering who would be getting off the train that day, she continued down the hill toward the depot.